A Ballad of Pretty Vipers

A BALLAD OF PRETTY VIPERS

D.T. BENSON

COPYRIGHT

A Ballad of Pretty Vipers

Copyright © 2024 by D.T. Benson

All rights reserved.

No part of this book may be reproduced in any form or by any electronic or mechanical means, including information storage and retrieval systems, without written permission from the author, except for the use of brief quotations in a book review.

BECOME A VIP

Scan the code to sign up for D.T. Benson's VIP readers' group and be the first to know whenever she has a new book out.

CONTENTS

Chapter 1	1
Chapter 2	15
Chapter 3	28
Chapter 4	47
Chapter 5	63
Chapter 6	76
Chapter 7	89
Chapter 8	104
Chapter 9	114
Chapter 10	130
Chapter 11	147
Chapter 12	166
Chapter 13	186
Chapter 14	199
Chapter 15	212
Chapter 16	225
Chapter 17	239
Chapter 18	251
Chapter 19	268
Chapter 20	284
Chapter 21	296
Keep Reading	305
Become a VIP	307
Books by D.T. Benson	309
About the Author	311

I

My mind is a blur of darkness interwoven with hazy memories. Brilliant blue eyes, flashes of glinting fangs and dark claws, elaborate faerie gowns. I'm barely lucid, my body consumed with a fierce fever that makes me shiver.

A week passes like a few seconds, then I wake up to dawn sunlight filtering through the window at my bedside. There's a welcome silence in my mind. I don't recognize the pale walls or thin, gray curtain, but the softly beeping monitors and sharp antiseptic smell tell me I'm in a hospital room.

The silence in my mind doesn't last long, as urgent thoughts tear through it.

I need to get back to Eraeon.

I need to find Kali.

I sit up. Somehow, I know that a team of nurses and doctors have been doing all within their power to keep me from slipping into a coma, or worse, death. They had no cure for me because I wasn't suffering from an ailment, but a magical hangover.

I endured magical attacks from Eraeon's Master of Divination and Chief Sorcerer. Even Jaxson's magic, which only invaded my body to defend me from those attacks, took a toll. Then came the bleak, debilitating magic that overpowered me in the forbidden north end. It was all too much for my mortal body. And yet I must return to that brutal realm of magic if I'm to find Kali.

There's only one problem. I don't actually know how to get to Eraeon. I know there's an underwater hideout off the shores of Maruga Beach with a portal that can take me there. However, without a faerie accomplice, there's no way I'll be able to find it.

Eraeon is somewhere in the Indigo Ocean, but that's halfway across the world. Not to mention that the Indigo Ocean is vast and surrounds many islands and countries.

First things first, I tell myself, *brush your teeth*—my mouth tastes dreadful—*then call Shearne to pick you up.*

Shearne will know I'm back—the whole country will. It's unheard of for a kidnapped girl to return. Everyone will want to hear my story.

As I climb out of the bed, the door to the room bangs open, and a man dressed in a coat and tails and a tall black hat walks in. Six men in black uniforms swarm in after him, formidable looks on their faces and guns hanging from their holsters. I can only stand there in my hospital-issued nightdress, gaping at them.

"Riva Myra Kadiri," says the man in the top-hat, "you are hereby summoned to Islington Palace by King Bastien the third of the United Kingdom of Rithelia. You have ten minutes to prepare yourself."

My jaw drops. I expected to have to give a statement to the police. I did *not* expect a summons to the Royal Palace.

But, of course, King Bastien will want to know everything. My information could stop the winter solstice snatchings once and for all. It could also help Rithelia with freeing the other human girls still in Eraeon.

The messenger and palace guards file out and I enter the bathing chamber attached to my room for a much needed shower.

Nykolas's face fills my mind as warm rivulets caress my skin and the cloying scent of the cheap soap fills my nostrils. Prince Nykolas, heir to the throne of Rithelia's most hated enemy nation, Eraeon.

If I withhold my information, I will be betraying my people, and the kidnappings will continue. If I give my information, I'll be betraying Nykolas.

King Bastien will want all the details about the faerie palace. He'll want to completely destabilize Eraeon by wiping out all their royals, starting with the king, then the Crown Prince.

I don't know what to do.

LORTHIEN SEEMS FRIGHTFULLY gray in comparison to the vivid colors of Eraeon. It's all plain, efficient architecture, stark naked trees, and people whose soulless eyes proclaim lives of quiet desperation. There's none of the flamboyance or pointless jubilation with which faeries approach life.

The fancy car that the palace sent to get me snakes through the ice-slicked streets. Its pale leather seats and marble interior are nice, but nothing beats Nykolas's golden carriage. A stern-faced guard rides in the backseat with me, while the others fill the car in front of us and the car behind us.

I sigh and my breath mists the window. I should be thrilled to be home. But, oddly, it doesn't feel like home. Maybe because Kali is still in Eraeon. Not to mention Nykolas.

Stop thinking about Nykolas, I berate myself. *Nykolas believes me a spy and a betrayer.*

As much as it hurts, I think fate allowed things to unfold the way they did. Nykolas and I had no future. It was best for things to end. I do wish it could have been under better circumstances, though.

We enter the commercial district and familiar shops and businesses come into view. I've walked these streets thousands of times on my way to and from Mug Shot, before Kali disappeared and I started driving her car.

My heart skips a beat when we glide past Mug Shot and I see Shearne and Grigor, through the window, wiping the small circular tables. The door sign is turned to 'Closed'. It seems like a lifetime ago that I worked there. And now that I know the truth about Jaxson, I can't believe I ever thought he was human—especially with his glowing golden skin and animal-like stillness. Shearne will be shocked when I tell her he's a faerie.

A gaping hole opens in my heart as we pass Betty's Bakery. I will never eat red velvet cake again. I don't think I can bear the reminder of a certain faerie prince.

The commercial district bleeds into a suburb, the type of place I once aspired to live in. Now, it looks painfully drab. The faded red brick of the houses. The barren yards. Even in full bloom in the summer, they'll never compare to the palace gardens in—

Stop! I tell myself. I'm going to drive myself crazy if I keep thinking about Eraeon.

On the outskirts of town, Islington Palace sprawls into view, a limestone mansion I once considered spectacularly opulent. I want it to blow me away, but as we draw closer, it just seems ordinary. Big but ordinary.

Ordinary is fine, I tell myself.

I've never been someone who grasps for the finer things of life so I will easily adjust back to life in Lorthien—although I do need to find a way to get back to Eraeon and find Kali. Or maybe I can speak to King Bastien about that and he'll instruct the military to get her.

The car crawls through the vast palace gates then slows to a stop outside the main entrance. The guard beside me gets out and holds the door open for me. I climb out and am ushered down a red carpet. The cold is jarring. I don't know how I ever endured this bleak weather.

You endured it with thick coats and fleece-lined boots, I tell myself.

I'm wearing no coat this morning, just a black pantsuit and thin cotton blouse. They were the smartest items of clothing I could find in the thrift store by the hospital. A kind nurse paid for them since I had no money on me.

The red carpet trails up the palace's porch steps and all the way to the enormous door of solid, black solathium.

Twelve guards are waiting for me in the entranceway. Silently, they fall into formation around me and escort me down a hallway of gilded walls and many-tiered chandeliers. The heels of my thrift store shoes are gratingly loud on the black and white checkered floor tiles, while the guards' steps are silent.

The hallway would have been beautiful once, when it was first decorated, but there's something dull and a little tacky about all the faded gold. I am, however, thankful for the warmth. It must cost a fortune to heat a building of this size. I've never been able to afford to heat my one-room apartment downtown satisfactorily.

The guards come to a halt outside an enormous mahogany door etched with intricate carvings of fire and the sun—clearly in honor of the solar storm that gifted us solathium. One of the guards opens the door then steps aside for me to enter. None of them follow me inside.

The throne room is gold and white. A dizzying mosaic pattern adorns the extraordinarily high ceiling. King Bastien, in his crown and with a golden scepter in his hand, sits on a gold throne atop a dais.

I've seen him many times on TV, so it's uncanny to be standing before him in the flesh. He's smaller than I expected, and his piercing blue eyes, a shade that matches the gemstones on his crown, glint with a cold shrewdness. The strong, defined features of his face are inscrutable.

I bob a curtsy—women don't bow here as they do in Eraeon. The only other people in the room are two guards, one standing on either side of the dais. King Bastien says nothing and as the silence in the room drags out, I begin to wonder whether I'm expected to speak first. Maybe thank him for the invitation?

A shadow shifts in my peripheral vision a split second before a solid arm grabs me around the shoulders from behind. Then there's a sharp prick in my neck. I know screaming would be futile. King Bastien is watching coolly from his throne. Clearly he has sanctioned this.

"What are you injecting me with?" I demand.

There's no response from my assailant. I hiss with pain as the needle is withdrawn from my neck. I turn as he releases me. He's another expressionless, black-clad guard. There's a red residue in the syringe he holds.

I turn back to face the king. He's watching me as though waiting for something to happen.

Have they injected me with poison? Am I supposed to die now?

The throne room is unnervingly silent. I stand there helplessly, terror rolling in over my heart like a fog, racking my brain for what I could possibly have done wrong to deserve whatever is going on.

"What is your name?" King Bastien asks finally.

"Riva Kadiri." But I'm sure he already knows that.

"Tell me everything about your capture and the faerie land."

I start at the beginning, telling him about how Kali was kidnapped last year and I vowed to find her, even explaining that I deliberately lured the faeries. Soon I find myself relaying what Frieve and Nykolas said about King Bastien knowing why girls go missing from Lorthien every year and how, if that's true, I think he's utterly despicable.

Then I pause. "They injected me with truth serum," I whisper.

"Indeed," King Bastien says. "Do continue."

I try to resist and my whole body trembles. Pain lances through my head, tugging on my memories. They spill from my mouth and I tell King Bastien every last detail of what happened in Eraeon. By the time I finish, I'm on my knees, sweating, tears streaming from my eyes. That was as bad as Jaxson's mind-reading powers. King Bastien is no better than him. Clearly, if he had magic, he would wield it just as brutally as any wicked faerie.

He nods to a guard behind me and I'm dragged out of his presence not a moment too soon. In the hallway outside the throne room, more guards are waiting. Chains are slapped around my wrists, binding them together.

"What are you doing?" I demand.

"Riva Kadiri," one of them says, "you are under arrest for the murder of your sister, Kali Kadiri."

"What?" I snap. "What are you talking about?"

"You will remain in the palace dungeon until your trial."

Fear and confusion surge through me as a guard tugs me forward by my chains. I try to resist, but his strength overwhelms mine. The other guards fall into formation around us as he drags me through a maze of corridors.

"I didn't kill my sister," I protest. "Ask King Bastien. He just used truth serum on me and I told him everything."

My cries fall on deaf ears. Panic bubbles in my chest when we enter a stone hallway. In stark contrast to the rest of the palace, it's plain and dimly lit, and an icy draft breathes against my face. At the end, we come to a heavy iron door. One of the guards unlocks it and pushes it open, revealing a descent into darkness.

"Please," I say.

But they shove me forward.

We descend stone steps that spiral downward for what seems like an age, the air growing cooler and denser as we go. The occasional spotlights barely illuminate our way.

At the bottom, there are more lights, but still nowhere near enough. I squint as the stoic guards lead me past cramped cells with desolate faces peering through the rusted bars. The stench of decaying flesh and mildew make me want to vomit.

Finally, we reach a section of empty cells at the heart of the dingy dungeons. A few cells in, the guards stop and one of them unlocks a cell door. It's a small, unlit space with straw covering the floor. My chains are unfastened, then I'm thrust inside. I stumble forward.

"No!" I cry as the door slams shut behind me, sealing me in the cold, unforgiving darkness.

THE NEXT DAY, I stand before a judge in a court room that's empty except for a few palace guards. By now, I understand what is going on. I know too much. King Bastien can't have me floating around out there, telling people the things I've told him—especially that humans stole the faeries' immortality and their royals have been unable to reproduce ever since, except with human girls, and that's why they snatch ten girls from Lorthien every winter.

I didn't know whether to believe Nykolas or Frieve when they claimed that King Bastien knew exactly what was going on. Now that he's trying to silence me, I believe them completely.

The courtroom clerk reads out my charge, and I can only listen in numb horror as the evidence of my crime is presented. Somehow, they've gotten their hands on a recording of that final fight I had with Kali. The one where we both said things we didn't mean.

I have no idea where this recording has come from. I can only assume we were loud enough for the hallway security cameras in our apartment building to pick up our voices.

Reliving the argument is excruciating. There are so many terrible details that time had snatched from my memory.

I remembered the *I hate yous* we snarled at one another in voices so contorted with rage, they hardly even sound like us. I didn't remember the *I never want to see you again* that I hissed.

She said it too.

She also said she wished I would die.

Usually, I never engaged when Kali got like that. But that night, I was tired and on the verge of burnout from working around the clock. I was also sick of Kali taking my sacrifices for granted and demanding money I had worked for months to save.

I threw her words right back at her and added that I hoped she would go to hades and burn for all eternity.

The courtroom is silent after the recording finishes playing. Shame eats away at my insides.

"Circumstantial evidence supports the charge of murder," the judge declares.

No, it doesn't. But he has been ordered by royal decree to send me to my death, so he must.

"You killed your sister on last year's winter solstice night so that it would be blamed on the faerie kidnappings," the judge adds. "Your execution will take place at the next available time, which is in two days."

"Murderer!" a drunken guard hisses, landing a heavy blow against my jaw.

I taste blood.

"You thought you could kill someone on solstice night and get away with it?" he growls.

The thick, hard soles of his boots make his kick to my belly almost a death blow.

I cower in a corner of my cell praying death will just take me. He's been doing this on and off all night. Alcohol clings to his breath, only worsening the pungent smell of death and decay in the cell.

The last time he came in, I thought screaming would help. Other guards came running, but they didn't drag him out. They joined him. All intoxicated. They were smart enough not to come in with their keys, though. Once shut, the cell door locks automatically; and when they were done feasting on my misery, other guards let them out.

I think they cracked my ribs. I can't even breathe without fiery pain lancing through my chest.

The guard grabs me by the scruff of the neck and lifts me clean off my feet. He turns me toward the wall then slams me against it. The pain is inexplicable.

But death doesn't come.

By the next evening, I'm praying for my execution day to come quickly. The palace dungeons are not a safe place. Bruises and gashes mar my skin. My nose is broken, as are my left wrist and numerous fingers. I only escaped the worst kind of violation because one of the guards' conscience kicked in and he yelled at everyone to get out of my cell and return to their posts.

The thought of more assaults tonight, after the guards get drunk, almost drives me out of my mind. I never knew such things happened in Rithelia. I always thought we were a fair, law-abiding people. But I stand accused of a crime that the king knows full well I didn't commit and I'm being preyed on by palace guards, no less.

Islington Palace might not have a torture room like the Royal Palace of Eraeon, but they are well-versed in the art of torment. I can't believe I ever saw the world as *humans good, faeries bad.*

Right now, only thoughts of one good faerie in particular keeps me from pain-induced madness.

Nykolas.

My mind travels back to that garden with trees whose blossoms changed colors. To the shade of the weeping willow where he opened his mind to me with magic and showed me his thoughts. To the kisses. To the 'I love you'.

I didn't say it back.

I could never have imagined that I would fall for a faerie. I thought love was a choice.

I didn't choose to love Nykolas. But…I do.

I'm going to die with two main regrets. That fight with Kali, and not telling Nykolas that I love him.

The bulky shadow of a guard appears at my cell door, and I sink deeper into my thoughts of Nykolas. Of his marine blue eyes and hair a myriad of browns threaded with gold. Of his subtle smiles and the beauty of his full-belly laugh. Of his power to control wind and rain. Of his voice; the deep timber that sounds almost like the thunder he creates.

I hardly even feel the guard's kicks and punches as my heart swells at the memory of the glamor that Nykolas used to fool people into thinking he was punishing me. And the ruby ring he gave me for protection.

I'm deep within myself, in a happy place, when a flash of hot magic fills the cell and snaps me out of my self-induced hypnosis. The air burns as the guard plants his hands around my neck, his intent to choke me written in his ugly expression.

That has been his sick delight. Choking me until I'm on the verge of passing out, then letting go. Just to do it all over again. I guess he would have killed me if King Bastien didn't want me to die by execution tomorrow.

The guard, his eyes gleaming with a deranged fervor, doesn't sense the flaming magic burning in the air.

Relief floods me as Jaxson ripples into view behind him. I can only see him with one eye—the other is swollen shut—but I'm pretty sure my mind isn't making him up.

There's a flash of steel then the guard's head falls clean off his neck. If I had any strength I would let out a scream as his headless body sags against me.

Jaxson sheaths his sword, then grabs the body and tosses it aside.

He gives me a cold-blooded smile. "Hello, sweet Riva."

2

I flop to the floor, unable to stand. Even sitting, I can't straighten my torso. My broken ribs are on fire.

Jaxson crouches before me, a small light orb appearing above our heads, illuminating our faces. I can feel the heat radiating from him. Not magic this time. He's hot-blooded. Nykolas told me it's because he's a demi-fae.

"You look terrible," Jaxson says.

Seriously? Is he here to kick me while I'm down?

"I know," I rasp with breath I can't afford to spare.

Breathing hurts so much that the little gasps of air I can take in are invaluable, but I just have to curse. I hiss a string of wheezy curses, although I don't know who I'm actually mad at.

Jaxson, for allowing himself to get knocked out at a critical moment while I was in the forbidden north end?

Kali, for getting herself kidnapped and setting off the chain of events that have led to this moment?

King Bastien, for being an evil, corrupt fiend?

Myself for...everything?

My cursing doesn't ruffle Jaxson in the slightest. In fact, he looks mildly amused.

"Heal me," I croak.

He snorts. "Do I look like your toy boy Nykolas?"

I forgot how infuriating he can be. What would it cost him to help me? Why would he *not* help when he has the power to do so?

I glance at the dead guard, hoping he brought his keys in with him this time, but the portion of his holster that they should be dangling from is empty. I don't have the strength to escape anyway.

"I'm not going to heal you," Jaxson says. "I will, however, enable you to breathe so that we can have a proper conversation."

The pain of my broken ribs wanes ever so slightly. Just enough for me to draw deeper breaths without white hot agony almost tipping me over the edge of sanity.

"I hope the purpose for which you took me to Eraeon and helped me to get into the forbidden north end was fulfilled," I say bitterly, sitting up. My voice is hoarse. I haven't had a bite of food or a drop of water since being locked in here.

"Not quite," Jaxson says. "Someone decided to frame you and got in the way of my plans."

That's why he's here. He doesn't care about my plight. He has some personal agenda and wants to use me to aid it.

Jaxson looks as deliciously dangerous as ever in a form-fitting black shirt that clings to his muscled arms, and I hate that I notice. His eyes, dark as smoldering chips of coal, were my undoing back when we both worked at Mug Shot. He looks right at home in the dungeons, surrounded by shadows, as if the darkness itself acknowledges him as a kindred spirit.

"Who framed me?" I ask him. "A part of me thinks it was you."

Jaxson cocks a dark brow.

"Maybe you weren't knocked out when I needed you. Maybe you just hate Nykolas so much that you wanted him to think the girl he was falling for had been plotting against him all along."

"It did cross my mind to do that," Jaxson admits. "But it wasn't me. I don't know who it was, but I'll find out. They not only framed you, they somehow knocked me out and I can't have someone with that kind of power walking around. Plus, they're guilty of treason."

I think it was Dabria, the woman Nykolas's parents want him to marry. But what does that matter anymore?

The rancid smell of the guard's blood is slowly taking over my cell, further poisoning the already disgusting air.

"How is...Nykolas?" Speaking his name is difficult. Tears rush forward, but I bite them back.

Jaxson waves a hand and a wispy image of Nykolas, formed of translucent light, appears between us. He's sitting alone in his tower, staring into space. His eyes are shadowed with depression and his lips are pinched together as though to hold in pain. A pallor has paled his skin. He looks...ill.

"Stop," I hiss, looking away.

I didn't ask to see him. I don't want this sad image of

Nykolas to be my final glimpse of him. I'd rather die with my head full of happy memories.

"I can help," Jaxson says. "I can prove your innocence to him by snatching a few of your thoughts and showing them to him. He's too noble to try and see them for himself."

"What if you tell him that I'll allow him to see them?" If Nykolas would come and read my thoughts before my execution, I can die happy, knowing that he no longer thinks of me as a betrayer—a spy who was just using him. Better yet, he might decide to help me get out of here.

"No," Jaxson says. "I'm not going to tell him that. Do you want him to see that you kissed me while wearing his ring? Do you want him to see all your sordid thoughts about me? There might be fewer of them these days, but they're still there."

"I'm not in love with you," I snap.

"But you are in lust with me. A little."

The arrogance!

"Here's the plan," Jaxson says. "I will select the right thoughts and reveal to Nykolas the truth about what happened to you in the north end. It won't be difficult to convince him. He desperately wants to believe that you love him and it was all just some kind of misunderstanding, or that you were somehow forced by your people to do what he thinks you did."

"What do you want from me in return?" I ask, knowing there'll be a price.

"A piece of your heart," Jaxson says without hesitation. Something dangerous sparks in the dark depths of his eyes.

He's mentioned wanting a piece of my heart before.

"What does that even mean?" I demand.

"I will reserve a portion of your affections for myself. A small piece no bigger than the size of a pea, taken from the very core of your being."

"Why?"

"So that a part of you will always love me."

"And why would you want that?"

Jaxson gives me a guarded look. "My reasons will become clear in due course. Now, faeries are not allowed to meddle in human matters, the only exception being winter solstice night, otherwise I would whisk you out of here. Instead, I will have to wait for your release from this dungeon in order to claim you."

"So even Nykolas couldn't rescue me?" I ask. "What if I told you they're going to kill me?"

Jaxson frowns. "Then I wouldn't waste my time trying to bargain with you. Is that true? Are you to be executed?"

I take in the utter coldness on Jaxson's face. He really would vanish, never to be seen again, if I told him I'm going to be executed tomorrow. And he would never tell Nykolas the truth about me. He doesn't do anything unless there's something in it for him.

He did heal Nydia and Ziani, I remind myself.

But Nykolas is involved this time and it seems there's no love lost between them. Jaxson would probably happily let Nykolas torment himself, believing lies about me.

"I-I'm to be released in two weeks," I lie.

Jaxson's chest falls as he heaves a sigh of relief. That dangerous look creeps back into his eyes. He thinks he has the rest of my lifetime to torment me with that pea-sized piece of my affections that he's going to take.

"I agree to the deal," I say. "A piece of my heart in exchange for you exonerating me before Nykolas so that he will have forgiven me by the time I get out of here."

"I cannot promise you his forgiveness," Jaxson snaps. "Only that I will give him the necessary information."

I know. I only said that to convince him the more that I'm not about to be executed. He thinks he has bribed me, but I've outmaneuvered him and he doesn't even know it. Faeries are supposed to be tricky, but I'm the trickster here, beating Jaxson at whatever game he's playing.

With a flash of blazing magic, Jaxson bursts into my thoughts and I quickly stop thinking about trickery. Instead, I think about Nykolas. I can't bear the thought of him never finding out the truth and thinking the worst of me.

Weakness settles into my bones as Jaxson mines all the relevant thoughts from my head about what happened in the north end. He also takes some about how much I love Nykolas. He doesn't seem to see anything in my mind about my impending execution.

"Thank you," I whisper when he finishes.

His magic is so draining, I feel like I've run a mile.

Without replying, Jaxson disappears into thin air.

Early the next morning my cell door opens and I'm ordered out by a guard. Five more stand behind him.

I can't get up. I can't move at all.

"We don't have all day," the guard snaps. "Your execution is in ten minutes."

I can only let out a whimper. That perverse guard with a penchant for choking the prisoners under his charge ruined my whole body. I'm nothing more than a piece of wreckage. Death has already begun for me. The execution will be a merciful end.

The guard enters my cell and kicks me. "Get up."

Then he sees the headless body of my tormentor and freezes. His gaze flicks to the severed head lying across the cell. I wish Jaxson would have made him vanish. That dead guard has been stinking up my cell all night.

All the guards are horrified and assume that I somehow killed him. I tune them out as they speculate about how I must have overpowered their comrade and sliced off his head with his own sword.

"She deserves the death she's getting," says the guard who entered the cell to get me. He drags me to my feet, igniting a cascade of pain all over my body.

Thankfully, he supports me as we walk out of the cell. He must want to get me to my execution as quickly as possible.

The six guards surround me as we walk down the dungeon corridor, one of them supporting me, since I can't walk unassisted. Each step is jarring, and I shuffle along, bowed over with pain. I hate that these guards' faces are the last I'll see. That I won't die a peaceful death with somebody I love beside me.

I've never thought of death much. I just assumed I would die in old age of natural causes, a gray-haired Kali at my bedside holding my hand. Though we're twins, I figured she'll probably live a good decade longer than me. She's smarter. Not to mention that, apart from her kidnap, she has lived the much easier life. I worried about food and bills so she didn't have to.

I wonder if she'll cry when she hears of my death. I think she will.

Nykolas might, too.

I hope he won't blame himself for blasting me out of Eraeon. He would have thought that returning me to my people would mean sending me to freedom and safety.

All at once, the guards go silent and stop walking. I can't straighten to see why. I figure we're at an elevator. But there's something odd about their absolute stillness. It's like they've been frozen in place.

It takes a supreme effort, but I manage to lift my head. Nothing could have prepared me for the sight of Nykolas standing before me.

I'm imagining this, I tell myself. *All of it. The still guards, the silence, the faerie prince.*

"Jaxson delivered your thoughts."

His voice sounds real. My imagination can't reproduce that deliciously deep timber so perfectly, or mimic all its subtle vibrations. I reach out hesitantly and touch his hand, just to make sure. His hand feels warm and solid.

This is no trick of my imagination.

"Nykolas," I whisper, lowering my trembling hand. "You're really here."

Tears slip down my cheeks. It feels like it's been eons since I last saw him. I didn't think I would ever set eyes on him again.

His magic ebbs around me, strengthening my body and numbing the pain. I sense it mending the cracks in my ribs and healing every injury. Soon, I'm strong enough to draw myself upright.

Nykolas, swathed in a red cloak, is a vision of royalty and power. "You didn't do it," he says.

I begin to smile.

"But I think you would have," he adds, "given the chance."

My smile dries up. "I've had chances. My people wanted information from me on the ship. I didn't give it until a few days ago when they used truth serum on me and I couldn't resist. For that reason alone, I told King Bastien everything—answered every question he had about Eraeon. You'll need to fortify yourselves."

Nykolas says nothing. He takes in my pantsuit, which is nothing more than rags now. Then he eyes my hair and face.

Jaxson was aghast at my appearance yesterday. I can only imagine how terrible I must look.

"Thank you for your honesty," Nykolas says. "I came to ask if you want to get out of this disgusting dungeon before they execute you."

"How do you know they're going to execute me?"

"Jaxson told me."

I frown, wondering how Jaxson knew. "Are you able to get me out?" I ask. "I thought faeries have a rule about not meddling in human affairs except for winter solstice night."

"Where did you hear that? We have no such rule."

I'm surprised. I guess Jaxson just didn't want to help me, then. Maybe he wanted to let Nykolas rescue me. But he could just have told me that and saved me from a night of worrying about my impending execution.

"Where will I go?" I wonder aloud. "Nowhere in the world will be safe. King Bastien will search for me until he finds me."

"You can come to Eraeon."

"They'll kill me."

"I have informed everyone of the truth about the attack from Rithelia, and an investigation has begun to find the true culprit. However I must also now inform them that you have told your king everything. I cannot guarantee whether or not they will decide that you ought to die for that, but I will fight any motion to kill you with my last breath, and help you escape if it comes to that."

His words have the ring of a vow, and in that moment, I fall for him a little bit deeper. Eraeon, for now, is safer for me than Rithelia. There, I will have a protector.

I consider telling Nykolas about Kali and my quest to find her. Then I fear that he might think she's the only reason I'm returning. To be honest, she kind of is. I do love Nykolas, but if Lorthien was safe for me I would be suggesting a long distance relationship right now.

I release the arm of the frozen guard supporting me, then step toward Nykolas. Lightning fast, he closes the distance between us and gathers me into his arms.

"The past few days without you have been horrible," he whispers in my ear.

"Same," I breathe. "I've thought of you constantly. You would have been my dying thought."

He touches a finger to my lips. "Let's not speak of death, my love. Only life, together."

Life with him sounds wonderful—if his people will allow it. For now, I can't worry about that. I can only gaze into his ocean blue eyes as he lifts me into his arms, cradling me against his chest.

Together, we vanish from the dungeons and reappear in the sky above Islington Palace. I squint as my eyes adjust. I haven't seen daylight in three days.

A bitter wind makes my teeth chatter, but a whisper of Nykolas's magic forms a pocket of warm air around me. I gaze at his beautiful face as he soars through the air in a wingless flight, holding me close. He gazes back, his eyes devouring me as though they'll never be able to get their fill of the sight of me.

Suddenly, Jaxson's face superimposes itself over Nykolas's and I twitch. Nykolas must think I'm still cold, because the air-pocket around us grows a few degrees warmer.

Jaxson's face drifts forward, toward me, an uncanny disembodied ghost crafted from wispy light. When Nykolas remains silent, I figure he can't see it. The apparition of Jaxson's face contorts oddly, morphing into the shape of an arrow. Then it launches itself at the left side of my chest. There's no pain, but pulsing heat fills me as the arrow enters my body. Then there's a sharp tug on my heart and a raw ache spreads through it—a deep, desperate yearning for Jaxson that I can't subdue.

But what I feel for Nykolas is infinitely stronger.

I clench my teeth, realizing why Jaxson lied about faeries

not interfering in human matters. He wanted me to think nobody could rescue me and death was certain. That way I would be more likely to sell my affection to him.

He must already have known I was to be executed. He just wanted me to think he didn't know, so that I would think I was ten steps ahead of him. The wretch! He tricked me while letting me think I was tricking him.

A twinge of worry skitters through me. Now, I'm wary of returning to Eraeon for more reasons than one. The wrath of the faeries who think I was King Bastien's spy might be the least of my worries if things get…complicated with Jaxson.

A circular portal appears from thin air before Nykolas and me, its rim glowing a vivid blue. We fly through it and emerge on the other side in the clear azure skies of Eraeon.

I push Jaxson out of my mind and snuggle closer to Nykolas, loving the feel of his strong arms around me.

"I love you," I tell him. Because never again will I hesitate to say those words when I ought to.

Nykolas presses his forehead against mine and his arms tighten around me.

My heart swells with emotion. "You're…my first love," I whisper. "And I love you so much, it hurts."

Later, I might regret baring my heart so openly, but right now, it feels appropriate. Or maybe it's just my relief at being rescued.

Nykolas closes his eyes briefly as though absorbing my words. Then he kisses my cheeks, eyes, nose, lips. "I love you, too, Riva. And I'm going to fight for us."

The Royal Palace of Eraeon comes into view and my

chest tightens at the sight of its gleaming pearl walls and the pointy spires that seem to pierce the sky.

Nykolas gathers speed and we reach it in no time. Above the entrance yard, he begins to descend, slowly.

Below us, dozens of guards are waiting, their weapons trained upward—on us. They're all on their knees, no doubt in apology to Nykolas for turning their weapons on him, although they must still carry out their duty—which is probably to kill me.

Alarm clangs in my heart. "Nykolas..." I say, my voice shrill with panic.

A sparkling blue shield appears around us, a radiant barrier of protective magic. Nykolas gives me a reassuring look. "Everything is going to be okay. Trust me."

When we land, my feet don't touch the ground. Three inches of what feels like bouncy air buoys me and it's pretty disorienting.

"What is the meaning of this outrage?" Nykolas demands, glaring around at all the guards.

A messenger dressed in scarlet, who is standing at the front of all the armed guards, bows low before Nykolas. "Your Royal Highness," he says, "forgive us. We are under the command of King Xander. Riva Kadiri has been summoned by the High Council and is not to set foot on Eraeon land until they have determined her fate. She is wanted in the Council Chamber at once."

3

Two thick marble pillars, festooned with white aurel roses, stand on either side of the ornately carved door to the Council Chamber.

A determined look fills Nykolas's eyes as we approach it. I sense a tidal wave of his cool, fluid magic, then the air around him crackles with static. Ethereal wisps of energy form a spectacular aura around him that shimmers in shades of pale blue tinged with burning red.

I gape at him, stunned. I know Nykolas is a faerie, but sometimes, it's easy to forget what exactly that means.

It means he's powerful beyond my imagination. It means he's ancient and mighty, made for an undying, never-ending existence. It means he and I have no business falling in love with each other.

Focus, I tell myself as the door to the Council Chamber opens for us of its own accord. The grandeur of the room on the other side is mind-boggling. Towering columns adorned with intricate gold leaf patterns line the periphery, supporting a vaulted ceiling that seems to reach for celestial heights. Sunlight filters through colossal stained glass windows, casting a kaleidoscope of colors on the polished marble floors, and gigantic paintings of ancient faerie kings and queens grace the walls, their vibrant hues contrasting with the gilded moldings that frame them.

Thousands of seats are set out in orderly rows, and faeries occupy every one, their loud chatter filling the air. I can sense a hodge podge of different faeries' magic and I miss the protective shield that Nykolas erected around us outside. Any of them could attack me with their powers.

But nobody does. At the sight of Nykolas, and the arcing, crackling light that surrounds him, a hush descends. Then everyone falls flat on the floor. They always bow before him, but this is different. With Nykolas flaunting the formidable power at his command, they're afraid.

Nykolas stalks through the room, his red cloak rippling after him like a banner caught in a tempest. With each step, the air seems to pulse with energy. Usually, when his subjects bow to him, he asks them to rise. This time he doesn't, and nobody dares to rise without his permission.

I trail him, trembling. Walking on air is odd. But at least it means my scuffed, thrift store shoes aren't clicking loudly in the cathedral-like silence. I button my tattered suit jacket, although I know that doing so still doesn't make me presentable.

A long rectangular table, surrounded by high-backed chairs on three sides, dominates the front of the room. There's nobody sitting at it, and I figure the High Council hasn't arrived yet.

To the left of the table are two seats occupied by two people who have dared to not bow. Maybe because it's the queen and Prince Jiorge, Nykolas's uncle.

And now I'm really afraid.

It could be worse, I tell myself before full-blown panic can set in. *At least King Xander isn't here.*

Quite frankly, I'm growing tired of formal situations involving royalty. Coming here, thinking I would be safe because of Nykolas, might have been a mistake.

"Everyone is still bowing," Queen Tarla says lightly, although her eyes are narrowed. Her blonde-brown hair is piled high on her head, and subtle makeup enhances her perfect features. She makes me think of diamonds. Pretty and sparkly, yet cold and rock hard.

Nykolas doesn't respond, but I know he'll have to listen to his mother—at least until he ascends the throne in two years.

Once we reach the front and center of the room, Nykolas faces the crowd of bowing faeries. "Rise," he says.

Slowly, they all stand.

"You may be seated," Nykolas adds.

I hover awkwardly at his side, while the crowd sits down in silence. As usual, everyone is dressed like this is some kind of party, rather than an ordinary day of court life. They're all wearing bold colors and the latest faerie fashions, which means many of the younger females just have bits of silk cast about their lithe bodies, plenty of golden skin on display. I want to disappear into nothing as all eyes turn to me. I'm the reason they're here.

I sense Nykolas's magic rearing, then a gold throne, encrusted with rubies, materializes from nothing.

"Don't you dare get *her* a seat, too," Prince Jiorge snaps. He eyes me with disdain. "That would be against the rules."

"Very well," Nykolas says. Then he gestures to his throne. "Sit, Riva."

There's a collective gasp around the room.

I appreciate what he's trying to do: show his solidarity with me. But I don't dare sit on his throne. It would be the utmost affront to the whole of Eraeon for a human to sit on a faerie throne. Prince Jiorge, or maybe even the queen, will probably kill me before my butt hits the plush, crimson seat.

"See how she refuses to sit on my throne?" Nykolas asks the room. "Yet, so many of you believe the lie that she is a betrayer seeking power."

He sits on his throne then tugs me onto his lap. He brushes my hair back from my face. That magical aura still surrounds him, coating him from head to toe, and the wisps of energy flickering around his hand tickle my cheek.

Slowly, the magical energy fades and he ceases to glow. Then he tips my chin. I tense. He had better not kiss me. If he tries to kiss me and I turn away, his subjects will say I've dishonored him publicly. If I kiss him back, they'll hate me for stealing the affection of their Crown Prince. It'll be a no-win situation for me.

"The accused stands in the dock," Prince Jiorge hisses, and a part of me is grateful for the interruption.

"The accused stands in the dock once the proceedings begin," Nykolas replies. "There is no rule against her sitting on my knee while we wait. That is my will and she is obeying it like a good girl."

I look at him, and, somehow, I manage not to glare. His subjects will like this little display of dominance he's putting on. He's committed the heinous crime of falling for a human girl, so he must be seen to be in full control of her. That's the only way they'll accept our relationship—even if they still don't like it. He wasn't supposed to fall for a human. Impregnate one? Yes. Love her? Never!

Nykolas smiles as a sprinkling of his magic splashes against my temples. Then his voice fills my mind. *You're being such a good little girl, Riva. Well done.*

Fuck you! I think.

Since I don't have magic, I don't know if he hears me until his laughter rumbles through my mind. *Fuck me? Only if you ask nicely.*

I almost let out a snort of laughter. Then I remember where we are. The last thing I want is to be held in contempt of their precious High Council.

A gentle creaking sound draws our attention to a two-leaved door at the very front of the room. It opens slowly, revealing twelve figures in floor-length, hooded, crimson robes. Their silhouettes are framed by a soft glow of light from the room beyond. As they enter the council chamber and their faces come into view, I realize they're all female.

Everyone stands—except the royals. I'm about to ask Nykolas if I should be standing when a burst of grating magic that feels like the scratch of sandpaper against my skin propels me to my feet. It emanated from Prince Jiorge.

The High Council stops walking suddenly and just

stands there at the front of the room, hands clasped before them in identical poses, their loose hoods framing their faces.

Nykolas rises, offering me his hand. "You have to stand in the dock and bow your head in respect until you're asked to look up. Come on."

I slip my hand into his, and he leads me forward. There's a rumble of low murmuring around the room and I guess he's breaking some faerie protocol. I can tell what they're all thinking. Why is he going to so much trouble for a human girl in rags?

Nykolas holds my hand up at almost shoulder height, like this is a ballroom and he's leading me to the dance floor. *Don't cower, Riva,* he says into my mind. *They'll take it as a sign of guilt. Stand tall, be courageous, and boldly defend your innocence.*

I straighten my back and hold my head high. The dock is a solid black stand, facing the crowd. I step behind it but I'm careful not to look at anyone.

Once Nykolas has returned to his throne, the High Council approaches the long table and takes their seats. As the rest of the room sits, I bow my head as Nykolas instructed.

"High Council, I present to you Riva Myra Kadiri," comes a loud commanding voice from my right. "Riva Myra Kadiri, you may look upon the Council."

I raise my head. The High Council is an intimidating sight. Their inscrutable expressions intensify the knots forming in my stomach. My fate is in their hands.

To my right stands a male in the same scarlet uniform as

so many palace officials. I assume he will oversee the proceedings.

"I exercise my powers of ordinance and command that no mind-reading, torture, or any form of coercion may be used on Miss Riva Myra Kadiri," Nykolas announces.

"We accept your ordinance, Your Highness," says a member of the High Council whose golden skin is lined with age. Wispy white hair spills from beneath her hood. "And we would like to add that we need not resort to such tactics to obtain the truth."

A prickle of discomfort spreads through me as I think of the fact that King Bastien did resort to such tactics to make me talk. The thought of faeries being more noble than my own people is...disquieting.

I cast a sweeping gaze around the room, then wish I hadn't. Pure hatred is written on every face. Humans and faeries have hated each other for a hundred and forty years, but this is more than that. They think I was behind the attack on Eraeon. That I summoned the human forces and gave away the location of their island.

I didn't. But if I had, wouldn't that be to be expected? Am I, and the other human girls, supposed to be happy for them to poach girls every year and not want to wipe them out? Why do they think we'll just sit back and surrender to captivity? None of them would do that, if the tables were turned.

They ought to expect no less than betrayal from a kidnapped enemy. The only thing is, it wasn't me.

"We all know what you are accused of so we will not waste time with outlining the charges," says one of the

High Council members. She has deep brown skin, and black ringlets frame her face from under her hood. "Convince us of your innocence or you will die where you stand."

Nykolas said I should be bold. I take a deep breath. "It wasn't me who disclosed the location of your country to King Bastien of Rithelia," I declare. "It was one of you. Kill me and you'll never find out who."

My words only seem to anger them. Voices rise in indignation all over the room and it's all I can do to not shrink into myself.

They will never believe me when I tell them who it was: Dabria. The woman handpicked to marry Nykolas and be their future queen.

Dabria came to the forbidden north end while alarms were blaring after the human attack. She tried to kill me, and in that moment I realized she had framed me. I was a threat to her desire to become Nykolas's queen, so she had gone as far as revealing the location of Eraeon to the outside world in order to seal my fate. She betrayed her people to ensure that she gets to rule them.

A pale-skinned Council woman holds up a hand to silence everyone. Then she looks at me. "Do tell us who it was. And please understand that, to verify your allegations, mind-reading will be used on whoever you accuse. If your claims are found to be fabricated you will die a slow, brutal death that we will make a spectacle of, inviting the whole island to watch."

I'm not sure if it's my imagination, but I think most of the faeries in the room lean forward in anticipation, as though the thought of such a spectacle is immensely tantalizing.

"I will speak nothing but the truth," I say as confidently as I can manage. "I went to the forbidden north end out of curiosity, which I understand is against the rules. That is my only crime. My mind was hijacked while I was inside. I know the feel of the hijacker's magic. It was cold and bleak. It left me feeling empty like it was feasting on my soul."

Prince Jiorge snorts. "Humans! So intimidated by magic."

"Do you not hear what she's saying?" Nykolas asks. "She's describing how that particular person's magic felt to her, not how all magic feels."

The High Council members frown.

"Are you trying to say that this...*girl* is a sentiae?" the white-haired member asks with a dismissive sniff. She appears to be their leader.

"She's a very powerful sentiae," Nykolas replies. "The second I summon my powers, she knows." He casts me a wry grin. "I can't even read her thoughts without her knowing I'm about to do it, which only gives her time to quickly clear her mind."

From the way the Council is staring at me, that is...unexpected.

"Each faerie's magic feels different," I add. "Distinct."

Stunned silence fills the room and people exchange dubious glances. Then the white-haired Council member rises. "Turn your back on us," she orders.

I obey, confused. A few silent moments pass, then Nykolas's power rears with an alarming intensity. I sense it gushing toward me like a raging tsunami.

I trust him, so I tell myself it isn't directed at me. But I know it is. I can feel it. It's a death blow. If it hits me, I'll be dead before I hit the floor. I let out a scream, then his magic vanishes. Palpitations wrack my heart. My breaths are coming in rapid gasps.

"Why did you scream?" comes the white-haired Council member's voice.

"I f-felt Nykolas's power coming at me," I stammer.

"I don't believe a word of it." That's Prince Jiorge's voice. "They've clearly rehearsed this."

Suddenly, power that sounds like nails on a chalkboard comes screeching toward me. It's the first time I've sensed magic as a sound and it's surreal. "No!" I scream, and the magic subsides.

"What is it?" asks the head Council member.

"I sensed someone else," I pant, wiping sweat from my brow. "Their magic sounded like nails on a chalkboard."

The hum of shocked whispers sweeps through the room.

Next, Prince Jiorge's magic rears. "Sandpaper," I call. "Prince Jiorge's magic is abrasive like sandpaper."

Different faeries summon their magic and I tell them how it feels. Then some repeat and I know they're testing if I really am identifying them individually.

"That was Prince Jiorge again," I say. "Nails on chalkboard. Quicksand. Breeze. Snowfall. Quicksand again."

"Okay, enough," says the head Council member. "She is clearly a sentiae. Turn around, Miss Kadiri."

I turn and face a sea of shocked faces. The tension in the air is palpable and I begin to wonder whether letting them in on my ability to sense their magic was wise.

"If you will allow me," I say into the silence, "I will identify the traitor in your midst by their magic. It was them, not me, who summoned the human army."

Queen Tarla's voice fills the room. "Why didn't you tell us she had this ability?" Her question is directed at Nykolas.

He shrugs. "It never seemed important."

"It never seemed important?" the queen asks slowly, an edge to her voice, and I realize that while I didn't know my abilities were anything of note, Nykolas probably did. And he purposely didn't tell anyone. Would they have killed me?

Jaxson also knows I'm a *sentiae*. And he kept my secret too.

"We have no choice but to arraign faeries before this *human*," Queen Tarla hisses. "In case anybody thinks they will get away with not summoning their magic for identification, I will tug on each person's magic so that the girl may evaluate it. She will have her back to us. She will also be blindfolded. I will compile a list of the main suspects so that we do not trouble the whole palace. If the culprit is not identified among them we will expand our list of suspects until everybody has been tested."

～

Hours pass and I stand at the front of the Council chamber, my back to the crowd, while the queen tugs on one faerie's magic after another. But so far I haven't felt that debilitating magic that struck me the night the Rithelian military showed up in Eraeon.

Jaxson was one of the first people they tested. It seems

they really don't trust him. They've also presented Neal, whose icy magic always makes me recoil, shivering. As much as I can't stand Neal, I called out "No."

His magic was followed by the warm tingles of Camran's magic, which were a welcome relief. Then it was a whole host of other faeries' magic that was unfamiliar to me.

I begin to worry that whoever hijacked me isn't at the palace today, or has left Eraeon entirely, never to be seen again. If that's the case, what will I do? They'll think I'm lying about the whole thing.

Nykolas? I think. But he doesn't respond. He isn't watching my thoughts. Of course he isn't. I can't sense his magic.

Jaxson? I think instead.

Immediately, I sense an odd connection, like a formless, yet very real, bridge. At first, it's made of wispy shadows that curl and unfurl like smoke, then it slowly solidifies into a solid, black expanse of gleaming onyx.

How can I help you? comes Jaxson's dark voice in my head as clearly as if he were standing before me.

I'm relieved that he's responded. Then concerned. *Have you been in my mind this whole time?*

No. But I built a connection between us the day you went to the forbidden north end, and I haven't severed it yet.

You've made it stronger, I reply. I can sense it.

Good. If you think my name with the intention to speak to me, I will hear you. Have you found the traitor yet?

No. What if whoever manipulated me isn't here?

Then you will accuse someone else so that you don't die.

Spoken like a true cold-blooded faerie. *I can't do that.*

Do you want to die? Jaxson asks.

No.

Then you'll have to do that. I have a few suggestions of extremely aggravating people you can choose from to condemn to death.

I'm about to give him some retort when I feel it. The magic I've been waiting for. It settles around me like a gathering night. Bleak, gloomy and soul-eating.

"Yes," I say aloud, practically shouting. The connection between Jaxson and me fades to nothing as he slips away. "That's it," I say. "That's the magic that hijacked me."

Hushed murmurs fill the room, but it can't be anybody too shocking or there would have been outright outrage. That means...it isn't Dabria?

The Council doesn't take my word for it the first time. They present others, then I sense the culprit's magic again. I call out immediately. This is done a third time, before they accept my verdict.

"Read his mind," comes Queen Tarla's voice. "Not you, Nykolas. Gatwyn, do the honors."

Gatwyn is the palace's Master of Divination, and I brace myself for the unleashing of his magic. It rockets forth like a dozen laser-guided spears. Thankfully, the target isn't me.

There's a cry. A male voice. Then something that sounds like knees hitting the marble floors. "Your Highness—"

"Don't you dare address me unless I speak to you first," Queen Tarla snaps. "Gatwyn, project his mind onto the wall so that we can all see."

I'm desperate to turn around, but I don't dare since I haven't been told to yet. Whatever they see in the faerie's mind will determine my fate. I hope he isn't super powerful with the ability to fool them all with false memories.

"His thirsty thoughts about numerous female courtiers are of no interest to me," Queen Tarla snaps. "Show me his thoughts from the evening of the attack."

I cringe on behalf of the culprit. Not only is he about to die, but his secret crushes have just been exposed before all.

Suddenly, all the whispers humming through the hall cease and a palpable sense of disbelief fills the air.

"What is your name?" Queen Tarla asks.

"Derne Masi," the culprit replies, his voice trembling with fear.

"Who do you guard?"

"Dabria Oderon."

"Why are there gaping holes in your mind? Why do you have no memories from the evening of the human attack?"

"I d-don't know. I swear I had nothing to do with it."

"Liar!" The word whips through the room with the force of a gale, and I suspect that Queen Tarla has weather related powers. That'll be where Nykolas got his, although I sense that she's nowhere near as powerful as he is.

Clicking footsteps echo through the hall. They're coming from the very back, advancing toward the front of the room. Whoever it is must be important since the queen is quiet while they approach.

As they reach the front of the room, I hear the unmistakable sound of the rustling of abundant skirts. Then the footsteps and rustling halt. "Your Highness," comes a cloyingly sweet voice. "As he is my guard, let me punish him for this crime."

Dabria.

"Make it painful," the queen hisses.

A suffocating feeling grips me as a powerful magic that steals the breath flows through the room. The guard cries out, but it's abruptly cut short. Choking sounds ensue. Then a gasp. Then a series of horrifying cracks that sound like bones breaking.

Now I'm glad I didn't turn around. And I'm thankful for my blindfold. I just wish I had earplugs too. The room is deathly silent as everyone watches whatever Dabria is doing to her guard with her magic.

I can't help wondering why a guard would commit such a treasonous act. Traitors usually stand to gain something, like more power, in the event of the kingdom's collapse. I guess that's why Jaxson and the other princes were among the first suspects. Maybe this guard was disgruntled about something and wanted to see his own people destroyed.

The human attack would have been something they'd been planning for at least a few days, not a spur of the moment thing. This guard would have had to have been watching me pretty closely, which makes me shudder. He even had the foresight to put my phone, which had been confiscated, in my hand.

Still, the niggling sense that something isn't right fills me. What if he's innocent and was manipulated just like I was?

There's a series of wet crunches, then a snap of bone. It's all punctuated with the guard's cries, which are beginning to sound more and more unhinged and desperate. Then there's a loud crack that echoes off the walls, and the guard's cries cease.

"Thank you, Dabria," says the queen.

There's the sound of Dabria's retreating footsteps, then someone removes my blindfold. It's the official in the scarlet uniform. "You can turn around now," he tells me.

I turn, and my eyes land on the bloody, broken mess beside the High Council's table. Derne Masi is nothing more than a pile of severed bones and spilled organs, his blue faerie blood smeared all over the pristine marble floors. A gasp gets stuck in my throat as I quickly look away. To think that Dabria did that...

I find her face in the crowd of faeries. Her glossy red hair pours down to her waist in delicate waves and contrasts stunningly with her jewel-green dress. She's the very image of innocence and beauty. The moment our gazes connect, I know the wrong person has been killed. What's more, I think Dabria knows that I know.

But what can I do? It wasn't her magic that knocked me out in the forbidden north end. It was her guard's. He must have been acting under her orders, though. No wonder she stepped up to kill him before there could be any further investigations and the truth could come out.

I drag my gaze away from Dabria. A few moments of silence pass, then the head of the High Council speaks. "We have discovered that Derne Masi was in collusion with Rithelia. He also hijacked the mind and will of Riva Kadiri, and manipulated her with his magic into going to the forbidden north end, using his magic to help her bypass the guards."

That second part isn't strictly true. I went to the north end on my own initiative to find information about Kali. I even told Nykolas that I'd been trying to find information about one of last year's human girls, although he refused to listen. Plus, it was Jaxson who helped me get past the guards. But of course, I'm not going to expose Jaxson.

"Derne Masi framed Riva Kadiri and also tried to use her to destroy the royal family's power sources."

I can't help another glance at Dabria, whose look of dignified disgust at what Derne Masi has done mirrors everyone else's. She really must have been desperate to get rid of me if she was willing to put the royal family's power sources at risk—desperate for Nykolas to think the worst of me.

When he blasted me out of the palace, she must have thought that would be the end of me. But now, I've returned. I had better watch my back since she is clearly willing to go to extreme lengths to get what she wants.

I would love nothing more than to expose her as the real betrayer, but I have no proof. Everyone will think I'm accusing her just because Nykolas's parents have selected her to be his bride and I want him all to myself.

"Riva Myra Kadiri is hereby declared innocent," announces the head of the Council.

Immediately, the three inches of air between me and the floor vanishes, and my feet finally touch down on Eraeon. I'd almost forgotten that I was practically levitating.

"We will not have a human overseeing faerie concerns or accusing us willy nilly, so Riva Kadiri will not be summoned for any further matters pertaining to our laws or judiciary processes. Everyone is to discount the fact that she is a sentiae. We will look into whether there is a way to strip her of that power."

Nykolas rises and all eyes turn to him. "Thank you, High Council, for a well-conducted investigation. I would like to honor Miss Riva Myra Kadiri for aiding us with exposing a traitor. What Derne Masi did was an unspeakable act of betrayal, and if not for Miss Kadiri, we would never have known that we had a traitor in our midst."

Nykolas turns toward me then clenches his right hand into a fist and touches it to the left side of his chest.

I wish he wouldn't make such a fuss. Even if he chooses me to be his human consort, we both know I can only ever be the mother of his children, not his queen. And I don't think I can accept that kind of relationship. I don't care about being queen. I do care about my lover being married to someone else while I'm just another girl in his harem.

"Miss Kadiri is to be held in the highest regard, and no harm is to come to her here," Nykolas orders, projecting his voice to fill the room. "I will personally hunt down and destroy anybody who might dare to hurt her." He lowers his fist from his chest then turns to face the crowd. "I give you, and all of Eraeon, my word that I will look deeper into this scandal and round up anyone else that Derne Masi might have been working with. We have been fortifying our island and will continue to do so. Now that Rithelia knows our location, they will be back, but we will be ready for them. Not a drop of faerie blood will be spilled by human hands."

Everyone bows their head in gratitude, and Nykolas resumes his throne.

The head of the High Council nods to the official on my right.

"This case is now closed," the official announces, his voice booming around the room.

Everyone rises, except the royals, then the High Council stands and parades out of the room. Once they've gone, loud chatter fills the air and people begin to flow toward the exits. There's one at the front so I'm instantly surrounded, although nobody looks at me. The fact that I'm innocent and helped them identify a traitor doesn't mean they have to like me.

I start toward Nykolas, but he's talking to the queen and Prince Jiorge, so I decide to go wait by his empty throne. As I press against the tide of faeries, a hand brushes against mine. I'm about to snatch my hand away, but the other hand holds on and presses what feels like a scrunched up piece of paper against my palm.

I glance back to check who it is just in time to see a young faerie girl hurrying away. Then others get between us and I lose sight of her.

A fiery headache burns around my temples, accompanied by a sense of fragrant earthy magic that makes me think of lush, damp soils after rainfall.

Sorry to speak into your mind without warning, comes a breathy, female voice. *Don't read that note until you're alone.*

Immediately, I slip the note into my pocket. Before I can respond to her, she vanishes from my mind.

4

"Doesn't she look atrocious, poor thing."

I would recognize that haughty voice anywhere. I'm halfway through the door, eager to get away from everyone and read the note, but I turn. It's Ivita, a snobby faerie girl who's been in many of the human girls' classes. She sashays past me with her posse of pals from the Guild of Ladies.

"She might be innocent," Ivita says, "but nobody wants her for Prince Nykolas, and nobody is pleased to have her return."

She's talking loudly on purpose so that I hear every word. I decide not to respond.

Frieve emerges from the hall after Ivita and her friends, looking pretty harried. Wisps of graying hair escape her bun, and the white apron she wears over her long, blue dress is slightly askew. "Girls, report for your lessons at once," she orders. "Riva, would you please go and change out of those appalling clothes! Lessons resume at eleven. Tonight is a big night. You don't have much time." Then she bustles off down the corridor, herding the other girls along.

I spot a bathroom further down the corridor in the other direction and hurry toward it. Thankfully it's a single room rather than the type with numerous stalls. I lock the door behind me, then take out the note that the mystery faerie girl gave me, curious to see what it says.

It might be some kind of threat, I think belatedly.

I unfold the note anyway.

Come to the whispering gardens at midnight.
P.S. No matter what we lose...

My heart skips a beat at that second sentence. It's something Kali and I, when we first started running away from foster parents, used to say to each other: *No matter what we lose, you have me and I have you.*

The note isn't written in her writing, but she had to have been involved with it somehow.

"It could be a trap," I whisper, stuffing the note back into my pocket. But my mind rejects that idea. It has to be from Kali. Nobody knows we used to say that to each other.

The only way to find out is to go to the whispering gardens, wherever that is, at midnight. But I can't afford another scandal. If this is a set-up and something terrible happens, like what happened in the forbidden north end, nobody will believe that I'm innocent yet again.

There's a knock on the door and I quickly flush the toilet, wash and dry my hands, then step out, hoping I look innocent. Like someone who was genuinely relieving herself in the restroom and not someone who was reading a secret note. I smile at the faerie woman waiting on the other side. She doesn't smile back.

"Ah, there you are, Riva." Nykolas is prowling down the corridor, the courtiers all parting like leaves yielding before a powerful gust of wind. "Someone told me they saw you head this way."

"I feel bad," I whisper when he reaches me. "I went to the north end to find records about last year's girls—"

"You were manipulated," Nykolas cuts in. "Let's not speak of that horrible evening when I thought you betrayed me anymore."

I open my mouth to say more, but he places a finger gently against my lips, silencing any further words. His eyes convey a mixture of understanding and reassurance. "Don't feel guilty about anything, Riva. It's all over now."

I nod slowly. He wants, so badly, to believe in my innocence, so I let him believe it. Even though I wish I could tell him about Kali.

Nykolas grabs my hand, then leads me toward a door hidden away in an alcove. He pushes it open, revealing a confined space. The shelves set into the walls are lined with cleaning products.

Nykolas has barely shut the door behind us before he threads his fingers through my hair and pulls my face to his. He presses a searing kiss to my lips, setting my heart into an instant tailspin.

Thoughts of the note and whether it's a trap are

consumed by a potent flood of desire. My passion echoes his as I kiss him back, cupping his face in my hands.

I gasp when his tongue invades my mouth. He strokes it slowly against mine, sparking a whirlwind of sensations that leave me breathless. Then he's nipping and biting my lower lip before sucking it into his mouth.

Our bodies draw closer, my softness against his hardness. The world outside the closet fades into insignificance, and the visceral hunger growing within me becomes all that matters.

Nykolas's his hands travel from my hair, down my back, then come to rest on my waist. He pulls me harder against him. Then, with a groan, he lifts me into his arms and sets me onto something solid. I know there was no table in here. I break the kiss and look down. I'm sitting on a slab of sparkling blue energy. Having magic really does come in handy for all kinds of purposes. I was so wrapped up in Nykolas's kiss that I didn't even sense him creating it.

"I've missed you," Nykolas whispers. "I'm so glad you're back."

I twine my arms around his neck and pull his head down, pressing a kiss to his lips. He kisses me back with the same fervency, and it's a heady feeling that Nykolas is as eager for this kiss as I am.

If I'm not careful, he's going to completely take over my heart. I've never been in love before, and this is all so new and frightening and wonderful. Things could have been so simple if I'd chosen to fall in love with some human man back in Lorthien. But no. I'm in love with a faerie. The Crown

Prince of Eraeon, no less. I can't see how this will end in anything but heartbreak.

I try to ignore that thought, but it persists. Soon, I'm doubting everything. Whether I should have returned. Whether Nykolas and I truly have a future. Whether I'm being recklessly naive in thinking that we do.

"Never leave me again," Nykolas whispers between kisses.

And I have to draw away.

"What's wrong?" Nykolas asks. The glaze of passion in his eyes turns to concern as he searches my face for an answer.

I shake my head.

"Tell me," he insists.

"I just...need some air." I force a bright smile.

His lips curve in a sexy, reciprocal smile as he buys the lie. "I have something for you," he says, slipping his hand into his pocket. He tugs out a small black box and hands it to me.

I open it to reveal two ruby earrings resting on a velvet cushion. Their vibrant red hue catches the soft light in a dazzling dance of color. Each one is sparkly and exquisite, hanging from a delicate gold hook.

I glance at the ruby ring on Nykolas's right hand. He gave me that for my protection the last time I was here.

"Are these earrings for protection?" I ask.

Nykolas lifts his shoulders in the most elegant shrug I have ever seen. "I guess they'll serve that purpose too."

"What do you mean?"

"Even without wearing rubies, everybody now knows

that you are mine. Word of me standing up for you in the Council Chamber will spread throughout Eraeon like a wildfire and nobody will dare mess with you, earrings or not. But if you wear them, it'll be a visual reminder."

"So, if these are not for protection, why are you giving them to me?" My voice is a tad shrill.

Nykolas looks taken aback. "It's a gift. Do your human males not give gifts when trying to court the affection of—"

"I don't need them." I snap the box shut. "I don't...I've never owned anything so valuable."

I sense a cool sprinkling of his watery magic on my ears, then Nykolas gives me a satisfied smirk. "They look perfect on you."

I touch my ears and feel the cool, dangly earrings. I open the jewelry box. It's empty. I scowl at Nykolas, although a smile is tugging on my lips. "Hey! You can't just force gorgeous, ruby earrings on me without my consent."

"You accepted my gift of red velvet cake without protest," Nykolas says. "Why is this any different?"

"That slice of red velvet cake cost two rhones. These earrings must have cost like..." I realize I have no idea how much the earrings might have cost, other than that they would have been very expensive.

"A hundred thousand enras," Nykolas supplies.

"What is that in rhones?" I ask, hoping their currency is weaker than Rithelia's, but suspecting that it's much stronger, and that I'm going to hate his answer."

Nykolas pauses. "The exchange rate is what? 0.05? Your currency is dirt compared to ours."

"How much is it in rhones?" I repeat slowly, although

I'm already doing the math in my head. I have to bite down hard on my tongue to keep from gasping in horror when I work it out. "I'm wearing two million rhones in earrings?" I curse under my breath, then set aside the jewelry box and reach toward my ears to take the earrings off.

Nykolas catches my hands. "You deserve so much more," he says fiercely, interlacing our fingers. "And more is coming. The royal stonecutter is still working on another piece I've commissioned for you."

"No, Nykolas. No more. Please."

His face falls. "Why, Riva? Why won't you let me spoil you?"

I don't understand why he wants to.

"I don't understand why you won't let me?" Nykolas replies.

I realize he's in my mind, his wet magic lapping against my temples. "Get out!" I hiss, and his magic retreats.

A few moments of tense silence pass between us. Then Nykolas lifts my hand to his lips and drops a kiss onto my knuckles. " I would have thought that a woman as beautiful as you would be used to such treatment."

Is he kidding?

"Hasn't anyone ever done anything like this for you before?" he asks.

I shake my head. "Princes willing to blow two million rhones on ruby earrings aren't exactly in large supply."

Nykolas grins. "Touché."

I really don't want the earrings but I can tell that it really is no big deal to Nykolas. He said I deserve them. My mind whirs with bewilderment. How can I deserve them when I haven't done anything for him?

It's different with love, I tell myself. *He's giving me these earrings because he loves me.*

But it's still hard to accept. Nobody has ever told me that I'm worth anything. I didn't have parents to tell me I matter, and I've never had a lover. The closest I've ever ventured toward feelings of being valuable was as a result of being responsible for Kali. She needed me. I took care of her; worked to put food on the table and send her to college. Provided everything she needed. That gave my life meaning.

I haven't done anything for Nykolas. I'm not even very presentable right now and he's all over me. I know that love isn't supposed to be transactional, and that gifts should be okay. But I still don't feel good about it. I'll never be able to reciprocate.

"Don't give me false hope, Nykolas," I whisper. "We can't be together. Your people—"

"Nobody will tell me who I can and cannot love, Riva. I love you and anybody who doesn't like it can go drown in the ocean of their own prejudices."

I smile despite the thick heaviness unfurling through my chest. "Ah, how poetically unbothered you are."

"I'm serious, Riva."

"But you have a duty to your kingdom, and there are rules that govern your life—"

"I don't believe in rules. I do believe in love. It's the magic that transcends rules, realms, and even species." He tips my chin. "Do you love me?"

I nod without hesitation.

"Then don't give up on us. Not without putting up a good fight. And not even then."

I lower my gaze. Looking at Nykolas hurts, because all of a sudden, I realize how much I want him. How desperately I want to believe that we can be together.

"I love you," he whispers.

"I love you, too."

"Then stop trying to reject my rubies and thank me instead. Preferably with a kiss."

So I kiss him. Hard. Even though I fear that I might lose myself entirely to him.

His kiss awakens a storm of emotions in my heart. And when his fingers tug on the button of my thrift store suit jacket, a wild need sweeps through my mind.

Once my jacket is undone, my fingers fumble with the fastenings of my blouse, their urgency matching the fervor of our kiss. The world shrinks to this moment, this overwhelming desire that threatens to consume us both.

Nykolas stills suddenly. Then he pulls away with a groan, cursing under his breath. He waves a hand and an image of Camran's face appears in the air between us. "I said I'm busy," Nykolas growls.

"Your father is demanding that you report to his throne room immediately?"

"Because I honored a human girl?"

"Well, he's definitely mad about that, but no. It's because our spies have reported back with intelligence about the Rithelian government infiltrating us."

A muscle works in Nykolas's jaw then he nods. "I'll be there in a moment."

Camran's face vanishes and I touch Nykolas's cheek. "Go. I'll see you later."

"Don't take off the earrings," he murmurs, dropping a final kiss to my lips. "Wear them all day."

"Okay."

Then he vanishes into nothing. Off to plot against my people. Alone in the storage room, I sigh.

If Nykolas was just an ordinary faerie, rather than the Crown Prince and Supreme Commander of the armies of Eraeon, we could turn our backs on both our people and pretend that a war isn't impending. But if war breaks out, he will be leading the charge.

I don't know if I could ignore that. But for all I know, King Bastien could deserve it, as he's clearly hiding something.

I slip out of the closet and am thankful to find the corridor empty. Frieve will no doubt be fuming at my lateness. I make my way through the palace, my feet skimming the marble floors and my every sense assaulted by the opulence. So much shimmering gold and vivid red, not to mention the glistening pearl walls.

Nothing in the palace is allowed to simply be functional. They must be beautiful too. Windowsills are engraved with intricate patterns, or polished to a high shine. Doorknobs are solid gold. In one corridor, the skirting boards are adorned with silver filigree. Everything is meticulously crafted for elegance and grandeur.

It takes me almost twenty minutes to reach my rooms. I open the door and almost crash into a display of flowers that's taller than I am. White roses, flamewood blossoms, baby's breath. Nestled among the flowers is a banner that reads 'Welcome Back', its golden script shimmering with a magical resonance.

Nykolas.

I guess I'm going to have to get used to his grand gestures.

I exhale and pick a flamewood blossom from the arrangement, tucking it into my hair.

"Why are you really here?"

I'm so startled, I jump. Then I spin toward the open door to the lounge so fast that my feet almost tangle.

Queen Tarla stands at the floor-to-ceiling window across the lounge, her back to me.

"Your Highness," I say quickly. I'm about to bow, but since she isn't looking at me, I decide not to bother.

I take an uneasy step into the lounge and see that she isn't alone. Dabria is standing at the other end of the room, her red hair like a halo of flames. The skirts of her emerald-studded, green dress are stained with the deep blue blood of the guard she killed.

"I, uh, I'm here because Nykolas invited me to return," I say slowly, addressing the queen.

"You did not bow," Queen Tarla hisses.

I immediately drop to the floor in a low bow.

The queen turns and looks down at me, her blue eyes simmering with open hostility. "So you would have me believe that you traded a life of freedom among your people for captivity here out of love for my son?" She lets out a soft peal of tinkling laughter, but her eyes continue to blaze. "I do not know the real reason for your return, and neither do I care," she hisses. "You are leaving. You will end your pathetic relationship with Nykolas and return to your people, or I will kill you."

I take in the barely leashed hatred etched into every inch of Queen Tarla's beautiful face, the ruthless gleam in her eyes, her tightly balled fists. That wasn't an empty threat.

"Send me back now," I whisper from the floor. "I need not stay another second."

"That won't work." The queen unclenches her fists and strolls slowly alongside the window, the train of her pale blue dress whispering after her. "My son will rend the universe to find you if you just disappear. You must break up with him and leave him with no hope of a reconciliation. Then I will see to it that you are delivered safely to Lorthien."

My heart begins to thud heavily. Could I do that to Nykolas? Purposely break his heart?

"You will have to be convincing," Queen Tarla adds, coming to a halt by a potted flamewood tree, its boughs heavy with fiery red blossoms. It's a new addition to the room. Probably because Nykolas realized I like them.

"Give Nykolas any hint that you have been coerced, or don't really want to break up with him, and I will explode your heart while it's still in your chest," Queen Tarla says, her sweet voice at odds with the sickening venom of her words. "A girl he loved has been manipulated and stolen from him before, so he's being extra vigilant about you. He's determined that nothing will come between you. Only you can put an end to it."

Nykolas has told me about some girl betraying him in the past. It makes the fact that he has forgiven the north end incident and doesn't suspect me of any wrongdoing at all even more touching.

"One would think that the last betrayal would make him more careful," Queen Tarla says, "but he's being such a fool. He's talking about fighting for you in ways he didn't fight for that conniving Aziza princess he fell for. You will have to be adamant. Give him no hope."

My legs ache from crouching, but I don't dare rise. The thought of breaking up with Nykolas shouldn't hurt so much. Especially when he hasn't actually even asked me to be his girlfriend. I didn't come to Eraeon for him. I came for Kali. But my heart is entangled in a web of conflicting emotions.

"I am traveling for four days," Queen Tarla tells me. "I expect your relationship with Nykolas to be over when I return. And do not think I won't find out if you tell him about this. Breathe a word about our little chat, and I will give you a sensationally slow and painful death. You are a dead woman walking, Riva Kadiri. The only way to not die is to leave my son alone. Is that understood?"

"Yes, Your Highness," I say around a tight, aching lump in my throat. My heart is hammering like it wants to break free from my chest and fly away to safety.

Queen Tarla heads toward the door, leaving her threats echoing through my mind, but Dabria lingers. Once the queen has gone, I drag myself to my feet. Dabria is watching me with a catlike intensity, so I clear all emotion from my face. I won't give her the satisfaction of seeing me shaken.

I want to ask her whether she thinks the queen would be fighting her corner so vehemently if she knew she was the true betrayer of Eraeon. But Dabria has magic and I don't. I don't know what her powers are, but just in case she can tweak my mind, I decide it's best to pretend I don't know what she did.

While Queen Tarla was here, Dabria was quiet, head bowed in a corner. Now that she's gone, she lifts her chin and her eyes are hard.

I sense that she's going to do something terrible a split second before I feel her magic lancing through the air toward me. It's suffocating; steals my breath in the most alarming way. I feel like I can't draw an inhale, even though I'm breathing. Her magic intensifies, choking me, freezing the air in my lungs.

Dabria steps toward me and I want to back away, but I find myself rooted to the spot. Frozen as though sculpted from ice. I couldn't move if Kali appeared in the doorway with an escape portal.

"Nykolas is yours," I choke out as she nears. My voice is tight with strain, and my head is beginning to go light. "When I leave, he'll be all yours again."

She snorts. "Who cares about Nykolas? It's not him I'm fighting for, but the queenhood." She gives me a smile that scares me more than if she'd bared her faerie fangs. Then she cups my face in her hands and darkness seeps into my mind, like ink swirling through crystal clear water. "Don't take this personally, sweetie," Dabria whispers. "See it as a favor, actually. I'm merely helping you to do what the queen has asked of you—so that you don't die."

Hatred swirls through my mind, borne by the invasion of

darkness. But it isn't directed at the queen, Dabria, or even Nykolas. I hate...myself.

I stare into Dabria's hazel eyes seeing everything I'm not. Her beauty. Her grace. Her elegance. And I sense, very acutely, my inadequacy.

What does Nykolas see in me when he has Dabria as an option? It can't be real love. He's playing some game with me.

I blink, realizing that these are not my thoughts. But they swirl through my mind anyway, strong and insistent.

Suddenly, I understand what Dabria is doing to me. She's bringing all my fears to the forefront, enhancing them, and adding a hefty dose of shame and self-loathing. I want to fight it, but her grip on my face tightens and I'm still completely frozen in place.

Fire lances through my brain as her magic digs in deeper, infiltrating the deepest recesses where my fears and inadequacies reside. It rouses the insecurities that I'm usually good at ignoring, and the doubts that have taken me a lifetime to sing to sleep.

I don't know how long we stand there, but when Dabria finally releases me, I collapse to the floor, my head spinning and thoughts swirling in chaos.

She turns to leave, then she spots something across the room and pauses. I watch her approach the lounge's other window and pick up a single aurel rose from the sill.

"Why do you have this?" she asks.

The truth—that Jaxson has been in my quarters and left it here—is out of the question.

"I just like them," I whisper, barely able to speak with

her suffocating magic only slowly dissipating from my mind and body.

Dabria places the rose back onto the windowsill and asks no further questions, but her eyes are filled with suspicion as she walks out.

I wait until I hear the door to my rooms shut after her, then I let the tears gathering on my lashes fall. It was foolish of me to return, thinking Nykolas could protect me. I don't belong in Eraeon, or in their royal palace, and I never will.

This is not my land and faeries are not my people. I must focus on my mission to find Kali then get the hell out of here.

It's urgent now.

I have four days.

5

Frieve stops talking when I arrive at the classroom. I'm an hour late, but that isn't why she's glaring at me. "You still insist on wearing gray?" she demands.

Ivita, who is sitting near the back of the room, scowls. "This is an affront to us!" she snaps. "After all that our Crown Prince has done for you, you refuse to honor our ways!"

I had every intention of wearing some pretty, brightly-colored frock, but after the queen's threats, what's the point? I can't let Nykolas fall for me any more than he already has. And I can't...encourage him. Wearing a pretty dress will make him think I'm trying to please him. I removed his earrings too. I'm not here for him. I'm here for Kali.

"Our Crown Prince has put his honor and integrity on the line for a girl who insists on laughing in our faces," says one of Ivita's friends.

I start toward my desk and realize that Seltie, another human girl, is sitting at it. Ziani and Nydia are now sitting side by side near the middle of the room. Thankfully, there's an empty desk beside Ziani. They both beam at me as I head over. I try to smile back, but I don't know if I succeed. I might just be baring my teeth.

Vielle, a sweet faerie girl, sits at the desk on my other side. She smiles, giving me a small wave. So does her friend Baila, who is sitting on her other side.

"Girl," Ziani whispers, "why the hell are you back?"

"She's here to save us," Nydia whispers.

There's a loud crash near the back of the room as Ivita leaps to her feet, knocking her chair over. "Do you hear what they're saying, Frieve? These human girls are nothing but ungrateful little—"

"Do control yourself, Ivita," Frieve cuts in.

"She's mad because Nykolas has never made a fool of himself over a faerie girl," Ziani says loudly, "but he's acting like he's completely lost his mind, all because of Riva Kadiri, human girl, citizen of Lorthien."

Ziani is clearly still as feisty as ever.

Faerie girls begin to talk all at once, their voices rising in anger, but a burst of Frieve's magic races through the room, silencing them. Us, too. I feel a tingling on my lips that seals them together. None of us can speak anymore. Ivita's chair is lifted upright by Frieve's magic, then Ivita drops onto it by force.

Frieve's magic isn't unpleasant. It swirls softly like a flurry of snowflakes, but it is clearly formidable.

"You can squabble after class," Frieve says. "For now, you must focus. Riva, you're just in time as Filpé will be here in a moment to provide more information about tonight."

I want to ask what's happening tonight, but Frieve's magical gag is still in place. She answers my unspoken question anyway.

"Tonight is the Ceremony of Official Declaration," she says. "Males make a formal declaration of who among you they intend to choose, and we'll be able to see how many are interested in any one girl and for what purpose."

Ziani rolls her eyes. I feel the exact same way. We've already had a stupid ball where we were paraded like objects on display in a shop window, and had to hope one of their males pinned a rose to our bodice, otherwise we would die —for no crime other than not being appealing enough to their highest ranking males.

The door to the room bangs open and Filpé strolls in, his eyes sharp with their usual hateful glint. I can't stand Filpé.

"I do believe Frieve has informed you all of what is happening tonight?" he says silkily.

"I have," Frieve answers.

The tingling on my lips fizzles away, and I guess we can all speak now, but nobody does. None of us likes Filpé, not even the faerie girls.

"Make no mistake that tonight is a competition," Filpé says, perching on the edge of an empty desk at the front of the room. "You must do all within your power to ensure that you stand out. I know some of you have made friends with one another, but tonight, your friend is your enemy. If she snags the male you want, you run the risk of snagging nobody, and being tossed into some randy duke's harem for the rest of your life, having orgies, instead of being with a partner who treats you with respect."

Ziani lets out a snort of laughter then quickly clamps her lips together.

"Is something funny, Ziani?" Filpé asks, his gaze narrowing.

"It was just you talking about orgies with such a straight face," Ziani replies.

Filpé's brows lift.

"By the way," Ziani adds, "orgies don't faze me. I've participated in a few. They can be pretty satisfying if you choose the right people."

Girls gasp, and poor, matronly Frieve looks shocked.

"Just kidding," Ziani says quickly, although I don't know if she is.

"Shut up," Filpé hisses.

Thankfully, Ziani obeys.

"Of course, the prize is Prince Nykolas," Filpé says. "He will give any female he chooses her own home, and she will be treated with respect, as our royals are known to do."

So...no orgies then.

"Do not be disheartened by..." Filpé's gaze flicks my way. "...recent events. Hearts are fickle things and can often be swayed. You must all use every weapon in your arsenal to try and catch his eye." He's looking at the faerie girls at the back of the room. "Use magic if you must."

He's openly telling them to try to snatch Nykolas from me. Well, that would mean I won't have to be purposely cruel and break his heart. Instead, he can break mine. Not that that would be any easier.

I notice Seltie glancing at me. It's not only the faerie girls who want to be chosen by Nykolas. She wants him too. She was popular with most of the princes at the ball, but it was clear that it was Nykolas that she had her sights set on.

With her dainty, voluptuous figure and shining blonde hair, I'll bet she's never not gotten a man she wanted. I was as surprised as anyone else when Nykolas bypassed her, Ziani, and all the pretty girls for me.

Especially when he can have as many of us as he wants. In fact, he only needs to say the word and he could have us all. He's to wed Dabria, but he needs a human to birth his heirs, and he's free to have as many playthings in his harem as he wishes.

Seltie is still watching me and I meet her gaze. She stares me down for a moment then looks away.

Pathetic!

Even without the queen's ultimatum, I refuse to be forced by Filpé to compete with other girls for the attention of a male, Crown Prince or not. How do Seltie and all the other status-hungry girls not see this as totally degrading? I guess they're all just trying to survive—and trying not to wind up having orgies in a duke's harem.

"Since the ball," Frieve says, "the choosing males have all had a chance to get to know you and make their final decisions; and for those still deciding, to at least narrow down their choices. If multiple males are still interested in the same female, we will hold negotiations between now and the Choosing Ceremony, which is in a week's time."

Nykolas and I will be over by then. I'll be back in Lorthien, or maybe I'll have moved to someplace else in Rithelia, living under the radar so as not to be executed. I wonder if Nykolas will select someone else at the Choosing Ceremony and who that might be.

Ziani and Seltie are easily the most beautiful of the human girls here, but I don't see him poaching them away from all the males who want them. Maybe he'll choose at random, or maybe he'll refuse to participate.

A loud snore interrupts whatever Filpé is saying, and he stops mid-sentence. Every head turns toward Emy. She's sitting upright, but is fast asleep, her head slowly drifting backward.

"Somebody wake her up before I kill her," Filpé snaps.

Keyta, a friend of Seltie's is sitting closest to Emy. She nudges her and Emy's eyes fly open. She stares around the room blankly, a bleary half smile on her lips as Filpé continues to talk.

I think of how Emy was brutally whipped for being late for breakfast our first morning here. She then spent a few hours in the infirmary and has never been the same since.

Eraeon has broken her.

The class seems to drag on forever, and I tune out as Filpé gives us tips for catching our desired male's eye. Apparently, letting a male know, in a subtle way, that you want him to choose you could make all the difference.

I know Seltie and Ivita will apply everything we're being taught to Nykolas.

Who cares? I ask myself, even as something cold trickles into my bloodstream.

I leave as soon as the class ends. The second I step out of the classroom darkness fills my mind and dark whispers of self-loathing bombard me; hateful words that I don't want in my head.

Dabria must have crafted her magic to stop working when I'm around others.

"Hey, wait up, Riva," Ziani calls, hurrying out of the classroom.

The voices in my head continue as she joins me, and even when Nydia, Vielle, and Baila catch up and suggest that we go have ice cream.

I revise my first conclusion. Dabria's magic doesn't stop when I'm around others. Maybe only when I'm around people with authority, like Frieve and Filpé?

"Tell us everything," Ziani says, linking her arm through mine. "You managed to escape. Why on earth are you back?"

"I didn't escape," I say distractedly, fighting the mental darkness. "Nykolas blasted me out to the human army."

They all stare at me, wide-eyed with shock. It dawns on me how beautiful they all are. Ziani with her flawless brown skin and long, gold-threaded braids; every feature fine and symmetrical and perfect. Nydia, with her unique white hair and blazing green eyes.

Vielle and Baila are faeries so of course they're stunning. The former's thick, brown tresses are twisted in an intricate braid that circles her head, and her cheeks and collarbone are dusted with a shimmery powder that highlights the golden hues of her skin. The latter's glossy black hair is curled and arranged in a side-sweeping updo.

I'm nothing, I tell myself. *I don't compare to them.*

I try to shake off the thoughts, but they have a tight grip on my mind.

Nydia speaks, distracting me from them slightly. "So how did you get back?"

Somehow, as Vielle and Baila lead the way to the palace's ice cream parlor, I manage to retain enough clarity to tell them about how Nykolas came to Lorthien to ask if I want to return.

Ziani gives a low whistle as we approach a vast entranceway. "You came back willingly? You must truly be in love with Nykolas, then. Are you willing to stay here forever just because of him?"

I'm not sure what to say. I didn't come back for Nykolas, but I can't tell anybody that. Neither can I lie that I did return for him because I've been ordered to end our relationship.

"That's sweet," Baila says, taking my silence as confirmation.

"Actually, it isn't," Ziani replies. "There's this psychological condition called Stockholm syndrome. It's when a hostage victim starts to empathize, or even fall in love, with their captor. There's nothing sweet about it. It's weird as fuck."

Vielle and Baila look shocked. "Ladies ought not to use such language," Baila admonishes, her gaze darting around in fear that someone might have overheard.

"Ladies ought to do whatever the fucking hell they want," Ziani retorts.

I look at Nydia. "Ziani is getting worse," she says with a shrug.

Ziani just snorts.

We step outside into blazing heat. I frown, sure it wasn't this hot when Nykolas and I flew in a few hours ago.

"Nykolas must be feeling happy," Vielle says. "We'd better get ready for a few unbearably hot days."

Baila sighs. "Thanks a lot, Riva."

"Can he not control his emotions?" Ziani asks. "Last week it was constant thunder and floods. He's like a hormonal teenager. Must the whole country suffer because of his mood swings?"

"It's only when he has extreme moods," Baila says. "He'll get control of himself before long." She picks up her pace, cutting through a meticulously manicured garden.

We gather our skirts and hurry after her. I note that our conversation has drawn me away from the chaos in my mind, and I determine not to let the chaos reclaim me.

We exit the garden through a gate in a hedge, and a charming, white cottage comes into view. Ivy vines with tiny, pink blossoms weave around the windows, and the thatched roof makes me think of storybooks.

"Nice," Nydia breathes.

Ziani glares at her. "Stockholm syndrome," she mutters under her breath.

"Just because you hate being here doesn't mean you can't appreciate anything," Vielle says, poking Ziani in the ribs.

Ziani bats her hand away. "Don't touch me, faerie."

Vielle grabs her and envelopes her in a tight hug. Ziani tries to break free, but she's chuckling now. She gives up and hugs Vielle back, then lets her take her hand and drag her into the ice cream parlor. My head is pounding as I enter, courtesy of Dabria's magic and the heat.

The smell of vanilla, berries, and freshly baked waffles wrap around me, and my stomach growls. I can't remember the last time I ate. I notice the soft music playing. Its haunting melody has to be somewhat magical, because my headache and dark thoughts instantly wane.

Circular tables fill the cottage, all spread with red tablecloths and surrounded by mismatched wooden chairs with plush, jewel-toned cushions that give the space a vintage feel. Thankfully, only a few of the tables are occupied.

I'm surprised when four guards at a window-side table with a lake view wave to us. I'm even more surprised when my friends head over and dump their books on their table. One of the guys pulls Ziani onto his lap, and she lets him. I glance at Nydia when Ziani drops a lingering kiss onto the man's lips.

"She's seeing like three guys," Nydia whispers. "So are Vielle and Baila. Don't ask."

The fact that Vielle and Baila don't deny it tells me it's true. Stunned, I follow Nydia, Vielle, and Baila to the counter where rows of ice cream tubs are encased in glass displays.

"I thought you don't want faeries touching you," Vielle says to Ziani when she joins us. You seem to enjoy Markus's touch quite a lot."

"I didn't know we're allowed to kiss random people," I say.

"We're not," Baila replies, "but who cares?"

"What would happen if you guys were caught?" I ask, worried on their behalf.

"A night in the dungeons probably," Baila says. "The Guild really wants us to get chosen and keep their track record good, so they'll pressure Frieve and Filpé not to tell the males who have shown interest in us. As for human girls, they'll probably just kill you."

Ziani's eyes narrow, but I know it won't deter her from sneaking around. I want to ask her if a few stolen kisses are worth the risk, but I don't want to sound like a bore, so I focus on the ice cream. I take scoops of familiar flavors: vanilla, cookie dough, and mint. Then Baila insists I add a scoop of a flavor called Starlight Swirl. It's bright purple with something that looks like glitter shimmering in it.

Ziani is much more adventurous and takes scoops of all kinds of new and strange faerie flavors. Nydia goes for three scoops of chocolate ice cream and refuses to be swayed when Vielle and Baila goad her to try others.

We add waffles and freshly baked cookies to our plates then return to the table of waiting males. None of them pays me any attention. They don't even look at me.

Because I belong to Nykolas, I realize.

I decide to move to the next table. The whole of Eraeon is probably waiting for me to make one false move that they can use against me. Sitting with other men could be handing them a reason to believe I'm dishonoring Nykolas, or am otherwise undeserving of his love and deserving of death. I have to be beyond reproach, as I need to survive long enough to find Kali.

Nydia follows me, clearly uninterested in flirting with the guards. I'm glad when Vielle and Baila come too. Ziani doesn't. She's kissing that guy again. Markus. I guess he's cute, with a deep tan and chiseled features. But she's being reckless.

"What's Dabria's power?" I ask Vielle as we all dig into our ice creams. "It was really terrifying the way she killed that guard," I add, so that she doesn't suspect anything.

"She has power over minds," Vielle replies. " She can give such pleasure. It's a shame that she chooses mostly to inflict pain." She pops a piece of waffle into her mouth. "I annoyed her once, when we were all still at the Guild of Ladies, and I spent the next few days hating myself with such a violent passion that Baila had to handcuff me so I wouldn't act on my terrible thoughts about myself."

Horror sweeps through me. I'm going to have to get help. But how do I do that without Dabria sensing that her hold on my mind has been broken?

"Be grateful that you didn't see what she did to her guard," Baila says. "She made him snap his own bones and contort his body until it broke."

Vielle makes a face. "He gouged his own eyes out—"

"Uh, I'm trying to eat here," Nydia interjects.

"Sorry," Vielle says, chortling. She nudges me. "Try the Starlight Swirl."

I scoop a little onto my spoon then take a tentative lick. A strong licorice flavor explodes on my tongue and a flashflood of pure euphoria blazes through me. I'm distantly aware of my friends laughing as I'm caught up in an intense wave of giddy joy.

Then as suddenly as the bliss took me over, it vanishes and I realize I'm standing halfway across the room. My friends are practically crying with laughter.

"Humans are so weak," Baila says between gasps of mirth. "Just one lick had her dancing her heart out!"

"Were those Lorthien moves?" Vielle asks.

"We dance much better than that in Lorthien," Ziani calls. Then she comes over, eyeing my Starlight Swirl. "What does it taste like?" she asks.

"A mouthful of magic," Vielle purrs.

Ziani leans across the table and digs her spoon into my Starlight Swirl, taking a huge dollop. She pops it into her mouth, and her eyes widen.

I laugh with the others as she bounds around the room then dashes out the door. Markus and the other guards are laughing too. The handful of other diners cast us censuring looks but we can't help ourselves.

In all the hilarity, I almost forget the death threat hanging over my head.

6

Evening comes too quickly and I find myself standing in line with the other girls outside the hall where the Ceremony of Official Declaration is going to take place.

Everyone looks stunning, as I knew they would. They've spent all afternoon in hair and makeup. The air hums with magic, as the faerie girls are using their powers to heighten their appeal. Ivita's skin is glowing like she has molten starlight running through her veins. It's impressive, but way too much.

Vielle's use of magic is more subtle. Her large, almond-shaped eyes are only slightly brighter than usual, and her brown hair glistens with a hint of enchantment.

Among the human girls, Ziani and Seltie look particularly stunning, as they always do. I was worried that Ziani wasn't going to make any effort as Markus spent the afternoon in her chambers and only left an hour ago. But she somehow showed up on time in a stunning gold dress, her makeup flawless and her hair braided and bejeweled.

I hope the pleasure he's giving her between the sheets is worth the risk. I wish she wouldn't endanger herself, but I suppose taking lovers is her way of coping with the stress of being here and no longer being in charge of her own life.

"Ready?" Frieve asks. She's been bustling around, straightening bows, powdering noses, and sprinkling magic. The magic was reserved only for the faerie girls.

She has ignored me completely. Maybe because she's disappointed that I'm wearing gray again, have no makeup on, and am wearing my hair loose and unstyled.

"It's time," Filpé snaps from his position at the doors. Then he nods to a guard who opens them.

Filpé marches into the hall and we all file in after him. It's one of the smaller, more intimate halls in the palace. Garlands of opalescent flowers drape elegantly from dozens of stands around the room, perfuming the air. The pale walls are lit from below by floor spotlights of pink and blue.

The choosers sit in two rows at the center of the hall. The princes in the five seats on the front row, and the six nobles in the one behind them. One seat is noticeably empty. Nykolas isn't here. Jaxson isn't either, but I didn't expect him to be since he isn't allowed a human partner. A crowd of about a hundred onlookers fills the seats behind the choosers.

At the front of the hall, sixteen daises have been set up, positioned in an arc. Each is decorated with a display of flowers and glittering jewels. A lone chaise longue sits on each dais. My dais is the plainest. I asked for roses, no jewels, and a white chaise, but only because Frieve insisted I must choose something. If she hadn't, my dais would have been completely unadorned.

"Princes, ladies, and gentlemen," Filpé announces. "I am pleased to present the Guild ladies and human girls. First up is Baila Allivre."

Baila minces forward and tiny specks of light shimmer to life all around her as she sashays to a dais with a display of silver and purple flowers. Her chaise is crushed velvet with two tones: purple and silver. She lounges on it in a pose that's going to be difficult to maintain all night."

"Ivita Ruvion," Filpé announces.

Ivita steps forward, looking every inch a faerie queen in a white dress with full, wide skirts that poof out from her waist. She raises her arms elegantly and the dress explodes in a cloud of pink smoke, making my heart stutter with shock.

When the smoke clears Ivita stands there in a black leather outfit that leaves little to the imagination. I doubt she can breathe with how tight the corset is, but it does give her a slamming silhouette as a halo of golden light shimmers around her.

The crowd bursts into applause, and Ivita strikes a pose, one hand on her hip, the other flicking a whip. Handcuffs dangle from a garter around her left thigh, completing her dominatrix-inspired aesthetic, and a long black train cascades from her waist to the floor for a touch of elegance.

The room is transfixed. The choosers look ready to salivate as Ivita turns and walks toward her dais, swinging her hips from side to side like the world is her runway. As she climbs the dais steps, her display of white lilies erupts into flames. A burning petal falls to the floor and her train catches fire.

The whole room gasps as the fire rapidly eats its way up Ivita's train. Soon she's completely engulfed in flames. Then they vanish and Ivita is wearing her white dress again.

The princes lead the cheering as she sits on her chaise and crosses her legs, her charred flower display the only reminder of her sexier, naughtier side. I exchange a look with Nydia and Ziani. Ivita has turned the ceremony into the Ivita Ruvion show and the crowd, and princes, are eating it up.

It's a good thing I don't care about being chosen. I'm also kind of glad that Nykolas is absent. From the way the other princes are now whispering excitedly to each other, they're impressed. I guess any male would be.

The rest of the faerie girls are called one after another, and although they all use magic, none of them puts on a show quite as spectacular as Ivita's.

Then it's the turn of the human girls. The hall is deadly silent as each girl walks, unceremoniously, to her dais. We might not have magic but some of us will be chosen anyway, as the princes need us in order to sire heirs—boring, non-magical processions to our daises regardless.

The names are supposed to be called in alphabetical order, so I'm surprised when Filpé skips me. He calls me dead last, and I feel the sudden shift in the atmosphere as everyone looks at me. It's like the air has grown a touch colder. Or maybe it's all in my head. As I walk to my dais, I pray I won't fall flat on my face in front of them all.

The walk seems to take forever and feels somewhat like a

walk of shame. Thankfully, I make it to my dais without embarrassing myself. As I sit on the chaise, I release a breath I didn't realize I was holding.

"Princes," Filpé says, you may now approach the women.

Music begins to play and the soulful tones of a saxophone fill the air. The princes rise, and all but one make a beeline for Ivita. I watch her flick her dark hair and giggle as she chats with them all, then I look over at Nydia whose dais is next to mine. At the same moment, she looks at me. We exchange small smiles, knowing that rolling our eyes or showing even the slightest hint of displeasure will only get us into trouble.

Ziani is a few daises over and she's positioned slightly ahead of us in the arc, so I can see that she's standing, rather than sitting. Sitting must make her feel helpless.

After a good thirty minutes, the princes are all still chatting with Ivita. They only move on to other girls when Filpé announces that the nobles will be allowed to approach the daises in five minutes. The princes immediately head for the human girls they're interested in—not that it's true interest. They don't really want any of us. They just happen to need us.

Over the next five minutes, all four princes talk to Ziani and Seltie. Nydia gets two. The rest of the human girls get one. I get none.

When the nobles are permitted to approach us, the princes linger, talking to more girls, just in case they're unable to get their first choice.

I decide to go for a bathroom break. We're allowed two over the course of the evening, mostly so we can freshen up our make-up, not because Filpé cares about the fact that we might need a breather.

A guard approaches my dais as I climb down the steps and offers his hand. I take it, although I'm not wearing heels high enough to make walking down the steps treacherous. Quite frankly, I'm surprised he's dared to help me. Everyone else is acting like I don't exist.

I look up into his eyes to smile my thanks and realize it's Markus. "Hey," I say. "Thank you."

He says nothing, just bows his head, and I guess the guards aren't allowed to speak to us. Only the choosers are.

I want to dash out of the hall as fast as I can, but I force myself to take measured steps. I head around the back of my dais and through a door that we were informed leads to a backstage area. Once through it, I relax my posture.

The backstage room is small and opulent. Its white feather couches look cloud soft, and the sheer, white wall drapes are studded with twinkling diamonds.

Frieve, Filpé, and a bunch of assistants stand before a big screen. It shows a table with all the girls' names on it, and the names of males who have declared official interest in each girl in a column beneath her name.

Ziani, Ivita and Seltie have the most names. I have the least at none.

"You poor thing?" Frieve says, bustling over to me. "Prince Nykolas isn't here as he's been sent on an errand for the king and forbidden to attend. If I'd known, I would have forced you to present yourself better so that a few males would drift your way and you wouldn't be left sitting alone on your dais looking so forlorn."

Forlorn?

"I'm fine, Frieve," I reply. "But thanks. Where's the restroom?"

She points to a door nestled between the wall drapes and I stride toward it, eager for a moment alone.

I exhale as I step inside. Then I look in the mirror. I look tired. More than tired. Completely fatigued.

I did only escape the dungeons of Lorthien this morning, after three days of being battered and abused. Nykolas took care of my injuries, healed every last one of them, but I'm far from okay.

I can't believe I've been back for less than twenty-four hours. So much has happened and I haven't had a moment to catch my breath.

Now that I'm alone, Dabria's magic whispers through my mind with an urgent intensity, subduing every trace of light and hope. I stare at my reflection as though seeing myself for the first time, taking in every flaw and imperfection that I usually pay no attention.

There are worry-lines at the corners of my eyes, etched by a lifetime of uncertainty and unrest as Kali and I were passed from one foster home to another. A small, faded scar stands out on the left side of my chin, a souvenir from the first night I went thieving and cut my hands and chin on the barbed wire atop the fence surrounding the wealthy home I targeted. My short eyelashes, unremarkable features, dull brown skin.

The bright lights over the mirrors don't help. They magnify every fault and blemish, and I can't help wondering what Nykolas sees in me.

I'm hideous!

Voices whisper through my head, too quiet for me to decipher their words, but as loathing swells in my heart, I suspect there's a level at which I do know what they're saying—subconsciously.

The longer I gaze at myself, the more imperfections I see, and the deeper the roots of my disgust sink into my heart.

With a yell that doesn't even sound like me, I slam my fists against the mirror. Pain bursts through my hands as shards of glass tear through my skin.

I don't register what I've done until Frieve and a bunch of other faerie women swarm into the restroom. Immediately, the voices in my head cease and the hatred I felt for myself vanishes. I stare at my bloody fists in horror, and then the broken pieces of mirror all around me.

The women begin to scold me, but Frieve just hurries me out of the bathroom. "We don't have time for rebukes right now," she says. "But tomorrow, you will explain to me exactly why you decided to vandalize palace property."

I can*not* believe what I just did. "I'm so sorry—"

"Hush," Frieve snaps. "Just get back to your dais immediately."

As I go, I sense her magic on my hands, and the blood and cuts vanish. My heart is palpitating as I enter the hall once again. It dawns on me just how vulnerable I am, and just how thin the line between sanity and a complete loss of control is. I can't let whatever Dabria did to me affect me this way. I'll have to be careful about being alone. And when I inevitably find myself alone, I'm going to have to be stronger.

I climb back onto my dais and sit on my chaise, hoping I don't look as shaken as I feel. It's not only the princes and nobles circulating among the daises now, other eligible males are too—the randy dukes Filpé warned us about included. They're obvious from the way they leer at the girls they're talking to, eyes gobbling them up.

I'm mortified when an elderly duke with a shock of wild, gray hair hobbles toward my dais, winking at me. Faeries don't age at the same rate as humans, so the fact that he *looks* old means he must be ancient—like a couple of millennia old!

"I can absolutely see why all common sense seems to have deserted Prince Nykolas ever since he met you," the man says. Half the buttons of his navy blue satin shirt are undone, revealing gray chest hairs, and his shiny black trousers are way too tight. "Seeing as he isn't here and you're not wearing any of his rubies, I wonder if you're back on the market. You could join my harem in time for my seven thousandth birthday next month. It's quite a milestone. I've lived seven thousand years of incredibly wondrous pleasure, and I could teach you a thing or two about the deepest intimate delights—"

The doors to the hall burst open just then, saving me from having to respond, and a blast of fanfare precedes the appearance of a messenger dressed from head to toe in scarlet finery. I recognize him as Nykolas's personal messenger. My heart skips a beat as he marches through the hall. It looks like he's heading in my direction.

The fanfare ceases when he reaches my dais. "A message from Prince Nykolas," he booms into the ensuing silence at the top of his voice. "I, Crown Prince Nykolas of Eraeon, wish to declare my official interest in Miss Riva Myra Kadiri of Lorthien, Prysha. I desire her alone, and I overrule any others who might have declared interest in her."

The six-thousand-nine-hundred-and-ninety-nine-year-old scowls and hobbles away.

Nykolas's messenger isn't done. "I present Miss Kadiri with this gift." A ruby necklace appears from thin air in his hands, each stone a deep alluring red, cut to precision. The messenger holds it up for the whole hall to see. The facets of each ruby catch the ambient light, creating a mesmerizing dance of crimson hues that seem to come alive in his hands. "It is a token of my affection, and a symbol of the eternal bond I seek to forge with her."

The expressions on the faces of the faeries in the hall range from bewilderment to shock. I guess nobody dares show outright anger.

I'm as bewildered as anyone else. Among the human girls there are beauties such as Ziani and Seltie, yet I am the one who has snagged the prize. I have no idea how, and it doesn't make me feel good. I only feel inadequate and unworthy. As Nykolas's messenger climbs up the dais, still holding the necklace aloft for all to see, I wish the floor would open and swallow me.

I realize that Frieve is at the steps to my dais, waving to catch my attention. She gestures for me to bow.

"Nykolas's messenger represents Nykolas himself," she whispers just loudly enough for me to hear.

I rise from the chaise and bow low. Then I glance at Frieve. She's gesturing for me to rise onto my knees. I obey.

Then Frieve comes to hold my hair out of the way as Nykolas's messenger places the stunning necklace around my neck and fastens the clasp. It's incredibly heavy and I don't even dare imagine how much it would cost in rhones.

Fanfare rings out once again as the messenger performs an abrupt about-turn then marches out of the hall. Only when the doors shut after him do people begin to talk again.

As I rise from my knees, a transparent blue bubble sparkles to life around me, shielding me from the rest of the hall.

"One more item is being cut for you," comes Nykolas's velvet deep voice, filling the bubble. "I apologize that they were not all ready at the same time. I only placed the order this morning and the royal jeweler has been working on the pieces ever since."

I'm not sure what to say, so I say nothing.

"I'm sorry I couldn't be there," Nykolas adds. "I'm...stuck in meetings."

"I know you were forbidden to come, Nykolas." I sigh. "You can dress me in rubies from head to toe, but it won't matter. King Xander isn't going to let me be anything more than a womb that carries your child."

"Once I am king, I will call the shots, not him. You will be my queen."

"Didn't you say that you run the risk of starting a civil war if you crown me?"

"Everyone just needs to get to know you," Nykolas insists. "Once they do, they'll fall in love with you as much as I have. We just have to take it one step at a time. The first step is officially declaring my intention to choose you. The next step is actually choosing you, which I will do at the ceremony next week. Then, we'll work on everyone accepting you."

I sigh. He really seems to think it's going to be that simple. He has no idea how adamantly his people, and even his own mother, oppose our relationship.

The sooner I can get out of here the better.

"Are you okay?" comes Nykolas's voice. "You sound kind of glum."

I stare at my hands. They were dripping with blood just a few minutes ago. The longer I stay in Eraeon, the less chance I have of leaving unscathed, and with my sanity intact.

"Are all the formalities draining you?" Nykolas asks. "You can leave, you know? Tell them I said so."

"Yeah, and let them hate me even more." I sigh. "Things really are very formal here. It's one ceremony after another."

"What are the courtship rituals of Rithelia?"

I roll my eyes. "We don't call them courtship rituals, but when you have a suitor, he or she gives you a bracelet to show that you're about to be taken. After you wed, he or she gives you a charm for your bracelet to show that you *are* taken."

"Interesting." Nykolas pauses. "And a little dull."

"Excuse me?"

Nykolas's rolling laughter fills the bubble. "I have to go now, but I hope to be back soon. I love you."

I bite my lip. If I'm to break up with him, I should stop telling him I love him.

"Riva?"

"Yes?"

"I have to go now," he repeats. He thinks I didn't hear him the first time. "I love you."

"I...love you, too."

The bubble vanishes and I cover my face with my hands, grimacing.

A bloodcurdling scream across the hall has me jerking my head up, hands falling away from my face.

Panic flashes through me and my blood curdles at the sight of a head on the floor, jaw-length auburn hair splayed around it, and eyes frozen in a glassy stare. It's Keyta, one of the human girls. Her body lies a foot away, by her dais. A faerie noble wipes his bloodstained sword on her pretty, lilac dress then sheaths it.

Filpé comes running through the crowd. "Whatever is the matter?" he demands. "Who did this, and why?"

"Drynne and I both want her," the faerie with the sword says, nodding to another male. "Instead of fighting over her, we agreed to kill her so neither of us can have her."

I stare at him in shock.

What?

7

Faeries have gathered around Filpé, the murderer, and Keyta's head and body. Every Guild and human girl is on her feet on her dais. I remain seated. I've witnessed many horrors over the past couple of days and I don't want to fill my head with any more.

Filpé sighs in exasperation. "Gentlemen, there are protocols to follow. You don't just take the law into your own hands and kill a human girl. We only have ten of them, remember? Can someone come and clean up this mess, please?"

Two stewards hurry over, one with a body bag and the other with a disinfectant spray and a mop.

I wait for the faeries who agreed to murder Keyta to be punished. They sentenced her to death for no reason at all other than their petty desire to have her and refusal to give in to the other.

But the crowd of faeries disperses, and they all get back

to their conversations as though what they just witnessed is no big deal—just a passing, mildly interesting, side attraction.

All the human girls are still standing, their faces drawn with fear. Seltie's face has gone as pale as the pearl walls. Even the faerie girls look aghast, and I know they're wondering if Keyta's death has been treated with such offhand callousness because she's human or because she's up for choosing.

Within five seconds, there's no evidence of what happened. Every hint of Keyta's existence is wiped clean. Her dais even vanishes. Then the rest of the daises, shuffle slightly, moved by magic, so that her space is gone. The steward with the mop sprays a floral scent that immediately pervades the room, overwhelming the smell of blood that was beginning to spread.

I never particularly liked Keyta, but what just happened is abominable. She didn't deserve to die. She did absolutely nothing wrong!

The weight of the faeries' mercilessness settles heavily on me, and a profound sense of disquiet grips my heart. Why must I and the other human girls contend with so much hatred? Whatever might be going on between King Bastien and King Xander is nothing to do with us. The young women of Lorthien didn't steal the faeries' immortality, but we are the ones paying the price for it.

Another scream brings the hall to a standstill. It's Emy. I realize it was her who screamed the first time, too. Emy, having been tortured way more than the rest of us, is much more fragile. She's shaking uncontrollably, and her low cut dress reveals just how hard her pulse is beating.

The way the crowd of faeries look at her, it's as though her scream is the true crime, not what the two faerie males did to Keyta.

"Silence," a random male scolds.

Emy quickly clamps her mouth shut and plops herself down on her chaise. But she's still shaking uncontrollably.

I don't dare glance at Nydia or Ziani. Tears are threatening and the last thing I should do right now is cry.

The faeries continue to mingle. I watch males approach Seltie and other girls, expecting them to pick right up where they left off and have the presence of mind to carry on flirting.

Emy lets out yet another shrill scream and I look over. A faerie male has approached her and she's clearly terrified. When he leans forward, smiling placatingly, she scoots backward on her chaise, her eyes terror-stricken.

The faerie male's smile fades and his eyes harden.

Filpé hurries over. "Quiet, Emy!" His voice is laced with threat.

But Emy is frantic. She recoils when the faerie male holds out a hand to her and slaps it away.

Gasps fill the hall. Suddenly the air is charged with tension. A hushed murmur ripples through the onlookers. I sense the burst of crackling, electric magic a split second before the faerie male beams white light from his eyes that strike Emy in the chest. Her body convulses uncontrollably then she stills on her chaise, two smoking holes in her bosom.

Filpé sighs. "She was just too weak," he mutters into the ensuing silence. It's an apology to the faerie male for having to endure being rejected buy a human girl, and an apology to the rest of the faeries for having to witness that rejection.

"Is this some kind of joke?"

Every eye turns to the human girl in the booth next to Keyta's. Her name is Tiona, and the only time I've ever spoken to her was the night Nykolas did blood rituals. "They get to just murder us like it's nothing?" she demands, glaring at Filpé. "No repercussions?"

The words have barely left her lips when she's hit with magic from all over the room as numerous faeries unleash their fury. She falls to the floor, blood gushing from her mouth. Silenced forever.

"Do any of the rest of you have anything to say?" asks a male dressed in opulent, multicolored robes. I realize it's Prince Jiorge. I hadn't realized he was here.

None of the human girls dares to speak. Prince Jiorge looks at Cardice, Tiona's friend, and I realize it's because while the rest of us are doing all within our power to stuff down our anger and fear, her rage shines clear as day in her eyes.

"Do you want to say something?" Prince Jiorge asks her. "Do feel free."

She says nothing, but the 'fuck you' in her eyes is obvious. Darna, Tiona's other friend, is trembling so hard, her mahogany curls are fluttering.

Once again, conversations resume as Tiona's body is collected and her dais vanishes. The ceremony was supposed to continue for an hour longer, but five minutes later, Frieve comes to close it, saying everyone has declared their intentions so there's no need to continue.

I think she just wants to get us all out of here before any more of us die, and I'm grateful that at least one faerie cares—even if it's only because she can't afford for too many of us to die when the royals so desperately need help with having offspring.

"Whore!" a voice cries as guards help us off our daises.

The crowd of faeries parts as a prince strides froward. He's tall and broad and dark, with a handsome face that is somehow completely unattractive. I realize he's glaring at Ziani, and my blood turns to ice.

"I've heard rumors of you consorting with various males," the prince bellows. "That guard included. How dare you!"

The guard helping Ziani down her dais steps is Markus. My heart begins to pound out an erratic rhythm.

She's going to die.

I don't want to look, but I can't help myself.

I expect Ziani to throw caution to the wind and give the prince the middle finger. Maybe even gather her skirts and moon the whole hall so that she dies insulting them. But she isn't quite that reckless. The wide-eyed look she gives the prince is the picture of pure innocence.

"This is untrue, Your Highness," she says. She looks up at Markus as though she's never set eyes on him before. "I would never do such a thing. I was very circumspect in my former life in Lorthien and I am even more so now. I happen to be a virgin. Furthermore, I do not take the interest of four princes of Eraeon lightly and I would never do anything to jeopardize such good fortune."

She must sound suitably self-abasing as another prince claps the accuser on his shoulder. "She's innocent," he says. "I've heard the rumors too, but they're not true." He nods to Markus. "Look at him. Why would she be interested in that when she knows she could have one of us."

Of all the self-aggrandizing things I've ever heard!

Throughout the exchange, Markus's face is inscrutable—devoid of even a hint of emotion.

I exhale when the princes walk away and Markus guides Ziani down the rest of the stairs then releases her hand and steps away from her.

I follow Frieve and the rest of the girls out of the hall, desperate to get away. None of us dares to speak as Frieve leads us through vast corridors and soaring archways, heading toward our chambers. The beauty of the palace seems cold and unforgiving all of a sudden. All the red decor reminds me of blood. The iridescent, pearl walls make me think of white-washed mausoleums. The fluttering wall silks are like ghosts, taunting us with their dance as they bide their time until they can consume our souls.

We might as well be locked in a cage with lions for how safe we are. We're all going to die. Every last one of us. None of us is going to survive very long here unless things change —which they won't.

At the door to our quarters, Frieve stops. She doesn't meet any of our gazes and I think she feels bad for us. "Go to your rooms," she says. "Change your clothes and rest for twenty minutes, then report to the dining room. We will debrief over dinner."

Nobody responds. We all just head to our rooms.

∼

THE LAST THING I want to do, twenty minutes later, is leave my room. But I must. I wear Nykolas's necklace and earrings. Whatever it takes to stay safe.

Six of the girls are waiting in the circular hallway outside our rooms, including Ziani and Nydia.

"We figured it might be safer to all walk together," says Lilise, a girl with wide blue eyes and jet black curls.

"Should we knock for the others?" I ask.

"We think they've already gone," says Darna, a girl with big, gravity defying hair and creamy brown skin.

We're probably no safer walking together, but we feel better for it. We make our way through the palace in silence and avoid locking eyes with any faeries.

When we reach the dining room, a sumptuous feast is set out. They've always fed us well here—or so I thought until I dined with Nykolas one night. Tonight's fare is better than usual and I realize it's because the faerie girls are dining with us. Usually, they dine separately.

There's a separate table set up for them across the room. It's set with cream and gold while our tablecloth is white lace—pretty, but theirs is prettier. They must remind us at every turn that they consider us inferior. Less worthy.

The faerie girls have clearly gotten over Keyta's, Emy's, and Tiona's deaths. They chat as usual as they pile their dishes high with roast potatoes, tender meats, baked fish in a lemon cream sauce, coconut-glazed vegetables, and more.

As hungry as I am, I know I won't be able to eat. Not with the coppery tang of blood still thick in my nose and bile churning in my belly. None of the human girls bother to eat except Lilise, who picks at a salad. Ziani serves herself a bowl of vegetable soup but just sits there, swirling her spoon through it.

Frieve arrives as all the faerie girls sit at their separate table across the room. "Is everyone here?" she asks.

My gaze drifts to Keyta's, Emy's and Tiona's empty seats. No dishes or cutlery was set out for them. No crystal goblet or napkin.

They're gone.

"Who sits there?" Frieve asks, nodding to a fourth empty seat where dishes and cutlery have been set out.

"Cardice," Nydia supplies.

She was pretty close to Tiona. She'll be freaking out in her room after watching her so brutally killed. We're all freaking out, but we're not allowed to show it. I glance at Darna. She's still trembling, and her dark eyes are red-rimmed.

"We'll give her a few moments to join us," Frieve says. "While we wait, look at the names of those who have declared official interest in you. If you have more than one, please circle the name of the chooser you would prefer.

"The final decision will not be yours. For the human girls especially, you are not allowed to reject a faerie. However, I will take your preference into account when Filpé and I are making the final decisions."

Single pieces of paper materialize from thin air before each of us, along with a pen. I glance over at the faerie girls. They have papers and pens too. As expected, my paper has just one name on it: *Nykolas Astoria, Crown Prince.*

I have no circling to do.

Ziani does, but she's just staring unseeingly at the list of names before her. Seltie, who still looks pretty pale, has already circled a name.

When everyone is done, Frieve begins to explain the process that she and Filpé will use to decide which prince should get which girl when multiple princes are interested in her.

She isn't making eye contact with any of us humans, and she hasn't said anything about us not eating. After a while, she pauses. "Where *is* Cardice?"

"Maybe she's run away," Ziani says. "We all would, if we could."

Frieve ignores her. "I can't locate her with my magic, but I'm pretty spent after expending so much of my energies today. Someone will have to go get her."

Darna begins to rise, but Frieve shakes her head. "Riva, do you mind going?"

I think she's chosen me because Nykolas's rubies will protect me as I walk alone through the palace.

I leave the dining room and make the long trek back to the human girls' quarters. Cardice's room is the one opposite Nydia's. I knock on the door. When there's no response I try the handle. The door is unlocked. I cautiously push it open.

Cardice's lounge door is open. The room is decorated

similarly to mine, but in peach and white, while mine is cream and gold. There's nobody inside

"Cardice?" I call, approaching her bedroom door.

I knock softly. There's no response.

A sense of foreboding tightens my chest as I remember the look of anger and disdain she gave Prince Jiorge not quite an hour ago. She was probably snatched on her way to dinner. She could be in the dungeon torture center right now. Or worse.

"Cardice," I call again, opening the door to her bedroom.

The dim glow of faerie lamps casts long shadows throughout the room. There's something on the bed. I frown, stepping closer, then I let out a cry of horror.

They didn't take her to the torture chamber. They killed her right here in her room.

An arm lies at the foot of the bed. A finger by the headboard. A pile of internal organs on the dresser.

I stumble backward, letting out another cry. As I dash toward the door I trip over a foot.

This is your fault, a dark voice whispers to me.

Guilt sours my stomach. This time, it isn't Dabria's psychological warfare trying to make me hate myself. It's true. The whole palace is seething with rage at me, but they don't dare hurt me, so they're taking their anger out on the other human girls for the slightest of offenses.

Today wasn't the first time Emy has screamed. Cardice isn't the first of us to scowl at a faerie. But after I got a faerie killed this morning and was honored by their Crown Prince, their patience with us has worn thin.

When I report back to Frieve, she's quiet for a moment,

as are all the girls. Then Frieve straightens and briskly continues her lecture about how girls will be matched to choosers.

I don't hear a thing.

~

OUR FIRST NIGHT IN ERAEON, Frieve told us we're not allowed in each other's rooms, but tonight, Ziani and Nydia insist on sleeping in my room.

"We're not safe in our chambers," Ziani says. "We could get attacked in our sleep. Nobody will dare to come into your room, though, since Prince Nykolas has made his interest in you official. We're staying with you."

Ha! If only they knew. I have a death threat hanging over my head from none other than Queen Tarla. But it's nice to have company.

The three of us change out of our gowns then get into my bed, which is big enough to sleep five. I turn out the lights, and we lie there in the darkness, silent.

The evil voices are back, whispering to one another in my head, but with my friends here, it isn't as disturbing as when I'm alone, and I find I care less.

I hope Ziani and Nydia sleep soon, as I have a midnight meeting to get to. But I already know that none of the human girls will sleep much tonight.

The soft chiming of the hallway clock filters into the room. Ten p.m. I'm wondering how I'm going to sneak out without Ziani and Nydia noticing when Ziani speaks. "They kidnap girls from Lorthien because humans stole their immortality. They're not immortal anymore. They've begun to die."

"How do you know?" I ask.

"Camran told me. I don't know if I believe him."

I sigh. "Nykolas told me the same thing."

"I'm inclined to believe them," Nydia says.

"Why?" Ziani's tone is sharp.

"Remember what Riva told us about how King Bastien treated her. He tried to have her killed before she could tell anyone else. He's hiding something."

I close my eyes as Ziani and Nydia discuss it, too weary to entertain such a heavy topic tonight. So many girls snatched from their lives. So many broken-hearted people who loved them, grieving the loss of their daughters, sisters, friends, lovers.

The enmity between humans and faeries began before even my unknown grandparents were born. The faeries who were alive then are still alive now, continuing the animosity, but that generation of humans is gone, so why must this generation continue to suffer the consequences?

"To think you willingly came back to this nightmare, Riva," Ziani says. "What were you thinking?"

I was thinking of Kali, so I don't feel foolish for returning.

"You've been talking to Camran?" I ask her. They must have been talking quite a lot for him to tell her about faeries losing their immortality.

"Not just talking to him," Nydia says with a snort.

"I haven't slept with him," Ziani protests. Then she adds, a tad sheepishly, "It's been just a few kisses."

"I can't believe you announced, before, that you're a

virgin," I say. I would laugh if my heart wasn't so heavy from what I saw in Cardice's room tonight, and from what was done to Keyta, Emy and Tiona. "That was dangerous, Ziani. What if they used magic to check if it's true?"

Ziani lets out a cackle. "I had Markus use his magic to make it look like I am. Don't you worry about me. I cover my tracks well."

"Not well enough if rumors are flying around the palace about you."

"Yeah," Nydia agrees. "You need to stop seeing them, Ziani. You could have died tonight."

"Well, I didn't, did I?"

"But that was a close shave," Nydia says. "You have to be more careful."

Ziani sighs. "I might stop seeing Markus and the others, but Camran and I mostly just talk."

Something about her tone makes me frown. "You actually like Camran?"

"He's sweet, not like all the other brutes in this place. Markus is too, but a boring kind of sweet that makes things feel pretty dull after a while. Camran is sweet but interesting."

"Well, you need to survive long enough to escape this place, so who cares?" Nydia says. "You need to stop seeing them all—Camran included."

Ziani says nothing and silence thickens the darkness.

I'm thankful for the space to think. How am I going to get out of here at midnight without raising their suspicion?

"I don't feel too good," I say into the silence.

"What a surprise," Ziani quips. "You only watched three

girls get murdered in cold blood, then walked in on a fourth that'd been butchered in her bedroom. Now, I wonder why you don't feel too good."

Over the next hour and a half, I make frequent trips to the bathroom feigning a turning stomach. Ziani and Nydia don't question me when, at twenty minutes to midnight I say I'm going to the palace infirmary.

"Do you want us to come with you?" Nydia offers. "Whatever they did to Emy after her whipping clearly didn't help."

"No, you try to get some sleep. I'll be fine."

"I wouldn't go to the infirmary if I were you," Ziani says. "I wouldn't trust them to actually look after me. They could slip poison into your IV so that Nykolas can't choose you."

"Thanks for that," I mutter. But it isn't far-fetched after what Filpé did two weeks ago, poisoning our breakfast to see if any males cared about us enough to heal us.

I've been in the infirmary once though and emerged unscathed. I don't remember any of it as I was completely out of it after being overwhelmed by Jaxson's magic.

"I hate this place," I whisper, rising from the bed.

"That makes two of us," Ziani mutters.

"Three," Nydia adds.

I move around in the darkness, throwing a gray dress on over my nightclothes, and digging my feet into shoes.

"Wear your necklace," Ziani says.

"Good thinking." I grab the ruby necklace then leave the room. As I head to the door, I look at the note again.

Come to the whispering gardens at midnight.

P.S. No matter what we lose...

You have me and I have you, I say in my mind, completing the sentence.

This could be a trap, but with how much danger I'm already in, I'm willing to take my chances.

The door to my chambers whispers open silently. I've fooled my friends. Now, I just need to make it to the whispering gardens without any trouble.

8

The palace is eerily still. Not a whisper stirs the air. Hallways that pulsate with activity during the day are shrouded with an unsettling silence that seems to permeate the whole building.

Our first night here, Frieve told us not to leave our rooms at night. It must be dangerous. I can just imagine the kind of trouble I would get into if I were spotted. I touch the cool rubies resting around my throat. They should protect me.

Jaxson, I think, heading down one of the main hallways. The lights have been lowered to a secretive dimness that casts murky shadows into alcoves and corners. The lights in the smaller hallways and corridors have been switched off altogether.

Jaxson, I think again, more urgently this time. There's no response. Maybe he's sleeping.

I linger at a vast hallway window, since I don't actually know where I'm going. I appreciate the dimmer lighting. If someone were to come, I could leap into the shadows cast by one of the hallway pillars.

I can see nothing through the window. The heavy darkness of night presses against the glass, turning it reflective. My own face stares back at me, and I draw my gaze away, afraid to look at my reflection after what happened in the bathroom earlier.

After waiting a few moments with no response from Jaxson, panic sets in. Instead of depending on him, I should have tried to find out where the whispering gardens are myself. For all I know, they could be an hour away on the other side of the palace, or miles away on the other side of the island.

But that's all the more reason why I figured I would need Jaxson's help. He can transport me with his magic.

Jaxson, I yell internally.

Whatever is Nykolas's sweetheart screaming my name for in the dead of night?

I find myself smiling. I can't pinpoint exactly when the dark timber of Jaxson's voice rolling through my head became something that feels...natural; comforting even.

You sound a little faint, I think in response. *Is that because you're half asleep? I didn't have you pegged as much of a sleeper. I imagined you as a creature of the night, stalking the darkness until the small hours, before finally turning in at say three a.m.*

Interesting. Well, I sound distant because I'm on a mission in Lorthien with your dear, delightful Prince Nykolas.

We both know he isn't mine and never will be. What are you guys doing in Lorthien?

Slaughtering humans and drinking their blood.

Drinking blood? That's vampires not faeries.

Ah, you know your supernatural creatures.

That's basic 101 stuff. Do you consider yourself supernatural?

No, we consider ourselves natural, but we know that humans consider us supernatural.

And what do you consider humans?

Most faeries consider them a lower, less powerful version of us.

So subnatural?

Your words not mine. There are faeries who consider humans to be equals. Just different.

I haven't met those faeries yet. What are you really doing in Lorthien?

Okay, we're slaughtering humans in their beds, but leaving their blood in their bodies for our vampire friends to drink if they so wish.

He isn't joking. This must be the errand that King Xander sent Nykolas on, too. In fact, Nykolas will be leading it, seeing as he's Supreme Commander of the military.

Is this in retaliation for the attack on Eraeon? I demand, my hands curling into fists at my sides. *That's hardly fair or noble. You're murdering innocent citizens when it's the king and the army you ought to fight.*

All's fair in love and war. Tell me, would the human armies have targeted only the king and our soldiers if they'd gotten into Eraeon the day they made their feeble attempt to attack us? No, they would have wiped out as many citizens as they could. Now, I need to raze a whole apartment building to the ground with my powers, so if you have called on me for a reason, get to it.

"No," I whisper. *Don't do it, Jaxson.*

I feel the faint brush of what feels like hot hands. Jaxson has remote touch. I knew that, but realize he could still do it from such a great distan uncurls my clenched fists. *Tell me why you called on me,* says.

Pleading with him will be futile. He will have to obey the command of his king and kill. Emotion clogs my throat and I force myself to focus on what I came to Eraeon to do. I can't stop the army and prevent the loss of lives, but maybe I can save Kali. *I need to get to the whispering gardens.*

What? The exclamation is pretty loud in my head and I'm glad Jaxson is all the way in Lorthien otherwise it would have been a deafening shout.

Why are you going there? he demands.

To meet someone. It's in connection with my sister.

Uh huh. He sounds like he doesn't believe me. *Just...don't get caught.*

I won't if you use your power to transport me there.

Are you fucking serious? Why would I do that?

Like I said, it's in connection with my sister.

You can stop saying that. I'm not judging you, okay?

No, it really is. I picture the note I received, and Jaxson falls silent as, presumably, he sees it in my mind and reads it. Then I explain the P.S.

Oh, Jaxson says. *You know nothing about the whispering gardens, do you?*

It's a garden?

His dark laughter rolls through my head. *You, sweet Riva Kadiri, are in for a big surprise.*

Before I can ask what exactly goes on at the whispering

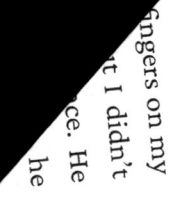

...ling takes over my body. Then dark... universe seems to shift and sway, ...nd me unravels and I'm outside, ...obblestone path in a garden of tall ...d of me stands a line of trees on the ...o which the cobblestone path ...appears.

I glance back and see the palace in the distance. The whispering gardens are on its grounds.

A breeze drifts by and I immediately understand why they're called the whispering gardens. The tall grasses rustle in the breeze, creating a whispering sound like hundreds of people murmuring under their breath.

Your meeting will probably be in the woods, Jaxson tells me.

Thanks.

I sense that he's about to slip out of my mind.

Wait, I say. *Spare Mug Shot, Jaxson. Don't hurt Shearne or her family.*

There's a brief pause, then Jaxson's voice fills my head. *Okay.*

Make sure nobody else goes anywhere near them either. Or ruins their business. That's their livelihood. Tell Nykolas to command it.

Very well. Is there anybody you do *want me to kill in cold blood?*

No! I don't want you to kill anyone. I want you guys out of my city!

Not even some high school bully or ex-boyfriend who dumped you? I could be your personal pet monster, you know? Unleashing my fury on all who have ever hurt you.

No!

So noble, Riva. Enjoy the whispering gardens. Stay out of the clearings in the woods or they'll think you're game. Next time you're going, invite me along and I'll meet you there. Show you a good time.

The weight of his presence vanishes from my mind and I step cautiously toward the woods. I remove Nykolas's rubies, sensing that I won't want to call attention to myself here. If I get into any danger, I can quickly put them back on again.

As soon as I pass the line of trees, the darkness seems to grow thicker. Magic hums in the woods so strong that the air feels almost effervescent. It tingles against my face.

The place is alive with a symphony of nocturnal creatures, their calls weaving through the cool air. The rustle of leaves are a constant stream of whispers that create an eerie yet captivating atmosphere in the velvety darkness.

At the first clearing I come to, I pause. Moonlight spills through the gap created by the brief absence of trees, revealing at least ten people intertwined in a tangled pile of heaving bodies and splayed limbs. Curiously, I can't make out their faces, even though I can see them.

For a moment, I'm confused as to what is happening. Then I suck in a sharp breath as I realize.

Instantly, I think of Ziani and what she said about having participated in orgies before. I have no idea if she was just fooling around, but I'm not going to tell her about these whispering woods. Ziani would get herself into all kinds of trouble here every night.

One of the people steps away from the others and holds

out a hand in invitation to me. I can't see their face but I know they're male from a glance below their waist. No wonder Jaxson said to stay away from the clearings.

Right now, anything that could distract me from the horrors of today is appealing, but my answer to the faerie's invitation is...no.

Cheeks burning, I hurry past, stumbling over twigs and stones in the thick underbrush.

At the next clearing, a couple is making out against a tree, her legs wrapped around his waist. She lets out soft moans as he slides in an out of her in a sultry rhythm that makes my heart pound.

Once again, their faces are oddly concealed, and I realize the tingling magic against my face must be concealing my features too. I'm anonymous in here. I could do anything with anyone and nobody would ever find out.

The couple falls to the ground, still matching one another's rhythm, his hands grabbing at her breasts, her nails digging into his back.

Jaxson's words swirl through my mind. *Next time you're going, invite me and I'll meet you there. Show you a good time.*

Is this what he meant? If so, I guess he was just taunting me.

And if he was serious?

I push that thought out of my mind. I have Nykolas.

Actually, you don't, I remind myself. Besides, I did want Jaxson before I ever met Nykolas.

Sordid images fill my mind. Wild thoughts of Jaxson. And I curse him for the words that have triggered them.

"No," I whisper, shaking my head.

As I pass the next few clearings, I don't check to see what is happening in them.

I'm wondering how to find whoever I'm here to meet when a tall male, naked except for a loin cloth, emerges from the dense darkness and steps into my path. "Starlight whispers, sing this song?"

I stare at him blankly. After a moment, he slinks back into the shadows and I realize it was a code. I didn't know the rest of it so he knew I wasn't the woman he was waiting for.

Two minutes later I'm stopped again. This time by a female in a slinky red dress. "Shall I burn the night and gild the stars?"

"Sorry, I'm not her," I mutter, stepping around her.

Then a voice up ahead calls, "No matter what we lose..."

The voice is male, and for a moment, I wonder if it's a trap. Have I been lured here by some faerie male who wants to take advantage of me?

But how would he know what Kali and I used to say to each other? Nobody but she and I know about it. So I hurry onward, and call out, "You have me and I have you."

A male steps out from among the trees. He's the first person in here whose face I can see. The tingling on my face remains, but it wanes slightly and I guess that others still can't see me, but he can.

The faerie is tall and stunningly handsome, with amber eyes that make me think of firelight, and full sensuous lips. His skin is honey-gold, and tousled black hair crowns his head.

Suddenly, I have the reckless thought that I wouldn't

mind if this was a trap. In fact, I would happily trap him and take him to one of the clearings. Then I give myself a mental shake. "Who are you?" I ask sharply.

He hands me a small, folded piece of paper then vanishes into thin air.

Frustration crackles in my chest. I'd hoped I would be meeting with Kali herself, but maybe she doesn't dare come to the palace. I can't say I blame her.

I unfold the note, but in the heavy darkness I can't make out the words written on it.

I retrace my steps, hurrying back through the woods and gardens. As soon as I reach the palace, I push through the doors and look eagerly at the note.

6 Achlys Drive
Red Heavens Midnight
P.S. I have you.

The first line is obviously an address, but I've no idea what or where Red Heavens Midnight is.

The P.S. makes me smile. Kali is clearly still as sassy as ever, omitting the 'you have me' part. I don't have her loyalty or affection the same way as she has mine, and we both know it. I want to think that had I been the one snatched by faeries she would have come to rescue me, but I'm not sure the thought would even cross her mind. She would mourn, and she would definitely miss me, but she wouldn't risk her life to find me. I guess it comes with the territory of being the older one. I've always felt responsible for her.

Footsteps in an adjacent corridor have me quickly donning my rubies, but the door to this hallway doesn't open, and the steps fade. As I hurry back toward my chambers, I piece together what tonight has told me about Kali.

First of all, she knows about the whispering gardens. Trust her to know of such a place. I'm not sure if she would join in with something like what I saw in that first clearing, but who knows? She was always pretty adventurous and had a revolving door of boyfriends. With faerie males being so easy on the eyes, she might not have been able to resist.

Secondly, she has faeries working with her—including some who can get in and out of the palace without raising eyebrows.

I need to find out where 6 Achlys Drive is and how to get there. I won't rely on Jaxson this time, in case I can't get hold of him. I'm under no illusion that it's going to be easy, though. Sneaking out to the palace grounds is one thing, but getting beyond the gates will be almost impossible. And after the Rithelian attack on Eraeon, palace security will be tighter than ever.

I'm almost at the human quarters when I slam into an invisible barrier. I'm thrown backward but manage to catch myself before I fall. I rub my forehead where I hit it, then reach out. There's absolutely nothing in front of me, but my hand rests on something that feels like a brick wall.

I glance over my shoulder and almost jump with fright at the sight of Dabria standing behind me.

9

I look around the hallway. It's empty. I'm completely alone with Dabria. And knowing that faeries can kill human girls with no repercussions, I'm even more afraid of her than I was this morning.

I'm wearing Nykolas's rubies, I remind myself. But suddenly, I realize they're no protection since Dabria has the queen on her side. She only needs to claim that my death was an accident and any punishment Nykolas might want to dole out would be overruled by the queen. Or maybe she'll frame someone else, just like she framed her guard. That way, Nykolas will still marry her, unaware that it was her who killed me.

"Nice necklace," Dabria says lightly. "I heard all about how it was presented to you."

"I haven't seen Nykolas since you and I talked this morning," I tell her. "I haven't had a chance to speak to him, but I will."

"The queen gave you four days, of which only three are

now left, but I doubt I can tolerate your presence for that long. Break up with him and be gone before my patience runs out."

Before I can reply, a blue-rimmed portal opens beside her, and she vanishes through it. This time, when I try to continue on my way, the invisible barrier is gone.

~

"Where did you go?" Nydia asks when I get back to my bedroom. "And why are you shaking?"

The lights in the room are on, and Nydia and Ziani are sitting up in bed. I mumble something about the infirmary and not feeling too great.

Nydia narrows her eyes. "We just went to the infirmary to check on you and almost got dragged off for a night of sin by a bunch of guards."

Great. I'm busted.

"Riva, you sneaky wench," Ziani says with a cackle. "Nykolas is away so you couldn't have gone to see him. Was it Jaxson?"

"Of course not," I say, even as warmth floods my whole face. "He's away, too."

"Well, who was it?"

"Nobody."

But Ziani will not be fobbed off. She hounds me until I give in and tell them about my search for Kali.

It took Shearne, my only friend back in Lorthien, years to earn my trust and get secrets out of me. I've known Ziani and Nydia for less than a month and here I am telling them things that could endanger not only me, but Kali too.

"You're a twin!" Nydia exclaims when I finish. "And your twin sister is a total badass!"

"She is," I agree.

"How the hell did she get out of the palace?" Ziani demands. "I've tried, and there's no way out."

"I have no idea, but I suspect she swayed some faeries to her side and got them to help her."

"I've tried that too," Ziani says. "Why do you think I've been sleeping with Markus? Because he's hot? I'm not as stupid and reckless as you think. I've been trying to get him to help me escape. He says he's working on it, but I think he's too afraid. So are Jayke, Deji, Lorenzi, and Neal."

"Neal?" I sputter. "Tell me you haven't been sleeping with Neal."

Ziani's shoulders slump. "I've only made that mistake once. Last night."

"You found him so aggravating that you actually bit him the night we were captured."

"Yeah. I bit him again last night."

Nydia snorts with laughter while worry floods me. Neal is an arrogant jerk. I don't trust him in the slightest. As for the other faeries Ziani mentioned, I have no idea who any of them are.

"I'm so inspired by Kali," Ziani says. "It means escape is possible. I'll keep trying."

"And now I regret telling you," I say, kicking off my shoes. "The more you sleep around, the more likely it is that you'll be caught, Ziani."

"I'll take that risk considering the size of the possible reward."

"You'll get yourself killed."

"Listen," Ziani hisses. "That cautious mentality is why you're stuck here in this waking nightmare while Kali is walking free with faeries at her beck and call."

I glare at her. She has no idea that she's struck a nerve, but she has. A big one. All my life I've lived in Kali's shadow. Everywhere we went, people's eyes would drift past me but linger on her. I would be treated with aloof politeness while she would be treated with warm respect. I was the responsible twin while she was the pretty twin. It never bothered me. I didn't let it. But right now, everything suddenly feels like too much.

"You call throwing my life away to come and rescue Kali cautious?" I demand. "Baiting faeries with my blood? Using Nykolas's blood key to get into the forbidden north end? Sneaking around the palace at night after seeing Cardice's butchered body and knowing it could very well happen to me? All that is cautious?"

"Nydia," Ziani says warily. "Does what I said deserve the way she's glaring at me and yelling?"

Nydia tactfully doesn't answer the question. "Riva," she says instead. "You need sleep. We all do. Come and lie down."

I stay right where I am. The powerful rage roiling through me wants release. I feel the same deep inadequacy that drove me to smash the mirror earlier and I take a deep breath, forcing myself to calm down.

"Whatever it was about that word 'cautious' that triggered you, just know it's okay," Ziani says slowly. "I wasn't trying to say anything mean about you. I was just impressed by your sister."

My fists clench involuntarily and Ziani's gaze lowers to them. "I'm sensing some complicated feelings about your sister. And I want you to know that having a badass twin doesn't make you any less badass."

I turn away and remove my rubies. I lie the necklace on the dresser beside the matching earrings, then I glance at my reflection. Quickly, I look away. I try to unzip my dress.

After a few attempts, Nydia rises from the bed and comes to help me get it off. For some reason, my hands aren't working. I'm wearing a nightdress underneath, so once the bulky dress is off, I roll into bed.

Nydia switches off the lights.

I already know I'm not going to sleep, but I close my eyes anyway.

"So, you did steal Nykolas's blood key?" comes Ziani's whisper in the darkness. "Not that guard?"

When I don't reply, she asks. "Did you know what you were doing, or not?"

"Maybe that story is for tomorrow night," Nydia says.

∽

IN THE MORNING, two more girls don't show up for classes —Lilise and Darna. I'm relieved when Frieve doesn't send me, or anyone else, to go check on them. They don't show up all day, and although Frieve and Filpé say nothing about it, we all know it means they're dead.

Filpé insists on a new seating arrangement whereby the faerie girls are dispersed among us rather than congregating at the back. "So that their good manners rub off on you humans," he says. "The Choosing Ceremony is in just a few days now."

He's lying. We're sitting like this so that the human girls can't talk to each other as much as usual and voice our anger at what is happening.

In the afternoon, Seltie shows up for lessons with her dress torn, having been manhandled by two princes on her way.

"Oh dear," Frieve says. "They really can't wait to get their hands on you."

I can't help narrowing my eyes. She's really going to try and spin this into something positive?

"All in good time," she says with a chuckle that sounds forced. "Just a few days to wait now."

Nydia raises her hand.

"Yes?" Frieve asks.

"What can be done to stop these attacks?"

Nydia must be really afraid if she, of all people, is daring to speak up.

"Yeah," Ziani snaps. "We thought faeries were more civilized than this. Are we just utterly defenseless out here, or is someone going to step up and stop the cruelty?"

The room goes terrifyingly silent. The rest of the human girls look afraid on Ziani's behalf, while the faerie girls scowl—except Vielle and Baila who are tactfully turning the pages in their notebooks, pretending to be reading. Thankfully, Filpé isn't here. He would have sent Ziani to the dungeon torture chamber for that.

Three of the faerie girls start talking at once, defending their males.

"I'm not afraid of any of you," Ziani calls over their voices. "And I'm not afraid to speak my mind. Your men are jerks. What use are you if you can't call them to order and teach them how to treat women, whether human or faerie?"

"Enough," Frieve says. She waits for everyone to pipe down then adds, "Our males respect *our* females. You are outsiders from an enemy land."

"Outsiders that you brought here," Ziani points out. "We could all just make a suicide pact and die. What would you do then? You'll have to wait until next year to get more girls. And what if they decide not to accept your barbaric ways and do the same thing? How will your blasted royals reproduce then?"

I raise my hand.

Frieve seems at a loss after Ziani's outburst. She nods at me. "Yes?"

"How about we have a representative who can raise our concerns, and any other issues we have, with a council of selected faeries, who can then advocate on our behalf with the rest of the faeries," I suggest.

"Excellent idea," Ziani says. "I'm happy to be that rep."

Frieve releases an exhale, brushing back wisps of graying hair that frame her weary face. "I will speak to Filpé and let you know what he says. Can we start the lesson now."

I don't know why she thinks we care about the lesson when our lives are at risk. If they got serious about ensuring our safety, they would get better compliance from us. How is that not obvious?

"A very important celebration is taking place in three days' time," Frieve informs us. "It's called Red Heavens, and will be followed by the Festival of Moons, which we call Moonblest."

I snap to attention. "Red Heavens?"

"Yes," Frieve says.

"What's that?"

"It's a temporal thinning of the barriers between dimensions, allowing the light of other suns to bleed into our world and turn the night sky blood red. Eraeon is the only place on the planet from which this phenomenon can be observed."

My heart beats into overdrive as, suddenly, I understand Kali's note. She wants me to go to that address on Red Heavens at midnight. With all the faeries distracted by Red Heavens, it'll be easier for me to sneak out of the palace, and easier still for Kali and I to find a way to escape the island.

"As for Moonblest," Frieve says, "the thinning of dimensional barriers means the moons of other realms are visible the night after Red Heavens. We tend to see two in addition to our own, and it's pretty spectacular."

"You say Red Heavens is in three days?" I ask, just to be certain.

"Yes," Frieve confirms. "Unfortunately, human girls are not invited as it's a rather wild night, but you may look at the sky from your room windows. The Festival of Moons is a much more dignified event. You are all expected to attend that one looking your very best."

It's all I can do to sit still for the rest of the class. In three days, I'll finally find Kali and we can both flee. Queen Tarla wants me to have broken up with Nykolas by the time she returns from her travels on Red Heavens. I'll do better than that. I'll be gone. I'll leave that night and be out of here by Moonblest.

After the lesson, I ask Frieve if there's a palace library, claiming to want to read more about Red Heavens and the Festival of Moons.

"Of course, dear," she says with an approving smile. "I'm heading to the kitchens. The library is on the way. Follow me."

I'm glad when Nydia and Ziani decide to go for ice cream with Vielle and Baila again instead of coming with me. I want to do my snooping alone.

I follow Frieve through a labyrinth of hallways and corridors, heading toward the very center of the palace. We pass the Grand Ballroom, where the palace's biggest, glitziest parties take place, and then a whole bunch of other entertainment rooms.

Frieve finally comes to a stop outside a pair of imposing ebony doors. The dark wood is a canvas for runes that glow with a faint blue light as we approach. Gold whorls trim its edges.

"Here we are," Frieve says. "Information about all our festivals and celebrations can be found in the culture section. Human girls are forbidden to enter the geography section. Have fun."

"Thank you," I say. The door handles are golden, crafted in the shape of antlers. I grasp one and push the door open.

A cavernous room yawns before me. Towering shelves line the walls, reaching upward for as far as my eyes can see, disappearing into thick darkness at the top. Glistening light orbs hover by them, illuminating thick tomes and ribbon-tied scrolls. Reading desks are scattered throughout the space.

The door heaves shut behind me as I step inside. The air smells of aged parchment. A rustle of silk draws my attention to my left, and I see a faerie woman in an elaborate burgundy gown rising from a desk.

"How can I help you?" she asks.

I guess she's the librarian. "Can you please direct me to the culture section?"

In a fluid, graceful motion, she points to my right. "Through that archway. Back wall."

In the distance, there's an archway adorned with vines. "Thank you," I say, then head toward it. The archway leads to another vast room. I make my way to the back wall and thumb through a couple of books about festivals and celebrations, just in case the librarian is watching me.

I know why they don't want human girls in the geography section. It's so we don't find maps of Eraeon.

As I explore the aisles, a light orb follows me, illuminating the book spines. I wander into the history section, knowing that geography must be close, and feign interest in a book on ancient faerie civilizations.

From the corner of my eye, I read the titles of the books across the aisle. They're atlases. It's the geography section. As well as atlases, there are maps and geographical scrolls meticulously arranged on the shelves. My gaze is drawn to a thick volume whose title is written in gold lettering: *Interactive Map of Eraeon.*

I dart across the aisle, grab it, then hurry back to the culture section and sit at a desk.

No sooner have I hidden the map book in my lap and opened a culture book on the desk than the librarian shows up. "Is everything okay?" she asks.

"Yes," I say distractedly, as though completely engrossed in the culture book's images of faerie girls who are wearing veils to conceal their identities on Red Heavens night.

"Did you go to the geography section?" she asks. "You're not allowed in there."

"Oh. I walked past it, but there wasn't anything of interest."

She nods. "Let me know if you need anything."

"I will."

She disappears around a bookcase and I wait until I can't hear her footsteps anymore before I take out the interactive map book.

When I open it, a 3D image of Eraeon projects from the first page like a hologram, along with a glowing keypad.

I scan the image for streets, but it's a very high-level map labelling only neighborhoods and landmarks.

I type *6 Achlys Drive*, and the image turns into a street map showing a network of lanes and houses. A glowing red dot indicates 6 Achlys Drive.

I find the Pearl Palace on the map and deduce that 6 Achlys Drive is a good ten miles away. I'll never remember the route to it, and I know that borrowing the map book is out of the question. Thankfully, I still have my lesson books and file folder on me. On the back of a worksheet about makeup color palettes that work well together, I sketch the map.

I've never been good at drawing, but it's only lines and angles. 6 Achlys Drive is by a river. There's also a forest nearby called Nocahya Forest. I add it to my map. It would make a good hiding place for Kali and me if we happen to need one. We'll need to steal a boat to get off the island. I'll have to look into that.

When I finish my sketch. I return all the books. Instead of venturing into the geography section again, I place the interactive map book in a section on the faerie religion of Oriya. Then I leave.

I still have an hour left before the final class of the day, and I'm planning to spend it plotting my escape. I'm so preoccupied that I walk into a solid wall.

Then I realize it isn't a wall, but a person.

"Whoa there, Riva!" he says, steadying me.

"Camran," I say, rubbing my forehead where I bashed it against his chest. "Hey."

He's beautiful. The vivid green of his eyes, the golden hair that flops over his forehead. The sculpted muscles that define his arms. There are way too many attractive men in Eraeon. It's little wonder that Ziani is making bad decisions, and more of a surprise that more of us human girls are not.

Camran isn't alone. Neal stands beside him, a sneer playing on his lips. As much as I hate to admit it, he's pretty easy on the eyes too with raven black hair, carved features, and golden skin that is slightly paler than most faeries. None of it matters since he's wanted to kill me from the moment we met. He's wanted to kill all of us human girls for no other reason than that he's a bloodthirsty fiend. I can't believe Ziani slept with him.

Further down the hallway, Nykolas is talking to a bunch of faerie men in military garb. My heart skips a beat at the sight of him. He's back.

He looks formidable in his Supreme Commander's uniform, weapons dangling from his holster. The thought of what he's spent the night doing in Lorthien troubles me.

Nykolas glances over at me and all the air seems to be sucked from the hallway as my breath catches. His brilliant blue eyes are shadowed and I can tell that whatever he had to do overnight in Lorthien, he didn't delight in it.

"I've been meaning to talk to you," Camran says.

I drag my gaze back to him. He gives me a boyish grin and I totally see why Ziani likes him.

"It's so nice to have you back, Riva—"

"Get to the point, Camran," I cut in.

Neal huffs a laugh.

"Okay," Camran says sheepishly. "Well, I was wondering if Ziani has mentioned being attracted to anyone in the palace."

"You mean you?"

Camran shrugs. "I don't get to be a chooser, but I could talk Nykolas into telling the princes to withdraw their interest in her so that I can have her."

Neal looks uncomfortable. He wanders away to a nearby window, and I realize Camran doesn't know about him and Ziani.

"Have her?" I ask Camran. "Is she an item on a menu?"

"That's not what I meant."

"You don't have to explain anything to this human," Neal says, shooting me a derisive look.

I shoot him what I hope is an equally derisive look. "In case you haven't noticed, I'm wearing rubies so don't talk to me and don't even look at me."

Neal bares his fangs although he averts his gaze. He would love nothing more than to strike me dead, but he doesn't dare.

Nykolas casts me another searing glance from across the hallway, and a thrill shoots through me. I'm supposed to be working myself up to ending our relationship, but I seem to be falling harder.

"I'll trade a secret for a secret," Camran whispers.

I tear my gaze from Nykolas and look at him, lifting a questioning brow.

"I'll tell you something Nykolas said about you," Camran offers, "if you tell me something Ziani has said about me."

I shouldn't want to know what Nykolas has been saying. I'm leaving in three days, so it doesn't matter. But my curiosity gets the better of me.

"Deal," I say. "You go first."

"He told me, last night, that he's going to do whatever it takes to be with you. He controls the weather and he's willing to cause unending darkness until his parents, and the whole of Eraeon, accept you."

No!

I shouldn't have let Camran tell me that. I can't let Nykolas go that far. If he forces his people to accept me, it'll be a grudging acceptance that will erupt in anger at any moment. They'll hate me more than ever. He needs to just let me go.

This time, when I look at Nykolas, he's watching me, clearly no longer listening to the soldiers around him.

"So, what has Ziani said?" Camran prompts.

"She says she hates faeries, and that the one they call 'Camran' is the most infuriating of all."

Camran chuckles. Then his face grows serious. "Tell me, Riva. What did she really say."

"She likes you. She thinks you're sweet and interesting, unlike other sweet guys who tend to be boring."

Camran is quiet for a moment, weighing the words. Then he shrugs, looking pretty pleased. "I can work with that."

"Is Jaxson back?" I ask him.

"Yes."

"Where is he?"

Camran shrugs. "He skulked off by himself as soon as we landed. I'll tell him you asked."

Just then, Nykolas breaks away from the soldiers and strides over. Every shift of his powerful frame exudes a raw magnetism that makes my heart race.

Camran and Neal make themselves scarce as Nykolas lifts me into his arms then presses me against the wall, his lips claiming mine.

But all I can think about is the fact that three days isn't a long time. I have to put my plan to break up with him into motion. Or maybe I don't. Maybe I can just fake my death or something. I can't bear the thought of breaking his heart like the Aziza princess did. Nykolas doesn't deserve it.

I pull away from the kiss and stare up into his electric blue eyes. "I still have lessons. Maybe we can go somewhere, alone, this evening?"

"Forget your lessons. We can go now."

"Okay. Let me go and freshen up."

"Meet me at the south entrance in an hour." Nykolas lowers me to the floor. "Don't be late."

10

I decide to go all out and get dressed up. This will be my goodbye to Nykolas, even though he won't know it's a goodbye.

Annha, my attendant, is happy to oblige and summons a hairstylist, makeup artist, and perfumer, then goes in search of the perfect gown.

I sit on the dresser chair, and the makeup artist begins to clean my face, while the perfumer mixes up a scent and the hairstylist plugs in a straightening iron.

"Why are you so excited?" I ask Annha when she returns bearing a red dress with a ruched bodice, lace sleeves, and full skirts. It'll match my rubies. She's also holding a shoebox.

"You don't deserve to be hated just because Prince Nykolas loves you," she replies, matter-of-fact. "And if you make more of an effort not to annoy everyone by wearing widow's garments, it might help when we begin a public campaign to improve your image."

"Is such a campaign being planned?"

"Yes. After the Choosing Ceremony, I'm to attend a meeting with Prince Nykolas himself, his advisors, and the top image consultants in the country. I imagine you will be there too."

I won't. I'll be long gone. My heart twists with melancholy, but even if Queen Tarla and Dabria hadn't ordered me to leave on threat of death, leaving is my best option. No image consultant can change the fact that I'm human. Faeries hate humans. And the feeling is mutual. I don't want to be Queen of Eraeon. I was nothing in Lorthien.

Annha lays the red dress on the bed then opens the shoebox, revealing a pair of red stilettos. "Besides," she says, "once the Crown Prince chooses you, I'll be the most successful palace attendant. Everyone will start consulting me. I could quit my job and set up shop downtown, advising women on style, grace, manners, and all things etiquette."

I don't roll my eyes—although I really want to.

"Or, I might get promoted here. I could even snag Filpé's job and oversee the whole human girl operation."

"If you do, treat them better. Filpé is a horror."

"Noted."

There's a knock on the main door to my rooms and Annha goes to answer it. She returns with Ziani and Nydia whose eyes widen at the sight of me being prepared for my date.

"What's the occasion?" Ziani asks. "Don't tell me there's some ceremony this afternoon that I've forgotten about."

"Nope. I'm going out with Nykolas."

"Oh. To where?"

"I don't know."

"What about classes?" Nydia asks.

"The Crown Prince demands my presence. What classes?"

Ziani snorts, then she comes closer, looking at my hair. "What are you planning to do with it?" she asks the faerie combing it out.

The faerie waves her hand and a wispy, translucent image of my face materializes in the air. In it, my hair is twisted in an elaborate updo. "I'll have to straighten it first," she says.

"Nice, but it's way too generic," Ziani replies. She looks at me. "I can do you some braids at the front of your head, then the back can be left in your natural curls.

The stylist waves again, and in her magical construction of my face, my hair changes to reflect Ziani's suggestion.

"Much better," Nydia says.

"Braids please," I agree, and Ziani comes to take over from the hairstylist.

Ziani's own hair is still braided in the intricate pattern she wore it in for last night's Official Declaration Ceremony. Her curls are tighter than mine so I guess braiding her hair makes things easier.

If not for my poverty I would braid my hair more often. Kali got hers braided all the time, something that frequently caused tension between us. As a result, her hair was longer and her curls more luscious, while my hair has never thrived.

Over the next thirty minutes, my appearance is totally transformed. I barely recognize myself when I look in the mirror afterward.

"I feel like something is missing," Ziani says, studying me.

"Yeah," Nydia agrees.

Are they kidding? I have never looked so good in my life. My makeup is in natural colors that enhance, rather than overshadow, my features. The unbraided part of my hair cascades past my shoulders in rippling sheets of bouncy curls. And the dress...it's perfect.

Annha studies me. "I think it's the makeup. It's very neutral. I feel like there needs to be a pop of color, otherwise her spectacular dress is wearing her, rather than her wearing it." She nods to the makeup artist. "Some red lipstick will do the trick."

The makeup artist immediately does her bidding.

Then Ziani clicks her fingers. "And something gold. Maybe gold eyeliner?"

Annha looks dubious.

"Trust me," Ziani says.

Annha looks expectantly at the hairstylist and she waves to create the spectral image of me, this time adding gold eyeliner.

"Lengthen the flicks at the corners of her eyes," Ziani says, and the faerie stylist complies.

Annha beams, clasping her hands together. "It's perfect. It adds a touch of regal glamor that is just wonderful." She nods to the makeup artist. "Gold eyeliner at once!"

The makeup artist selects a gold liquid liner then looks at my eyes and there's a tingling along my lash line. "I'm just removing the black eyeliner I used," she explains.

"That's one thing I appreciate about faerie magic," Ziani

says. "You can mess up your makeup and just use magic to fix it. So awesome."

"I feel like the gold kind of stands alone," Nydia says after the makeup artist has lined my eyes afresh. "She needs...something more."

"I was about to say the same," Annha agrees. "How about some gold body oil for her shoulders and décolletage. It'll bring out the warmer undertones of her skin and tie everything together nicely."

A pot of shimmering gold body oil appears in the makeup artist's hand from thin air.

"I think you're ready," Annha says once it has been applied.

Everyone agrees, so they begin to pack away all the makeup, hair products, and perfume oils.

Ziani and Nydia have to get to class. They leave grudgingly with Annha and her team.

As I step into my shoes, a whisper of a touch, like a soft caress, tickles around my temples. I already know it's Jaxson before his voice fills my head.

I'm at your door, he says. *I just saw a bunch of people leaving your rooms. Are you alone now, or should I come back later?*

I'm alone, I reply.

I turn toward the door to go and let him in, but he materializes from thin air before me. I'm so startled, I stumble backward. "Hey! Don't just appear like that. I could have been indecent!"

"If only," Jaxson replies with a slow smile. Then his gaze sweeps over me and he just stares, his jaw dropping slightly.

"What?" I ask.

He blinks then clamps his mouth shut. His throat bobs as he swallows. "You look...uh..." He clears his throat. "No gray today?"

I hesitate. For some reason, I don't want to tell him that I'm going out with Nykolas.

"Well, Nykolas will be pleased." Jaxson's tone is mocking, and I'm glad I didn't mention Nykolas. "A word of caution: You might not want to ask around the palace for me. I'd rather not have to deal with his suspicion."

"Nykolas was suspicious?"

"His messenger just paid me a visit asking if I need to be castrated or if I think I have the decency to keep...certain body parts away from you without his intervention. So, yes, I'd say he's suspicious."

I imagine Nykolas's messenger making that announcement in his loud, formal voice and I can't help a snort of laughter.

Jaxson looks unimpressed.

"Well, where are your chambers?" I ask him. "In case I ever need to find you."

"I don't live here." Jaxson slides his hands into his pockets then perches on the edge of my dresser. In all black he makes me think of a big, dark bat. A broody aura hovers around him. "I have my own palace. I'm a prince, remember?"

I study him for a moment, and he stares back at me with dark, searing eyes. "What's wrong?" I ask.

Jaxson's gaze drifts to the window. "Mug Shot was spared. Shearne and her family live."

A tension that has been tightening in my chest ever since

he told me they were in Lorthien loosens. "What happened?" I ask softly.

A muscle works in Jaxson's jaw as he continues to stare through the window. "I had to prove myself. I always have to prove myself. They gave me a bigger quota of kills to fulfill than the others."

"Because you're half human?"

He doesn't respond, and he doesn't ask me how I know. After a few moments of silence, he looks at me. "For once, I wasn't the only one. Nykolas also had to prove himself. Now that he's pretty much announced that you're more than just a surrogate and he's actually in love with you, he's on thin ice. The king insisted on this mission because we need to retaliate for the attack on Eraeon, but he also wanted Nykolas to prove that loving you will not stop him from doing his duty as Supreme Commander."

Horror splices through me. Their night of killing in Lorthien was because of me? I step backward as though I can escape the words. But they hang in the air between us, heavy and accusing.

I have to leave. I *have* to.

"I'm leaving in three days," I blurt.

Jaxson lifts a dark brow.

"I've made contact with my sister—"

"If you leave this palace you will be lynched in the streets."

"Everyone knows about me?"

Jaxson nods. "The whole of Eraeon is buzzing with word of the human girl who has turned their beloved Crown

Prince's heart upside down. You're all over the news. The fact that you're a sentiae is even more aggravating. Faeries hate it when humans have abilities—especially abilities that could police us."

My pulse races as I absorb this information. It's a good thing it'll be night when I leave. I won't be immediately recognizable in the darkness. Plus, everyone will be focused on celebrating Red Heavens. But maybe I should take the extra precaution of wearing some kind of disguise.

"I'll need a solathium knife," I tell Jaxson. It's the only way I'll be able to defend myself if I'm recognized. "Can you get me one?"

"That would be treason."

"Will you do it?"

He gives me a slow, dark smile. "Of course, sweet Riva."

"Thank you," I whisper.

This is how Kali must have escaped. Some faerie helped her. And now I have a helper too. "I don't know how I'll ever repay you," I tell Jaxson, my heart flooding with gratitude, "but if you ever happen to be in Lorthien, I'll buy you a drink."

"Another empty promise. Like the date that never happened."

I pause. I totally forgot about that. I figure he's just teasing me. He doesn't really care about the date. Does he?

"What else do you need?" Jaxson asks. "I can get you an escape pack and hide it under your bed, magically guarded and invisible. Even if someone were to check under your bed, they wouldn't see it."

"Why are you helping me?" I ask.

Jaxson is quiet for a long moment. Then he gives me a dark smile. "If I can't have you, why should he?"

I stare at him. He stares back.

I look away first, flustered. I'm not sure how to take the words. Jaxson is not in love with me. This is just about his rivalry with Nykolas. I get the feeling he doesn't like him very much.

"You haven't asked me why I'm not a chooser."

"Nykolas told me you're not allowed to be with a human girl."

Jaxson's brow furrows. "You and Nykolas make time, between staring into each other's eyes and whispering sweet nothings, to discuss me?"

"Don't flatter yourself. It was only once. And only because he was mad that you touched my back while I was wearing his ruby ring."

Jaxson snorts softly, then gives me a dark smile. "I could touch you elsewhere and really give him something to be mad about. Would you like that, Riva?"

Heat climbs up my neck. Once again, I know he's just teasing me, but I still feel hot and itchy all over. "Why aren't you a chooser?" I ask, steering the conversation back on track.

"They think a human lover would inspire pity in my cold, black heart, and turn me against my own people."

"Both faeries and humans are your people."

"Humans are not my people. Do I seem remotely human to you?"

He's right. He has magic and he's just as deadly and

ruthless as the rest of the faeries. There is nothing human about Jaxson.

"But that's because you live among them," I say. "If you'd been brought up among humans, you would be more like us."

"I have magic."

"I, apparently, have...abilities, too."

Jaxson huffs a laugh. "Mine are not *abilities*, sweet Riva. I'm more powerful than anyone in Eraeon."

He lowers his voice on that last part, like he's sharing a secret.

"Do they know that?" I ask.

"Of course not. I don't have a death wish." Jaxson rises and prowls slowly to the window. "You've heard of the ritual they do to turn demi-fae into full-bloods?"

"The cleansing ritual?"

"I don't like that word," Jaxson says.

"Neither do I."

"Well, faerie royals have never found it easy to sire offspring, so they used to seek willing human women. That's what most of the kings did, even before our immortality was stolen. It was just easier with a human. Something about their weakness makes them more susceptible to our will when we make love to them. The ritual, for some reason didn't work on my grandfather, father, or me. So the crown passed to Nykolas's grandfather and has stayed with that line."

And now I understand the bad blood between Jaxson and Nykolas. "You're supposed to be the Crown Prince?"

Jaxson nods, his back still turned to me. "If I can get the ritual to work."

"You're still trying? I thought it's only done on children."

"I'm still trying," he confirms. "And I'm petitioning against the ruling that forbids me from being part of the choosing ceremony. They can't stop me from having heirs."

"Even demi-fae struggle to conceive with faeries?" I ask. "Shouldn't your human side be susceptible to a faerie female?"

"No royals can conceive. It isn't a struggle anymore. Since our immortality was stolen, it's become impossible—except with humans."

"Well," I say, "I'm glad I'm getting out of here. I don't want to have children, and I won't be forced to birth some faerie's offspring."

Jaxson turns. "Why don't you want children?"

"I…" I shake my head. "It's personal."

"Something to do with being an orphan?"

I don't know how he knows that, but neither am I surprised. He lived in Lorthien, eyeing up girls for the palace. He probably looked into many girls' backgrounds as he decided on who to kidnap, including mine.

"I understand," he says quietly, but his voice still sounds dark and dangerous. "Sometimes, I too wonder whether I really want to bring an innocent new life into this cold, brutal world."

I'm stunned. He has summed up my feelings perfectly.

"But with the right partner, we could create a nurturing environment and shield them from the darkness." His gaze bores into mine.

I notice the way the daylight streaming in from the window beside him sets his golden skin ablaze and gutters in his dark eyes.

Since meeting Nykolas, I haven't allowed my thoughts to linger on how breathtaking Jaxson is. And I don't allow them to do so now.

I screw up my nose. "Selecting a partner based on how good a parent you think they'll be is pretty icky. Such a relationship is doomed to failure once the children grow up and leave." I cross the room, open my file folder, and grab the map I drew. Then I approach Jaxson and hand it to him. "Kali wants me to meet her at 6 Achlys Drive. Is there an easy way to get there? Tell me there are taxis in Eraeon. If so I'll need money to pay."

I cringe. I hate having to ask him for help—especially the money part. I hate having to rely on anybody. I've always been completely self-sufficient.

Jaxson isn't looking at the map. He's looking at me. His dark eyes sweep over my braided hair and the curls that ripple past my shoulders. He opens his mouth to say something, then his gaze catches on Nykolas's rubies dangling from my ears and encircling my throat. He promptly turns his attention to the map.

If I had magic, I would break into his mind to see what he was about to say. But I don't, so I'll have to be content with not knowing.

As he stares at the map, a whisper of his smoky, fiery magic rolls through the air, and the wonky lines I drew begin to straighten. Colour fills my sketch. More labels appear.

"Thank you," I say.

"Go back to where you were standing." Jaxson's voice is sharp. Terse.

I frown.

His dark eyes narrow. "I said go back to where you were standing."

I remain right where I am. "I heard you the first time, and my response is no. You don't get to order me around."

"You either take my orders, or bow to my magic," Jaxson says softly.

His smoky magic rears, and I feel a force begin to push me backward. I stand my ground, scowling. "You're never a ray of sunshine, Jaxson, but you're even worse than usual today. Are you just rude, or is it because you've been killing people all night and you're on edge?"

His magic peters out and he shoots me a burning look that spikes my heart rate. "If you must know, it's because your nearness is giving me all kinds of filthy ideas that could get me castrated. Now, move before I do something that Nykolas won't be pleased to hear about."

"You move, if you're the one with the issue," I retort. But his words light something inside me that really shouldn't be lit. Not by him. Suddenly, I'm all too aware of our utter aloneness. And the huge bed in the room.

He shouldn't be in my bedroom.

Jaxson gives me a slow smile. "Are you testing me, Riva?"

"Can we focus on the map?"

"And are you saying you have no issue with our closeness?" Jaxson asks, completely ignoring my request. "You don't feel the smoldering chemistry crackling between us."

I just look at him.

"What would you do if I were to draw you closer and—"

"Jaxson."

He lifts a dark brow.

"Can you try to be noble and not proposition the woman your cousin is in love with?"

Jaxson's smile is completely wicked. "I am not noble and there is nothing noble about my desires right now. Make no mistake, sweet Riva, I am a filthy, rotten soul, and the things I want to do to you...the things I've been dreaming of doing to you, are completely depraved."

A rush of heat burns through me. I steel myself against it. "I'm not interested."

"Liar," he hisses.

"If any part of me is interested, it's only because you have inserted yourself into my heart. Since I'm leaving Eraeon soon, I trust you'll undo whatever you did?"

"It will wear off after a few months," Jaxson replies. "But if you ever return, I will take a piece of your heart again. I brought you to Eraeon for a reason, but I know better than to stand in the way of fate. If you want to leave, I won't stop you."

"Why did you bring me to Eraeon?" I ask, although I already know he won't tell me.

He looks down at the map, avoiding my gaze. The map is no longer the pencil sketch I drew. It's full-color and highly detailed.

A dull ache of desire ripples through me as I watch him, my gaze trailing over his powerful, male form. Frustrated with myself for my weakness, I move across the room, putting distance between us.

"Thank you," Jaxson says, not looking up. "It's going to be almost impossible for you to sneak out of the palace. Security was stepped up last year. I didn't know why at the time, but it must have been because of your sister's escape. It was stepped up again when this year's cohort of human girls came. And after the human attack, the palace is on high alert. We're surprised there hasn't been another attack yet, despite humans now knowing our location. We think they're planning something big."

"After what you did in Lorthien overnight, I wouldn't blame them."

He looks up from the map and studies me. "Does it bother you that Nykolas spent the night killing humans?"

"Yes."

"But you can overlook it since you're leaving anyway?"

"Exactly."

A powerful wave of raging desire swamps my senses, and I have to look away from Jaxson. I used to be helplessly attracted to him. I spent many slow moments and lunch breaks at Mug Shot indulging in all sorts of steamy fantasies about him, but I thought I was over that crush. Clearly not.

"You are so hot for me," he whispers.

I don't know how he knows. He isn't in my mind right now.

I want to deny it, but another ripple of desire washes over me, too strong for me to fight. I find myself taking a step toward him. What would it hurt to indulge in just a few stolen moments of pleasure? We wouldn't go too far. Just enough to break the electric tension hanging between us.

Jaxson watches me approach him. Only when his

sensuous full lips twist in a smirk do I realize I can sense the subtle heat of his magic stirring my desire.

I blink, shaking my head. "You're toying with my emotions."

"And that dress is toying with my restraint."

"Jaxson, stop this!" I hiss.

He sighs, but I sense his magic withdraw. The raging hunger I felt for him vanishes so suddenly, it's like I imagined it.

"The best time to sneak out is at five minutes to midnight, during the changing of the guard," Jaxson says.

The abrupt change in topic is dizzying, but I welcome it. This is why I wanted to speak to him. I need help with sneaking out.

"There are secret passageways all over the palace," he adds, "including a deserted one that nobody knows exists. I will get you a map of them. If I could, I would transport you out of the palace so that you bypass all the security measures altogether, but there are magical wards in place to stop that. I have the power to bypass them, but I'd rather save such flagrant acts of defiance for when there is no other choice. The passageways are your best option."

"Really?" I ask. "Nykolas transported me to the beach."

"Nykolas is trusted so he's one of only a few people who have special permissions. Nobody trusts me."

"And they shouldn't," I say, although I soften my words with a smile.

Jaxson holds my gaze for a moment, then he holds up my map and points to the forest near Achlys Drive. "Stay away from Nocahya Forest. Whatever you do, do not go in there."

"Why?"

"It drives human girls mad."

I'm about to ask him more about it when the room seems to vanish around me, and I find myself somewhere else entirely.

11

I turn and realize I'm standing in one of the palace's entrance halls. Nykolas is waiting in the vast doorway, staring into the distance, his hands in his pockets.

Whenever Jaxon transports me, it's like tumbling through a dark abyss, but Nykolas's transporting powers give no dark interlude. The transition from one place to the next is seamless, like stepping through a portal into another world.

"You're late," Nykolas says, turning. He's wearing a regal ivory shirt and matching trousers that are tucked into polished black riding boots. An ivory cloak, embroidered with gold, drapes gracefully from his shoulders.

At the sight of me, he stills.

"Sorry I'm late," I say.

He gapes, his eyes trailing over me from head to toe. I wait for him to say something, but he's just staring.

"Okay," I say slowly. "I don't look *that* good."

"Oriya help me," Nykolas says, finally finding his voice. He gives a low whistle as he holds out his hand.

I take it, and a spark of what feels like pure electricity zips through me. It's vastly different from the frenzied lust I felt for Jaxson moments ago. This has depth. Authenticity.

"I'm trying to hold out until the night of the Choosing Ceremony," Nykolas murmurs as we step outside. "But how will I resist you in this dress?"

"You'll just have to try your best," I joke to deflect the compliment, but Nykolas doesn't smile.

A saddled white horse waits in the yard. Nykolas lifts me into his arms and floats upward a few inches then positions me sideways on it. Then he climbs on too and reaches around me to take the reins. "Hold on to me, my lady."

I wrap my arms around his waist as he eases the horse into a canter. Its hooves clomp loudly as he navigates through the palace grounds. Everyone we pass stares. Nykolas really doesn't seem to care what anyone thinks of him for loving me.

What terrible luck for me to find someone who truly loves me and have to let him go.

Soon, the palace's back gates come into view. I hold a breath as they slowly slide apart for us. The high security measures make no difference to Nykolas's movements. He can come and go as he pleases.

Once we're through the gates, he flicks the reins and the horse begins to gallop. My skirts flutter in the breeze. I clutch Nykolas tighter. He smells of some crisp, woodsy fragrance that makes me want to sit here forever, breathing him in.

We speed over miles of rolling hills that surround the palace, until I spot a sparkle of blue on the horizon. He's taking me down by the sea.

When we get there, Nykolas brings the horse to a halt and ties him to a nearby tree, then leads me down to a promenade, his hand at the small of my back. It's completely empty of people. An opulent, low-lying couch of deepest crimson sits facing the water. It's scattered with plush, jewel-toned cushions.

"I thought we could watch the sunset," Nykolas says, steering me toward the couch. "Servants are on standby with refreshments, but I told them not to bother us unless we call."

I sit and my dress drapes elegantly around me. The couch heaves as Nykolas sits beside me. It crosses my mind that I could run. Try to escape. But despite the fact that Nykolas would easily catch me, I don't have my map or the solathium knife that Jaxson has promised to get me. I'd be utterly vulnerable without a weapon.

I glance at Nykolas and find him watching me. I drag my gaze to the sea and focus on the way the sun sparkles off it, making the waves glisten. And I wonder how he can truly love me and yet hate humans enough to slaughter them in their sleep all night.

A boathouse further down the promenade catches my eye. A few anchored boats bob on the water outside it. They look like motorboats, which would be perfect for my escape with Kali.

I can feel the heat of Nykolas's gaze still on me. I look at him, and he chuckles softly. "I'm sorry," he whispers. "I can't seem to take my eyes off you."

If I were staying, if I were going to try and make things work between us, I would ask him about last night. I would tell him it hurts to know that he has human blood on his hands. I would let him know I can't give myself to him wholly if he is an enemy to humans.

Nykolas takes both my hands in his. "Riva, you must have heard about last night. I want you to know I didn't kill any innocents."

"You didn't?"

He squeezes my hands. "I didn't. No regular citizens died. We went to the barracks. When my father realized what we were doing, he ordered that we go to downtown Lorthien. But I came up with a workaround. I used this painstaking process to find off-duty soldiers, and we targeted them. I did my best not to spill any civilian blood."

Soldiers are people, too. They're lovers, parents, siblings, and children. Prysha, and indeed the whole of Rithelia, will be mourning. But this helps. *Really* helps. Nykolas didn't have to do that. It tells me he isn't just a callous, bloodthirsty faerie, and that things might actually change when he becomes king in place of his father.

Sincerity shines in his eyes. Eyes that are somehow a more vivid blue than the sea before us. The sun amplifies every hue of his blonde-brown hair, making me think of nurturing soils and gold mines.

"I heard what happened at the ceremony yesterday," Nykolas says. "I've been so worried that someone might attack you in my absence. I can pull you out of lessons if you want. After the Choosing Ceremony, I'm getting you out of this palace. You'll have your own home. Maybe a castle on a hill with a personal battalion of soldiers for protection."

Warmth fills my heart. I lift a hand to cup his face. "I love you, Nykolas."

"I love you, too," he replies, covering my hand with his. Then he turns his face toward my hand and brushes a kiss to my palm.

"Nobody would have a problem with our relationship if I was treating you poorly," he says tersely. "They're mad because I actually like you and I'm treating you well. But I plan to treat you even better than I have so far, so they'd better get used to it."

"What about the other human girls?" I ask. "I'm terrified that something will happen to Ziani or Nydia."

"When I am king, everything will change. I'll stop the kidnappings."

"Really?" I ask, dubious. "But your royals need us."

"We don't have to snatch girls from their homes at night like Neanderthals. I've been considering initiating a scheme with human nations around the world—places in which there is less of a bias against faeries than there is in Rithelia. Any prince who wants heirs can go and court a human female, then reveal that he's a faerie and ask if she'll come to live here. What do you think?"

I stare at Nykolas, moved by his desire to do the right thing, even if it means tearing down the current system and causing upheaval. "That could work."

I lower my hand from his face, then rise, my heart feeling full and heavy, and a bittersweet ache settling in the depths of my being. How do I let Nykolas go when he's so wonderful? When he's pulling out all the stops to please me and put things right between faeries and humans, despite King Bastien stealing something so precious from his people?

I sense Nykolas's magic rising powerfully around us. My heart skips a beat, but I force myself to stay calm. If things were different and I was going to stay, being in a relationship with someone so powerful would take some getting used to. It would also take a lot of trust.

I look down at him. "What are you doing?"

"You can sense my magic?" he asks.

"Yes."

"Good. I was just testing if you could. The High Council tried to strip you of your sentiae abilities overnight. They said it didn't work, despite them using a ritual that reliably works whenever it's used on faeries."

They really do hate that I can sense their magic.

An almost imperceptible whisper of Nykolas's magic skims my cheeks. "I sensed that too," I tell him.

Nykolas beams. "I'm relieved that your abilities are unaffected. They are incredibly valuable. They just can't see that yet, simply because you're human. When we are king and queen nobody will be able to commit magical crimes on your watch."

I approach the balustrade on the edge of the promenade and look down into the water.

Nykolas doesn't allow me to stand there alone for long—as I'd known he wouldn't. He comes up behind me moments later and wraps his arms around me. I can feel the solid beat of his heart against my back.

"What are you thinking my fire girl?"

"Are you ever going to let me forget that I set you on fire the day we met?"

"Nope. I plan to make you feel guilty about it forever."

Forever.

Tears rush to my eyes, but I manage to hold them back. Blink them away. "I'm not thinking anything," I say in response to Nykolas's question. "What are you thinking?"

"That you're the one. The one I loved before I ever even knew you. The one I've been waiting for my whole life."

His words tug on my heart. A heart that Jaxson is supposed to have stolen a piece of. If so, why are my feelings for Nykolas so profoundly fierce? Especially when he isn't using magic on me.

"I have something for you," Nykolas says.

I shake my head. "No. No more rubies."

"It isn't rubies this time."

I turn in his arms and look up at him. "What is it?"

"Close your eyes."

I obey, and his arms leave my waist. A few seconds tick by.

"Open your eyes."

I open them to find him dangling a courtship bracelet from his finger. My jaw drops. It's a platinum one, the best kind. And a heart-shaped diamond charm hangs from it. "I was in Lorthien, so I figured I would pick one up," Nykolas says.

I shake my head. "You don't know what this means. If you give me that, you're proposing marriage."

"Nope. I've added a charm so it means we're already wed."

"Yeah. But we're not."

"But we will be."

"The Choosing Ceremony is not a marriage," I remind him. "It's an arrangement where I just give birth to your offspring."

"And sleep with me whenever I want," Nykolas adds. "Don't forget that part?"

I ignore the flirtation in his tone. "Yeah," I say. "That's not a marriage. It's surrogacy and servitude."

Nykolas sighs. "Don't you get it, Riva? Haven't I told you I want you as my queen? I want to marry you. Our faerie customs hold no weight for you, so I will do it the human way if I must. I also got you more of that horrifying cake you like. I bought a whole platter. It'll be delivered to your room before you get back. The baker also agreed to send a monthly supply."

I grab his face and kiss him.

I'm not in charge for long. Nykolas slips the courtship bracelet over my wrist, then his hands are in my braids and curls, pulling my face closer, pressing my lips harder against his. His kiss is as fiery as the desert heat he creates in southern Eraeon, and as potent as any drug. My head is spinning, my heart thrumming.

Nykolas pauses, touching his nose to mine. "You're so beautiful, Riva," he whispers. "So so beautiful."

Then his lips claim mine again. Still kissing me, he guides me back to the couch and we fall onto it.

My mind whirs as I realize I've never heard those words

before. Never. Beautiful was what Kali was. What Shearne was. What other women were. Not me. That word, given as a gift to me, is like spring rains on parched land. I don't know how he can possibly mean it when there are many much more beautiful women at the palace, both human and faerie. But, today, I choose to accept it. I'm beautiful.

His magic laps against my mind, and I know he's about to speak into it.

Stop worrying about the future, my love.

The mind connection heightens the intimacy of the kiss, and I gasp against his mouth.

Just enjoy this moment, he says. *It's just you and me. Nothing matters, except this kiss.*

My back hits the couch cushions and I pull him closer, needing all of him pressed against all of me. He hikes up my skirts and I wrap my legs around his waist, and use my heels to urge him closer.

Groin to groin I feel the stiff hardness of his desire. I freeze.

"You seem surprised," Nykolas murmurs against my lips. "Do you truly have no idea what you're doing to me, Riva?"

I don't. I doubt I've ever inspired such passion in anyone. The knowledge of how much he wants this, how much he wants *me*, is electrifying.

My breath hitches when he presses against me, his firmness against my softness, sending a thrill shooting throughout my whole body.

Then he presses his nose to my neck, and groans, his fangs sliding out from between his lips. I tense. I've only ever glimpsed his fangs twice before. The day we met, after I set him on fire, and the first morning I woke up in his quarters when he was supposed to be 'punishing' me.

"Sorry," Nykolas says, retracting them. "That tends to happen when I'm...losing control." His eyes search mine. "You're afraid."

"No," I say, touching his cheek. "Keep them out if you want."

Making out with a man with fangs is...different. But love is nothing without acceptance. If I'm going to be in love with a faerie, I can't make him hide parts of who he is from me.

His fangs protrude once more, and I reach up and kiss his lips, careful to make sure I don't cut myself on his sharp canines.

Nykolas trails his nose down my neck, taking a deep inhale. I want to ask him what he's doing, but I hold still as his nose continues its exploration, not quite touching my skin. He lingers at the base of my throat, and draws in a deep breath. "Riva...you smell amazing."

I find my voice. "This is kind of weird."

He laughs softly.

"I thought it's the morning scent that faerie males like."

"Your scent is always stronger in the morning, but it's there all the time. Even all the annoying perfumes you've been drenched with haven't masked it." His eyes are liquid with hunger, and his voice lowers to a whisper. "It's driving me so wild."

I realize Jaxson has scented me too. The night of the winter solstice when I asked him out on a date. His nostrils twitched and I knew he was sniffing me, but I didn't know why.

It's so ridiculous, I want to laugh.

"May I?" Nykolas asks, short-circuiting all thoughts of Jaxson. He gives a sweeping nod, indicating the rest of my body.

He wants to smell me all over?

"Sure," I say slowly.

"Everywhere?" Nykolas asks.

"Go on, you animal. Hurry up before I change my mind."

He chuckles softly then begins at my hairline. He trails his way down the side of my face. Down my neck and the top of my chest.

"Are you sure you're okay with this?" he asks.

"Uh huh."

He buries his head between my breasts and I stop breathing.

Nykolas makes a growling sound at the back of his throat as he breathes me in. Then he's sliding downward.

My mind stutters with shock when he bunches up my skirts, exposing me from the waist down. Surely he isn't going to...

He nudges my legs further apart, then his nose is trailing my panties.

"What in hades are you doing?"

"You said anywhere."

"I didn't think you would...Never mind just be quick."

"Say the word and I'll stop."

I say nothing, and he continues, letting out another of those throaty groans.

"Did you say there are servants around?" I ask, suddenly worried that we have an audience.

"They wouldn't dare speak of this."

He lingers between my legs until I nudge him. "Move on, please."

He chuckles as he obeys. But after working his way down to my feet, he's back between my legs. He slides his finger over the thin silk of my panties and a deliciously powerful shiver racks my whole body. I choke back a small cry. I've never felt anything so beautifully thrilling.

More of that. I *need* more of that. He's back to sniffing, but I want his touch. I'm desperate for it.

"Riva..." Nykolas whispers on a ragged breath. He curses softly. "You're completely wet."

I tug at my panties and Nykolas catches my hand. "No," he whispers. Then, with a tortured groan, he lifts himself up onto his forearms. "I want...all of you. Trust me, I want this so badly. But we should wait."

I lift my head from the cushions so I can see his face. "Why?"

"Unless you're ready to have my child, we can't. There's no birth control for humans here. It's outlawed."

"That makes no sense. If they're bringing human girls here, why wouldn't they want to get birth control for us?"

"It's on purpose," Nykolas explains, "to take away your power."

I flop my head back against the cushions and glare at the skies. Of course, the ability for a woman to resist pregnancy is power.

"Funny how it's the opposite for males," I growl, "how their power is in the ability to impregnate."

I curse. Their stupid rules, designed to make us

completely subservient, are all that stand in the way of Nykolas and I making love right now.

"It's not strictly a gender thing," Nykolas tells me. "We've only ever kidnapped human girls because our princesses aren't interested in having offspring yet. When they're ready, human males will be kidnapped for them, and they will not be allowed to use any birth control methods either. It is frustrating for faeries too, as it limits how much we can make love to humans for pleasure. The whole point is to make sure we don't get too fond of each other. Obviously, the law will have to change once you're my queen. I plan to fuck you as often as your mortal body can take it."

"Shut up, Nykolas." He can't say things like that if he isn't planning to make good on them immediately.

He chuckles. "You are delightful, Riva." Then he's back to sniffing me.

Sunset has begun. Ribbons of color grace the western sky, and the sun is a molten ball of fire at the center of the grand display.

I realize I want to make love to Nykolas before I leave. I want it with an intensity that shocks me. This is probably the last time that he and I will be alone together like this. It's our only opportunity.

It will be my first time, and who better to create such a memory with? What better way to say goodbye?

"What if I don't care about the lack of birth control?" I ask Nykolas.

I can find emergency birth control when I get back to Lorthien.

"Let's wait," he replies. "The Choosing Ceremony is just a few days away, then we'll be together officially."

"Surely there are magical ways to prevent pregnancy."

"I would have to look into it. Even then, I wouldn't want us to do it. Not here and not now. Our first time should be special. I plan to blow your mind."

I want it now because I won't be here, I want to scream at him. But I can't tell him that. So I will forever wonder what it would have been like. How wonderful it would have felt.

"Now, all this talk is distracting me," Nykolas says. "I need to focus on your scent."

I laugh softly.

When he finally comes to lie beside me, his eyes are the color of storm-tossed waves.

I pull him on top of me and kiss him. His groin presses against mine. He's even harder now. I let out a moan as he rubs against me. My mind floods with a frustrating blend of blissful pleasure and deep yearning. Every cell in my body is crying out for more.

My dress feels like an obstacle. There's too much material between us. The raw intensity of what I'm feeling scares me. If I were to stay in Eraeon forever and marry Nykolas, he would consume me completely. I would lose myself to loving him.

As good as his body feels pressed against mine, a part of me is glad when he rolls away, breaking the kiss. We lie there, side by side on our backs, panting. A much appreciated breeze whispers by, cooling my cheeks.

Seconds turn to minutes, then an hour, as the sun glides toward the horizon.

Nykolas props himself up on his elbow then traces my jawline with his finger. "What do you know about faeries?"

"I know that you're all crafty, brutal creatures."

He grins. "I forgive you your misconceptions. What else?"

"They're soon to be ruled by the sexiest faerie to have ever lived."

"Interesting. I shall request an addition to my formal title: His Royal Highness, Crown Prince Nykolas, Heir to the Throne of Embers, Sexiest Faerie Ever."

"It has a ring to it, don't you think?"

"It does."

I smile. "I also know that faeries are powerful and strong—although they seem to mostly use their power for ill."

"Another misconception that I will forgive. Do you know about how we like metaphors and symbolic acts?"

"Yes. I've heard of that."

Nykolas rises, tugging me up with him.

"Where are we going?" I ask as he leads me toward the sloping hills behind us.

"I was going to do this the night before the Choosing Ceremony, but that's the Festival of Moons, so I'll do it now."

I fall silent. If all goes to plan, Kali and I will be back in Lorthien by the night of the Festival of Moons—although I don't know if Lorthien will be safe with King Bastien wanting me dead. But where we go when we leave Eraeon is something to consider later. For now, I give the beautiful faerie beside me my full attention.

We walk down a path that winds through the landscape,

hillsides sloping upward on either side of us. I kick off my shoes after a while and Nykolas carries them for me.

Eventually, we come to a grove of ancient, towering trees. The path continues through the midst of them, shaded by the tangle of their branches overhead. Shafts of sunlight pierce through the dense foliage of the intertwining branches, casting a dappled golden glow on the vibrant wildflowers that carpet the ground on either side of the path.

Halfway down the path, Nykolas stops and places my shoes at the base of a tree. Then he removes his cloak, drops it to the ground, then begins to unbutton his shirt.

"What are you doing?" I ask.

"I know this might not mean anything to you," he says, "but it's something we do here to show openness and complete commitment."

I clasp my hands together as he shucks off his shirt, revealing acres of smooth, golden skin rippling with muscle. He tugs off his boots, then my brain stutters when he drops his trousers.

He hooks his thumbs into the waistband of his boxers and tugs them down. I glance away, my cheeks warming.

"You have to look at me," Nykolas says. "That's the whole point."

So I drag my gaze back to him. He's completely naked. I want to focus on his face, but my good intentions last all of a second before my eyes travel lower, over the broad expanse of his chest, the rippling muscles of his abs. Then lower. I clench my jaw at the sight of his rigid, aroused flesh. That sight all but paralyzes me.

"Sorry," he says. "I'm not supposed to be, well, so turned on, when I do this, but can you blame me?"

I feel like I'm about to come apart at the seams. I swallow around a knot in my throat and make my eyes travel down his powerful thighs and all the way to his feet.

I release a breath I hadn't realized I was holding. "You're beautiful, Nykolas."

His skin glows like the setting sun; his eyes are the jewel blue of the ocean and just as deep; his muscle-bound form is the stuff of fantasies.

"Explain again why you have to be naked," I say. "I feel like you're flaunting yourself to tempt me, while insisting we can't go further than a kiss."

"No." His eyes blaze intently. "This is a symbolic act to show openness. No secrets. No lies."

No secrets.

No lies.

Guilt threads through my heart, weaving a tapestry of conflicting emotions. I want to stay with Nykolas. But I have to go. On threat to my life I have to go.

I sense his magic sprinkling around us. "What are you doing?" I ask.

"I'm going to show you my heart. It's part of the whole thing. I will bypass your ears and communicate directly with your heart."

"Okay," I say slowly.

Then I gasp, my eyes fluttering shut, as...I see.

I've been in Nykolas's head before, and seen myself through his eyes. Now I'm in his heart, feeling...everything.

I stumble backward, my back hitting a tree, at the full force of his emotions.

The love. The desire. The passion. The devotion.

Nykolas loves me.

Me.

Deeply.

Tears spring to my eyes as the waves of his love carry me on a voyage through his innermost feelings. I know he's showing me everything when I feel his uncertainty and fear too.

He worries that the ancient hostilities between our races will ruin what we have. That he might have to give up everything to have me. That he can't have both his kingdom and the woman he loves.

I explore every sensation, navigating their depths. There's so much passion. So much tenderness.

When it's over, I sink to my knees, tears slipping from my eyes. I'm going to have one hell of a magical hangover after this, but it'll be worth every second.

That was...profound.

Nykolas leaves me to my thoughts, and I don't know how long I kneel there, recovering. Trying to process it all. I'm shaking when I eventually drag myself to my feet.

"This is the part where you would strip down and show me your heart too," Nykolas tells me softly. He smiles. "Then we would feel all close and connected to each other," there's a dry humor to his tone. "But you're human so you can't show me your heart. And if I were to try and use my magic to see it, it would be a poor reflection of your true emotions."

I go to him, and take his hands.

"Words feel so inadequate after that," I whisper. "But my words will have to suffice. I...love you, Nykolas. I love you with all my..."

I pause. If I tell him that I love him with all my heart, would I be lying? A piece of my heart has been stolen. At the same time, the rest of it burns with a passion that is all for him.

"I love you with all my heart," I tell him. "And what you've just done is not at all meaningless to me. It means everything."

The air between us grows charged, but with more than just the physical desire we felt on the couch. It's a palpable, all-consuming love that threatens to pull me under.

I kiss him, hoping I'm conveying everything I feel for him in my kiss. Nykolas's eyes are slightly unfocused when I pull away and I think I did. I watch him seem to pull himself together. It's shocking that I affect him so.

When we emerge from the grove, Nykolas now fully dressed, the sky is a brilliant but unnatural shade of purple, and stars twinkle like scattered diamonds.

Nykolas curses.

I laugh shortly. Everyone will now know that he's been caught up in a romantic moment.

There's a powerful burst of magic from him, then the purple rapidly clears, revealing the sunset again, and the stars fade.

Nykolas takes my hand and brushes a kiss to my fingertips. "Five days," he murmurs. "Five days, and then I will show you all the ways in which women are designed for pleasure."

12

When I get back to my chambers, Ziani and Nydia are having dinner in the lounge. The place smells of freshly baked bread and a hearty meat and vegetable stew. There's also a platter of red velvet cake.

"We brought you some dinner," Nydia says, nodding to a dish covered with a chrome bell jar.

I sink onto the couch and uncover the dish. Nykolas and I were so preoccupied with...other things. We didn't get around to summoning the servants he spoke of to serve us anything to eat. He's now in a military strategy meeting. "Is dinner no longer served in the dining room?" I ask.

"It is, but we refused to go," Ziani replies. "If they won't make sure the palace is safe and won't let us have a representative who can advocate for us, then we shouldn't be forced to walk around the palace unnecessarily. We can eat in our rooms."

"They won't let us have a rep?"

"Nope. Filpé said no."

"They hate us," Nydia hisses. "They really do hate us."

Worry snakes through my mind. I have plans to get out of here, but what about everyone else? Could I just save myself when they're in so much danger?

"Anyway, where did you and Nykolas go?" Ziani asks. "You looked sickeningly happy when you walked in."

I bite on my lower lip, trying to hold back the smile that wants to break loose. I don't know if I succeed. I will cherish the memory of the afternoon that Nykolas and I just had forever.

I'm not sure how much to share with my friends, but as I tell them, between bites of bread and mouthfuls of stew, they goad me for more and more, until I've laid everything bare. They seem as stunned by it all as I am.

The only person I ever used to be so open with was Kali. I can't wait to see her again.

"On your next naked meetup," Ziani says, as we savor red velvet cake and sip on sweet tea after our meal, "ask him to do something about the killing."

"I will," I say, although I don't know whether Nykolas and I will see much of each other before I leave. He's so busy preparing Eraeon in case of an attack from Rithelia.

He has many plans for when he ascends the throne, but that's two whole years away. By then, twenty more human girls will have been captured, and who knows how many more might have died.

I leave my friends in the lounge and go to change out of my fancy dress. Inside my bedroom, I drop to my knees and check under the bed. There's a small backpack waiting for me. I pull it out and unzip it. Inside is a sword with a black blade that is warm to my touch. As promised, Jaxson has gotten me a solathium sword.

My map is tucked into one of the inner pockets, along with a small flashlight and another map showing the palace passageways. They're a vast network of tunnels that snake through the palace walls like veins. One of them is highlighted in red. It must be the forgotten one that Jaxson spoke of. The one nobody knows about. The closest access point is in the hallway outside the human girls' chambers. It'll be easy to slip inside.

Finally, there's a small tub. I open it and it sprawls into a silver platter of various foods. Jaxson's voice fills my head, although I don't sense his presence in my mind, so I guess it's some kind of pre-prepared message: *All the food is spelled to last a week. Keep the tub closed and don't open it again until you're on the run and actually need to eat.*

I didn't even think of packing food. And I wouldn't have expected such a thoughtful gesture from Jaxson. There's a whole roast chicken, a loaf of sweetbread, a wheel of cheese, apples, a handful of cereal bars, a bottle of water, and a flask. I open a flask and peer inside. The scent of tomato soup wafts from it.

I wonder how to stuff everything back into the small tub. Jaxson must have done it using magic. I begin to close the lid to the tub, hoping that will do the trick, and another pre-prepared message rolls through my mind.

To trigger the charm, say 'Jaxson is the sexiest male alive'.

I roll my eyes. Of course the password would be that. "Jaxson is the sexiest male alive," I growl, although a grudging smile tugs on my lips. The platter and everything on it vanishes back into the tub and I shut the lid.

I'm all set to get out of here. I just have to wait for Red Heavens.

∽

THE NEXT FEW days pass in a blur of tedious lessons and secret preparations for my escape. The entrance to the tunnels proves difficult to find, but I eventually discover that behind the cascading white wall silks in the corridor beyond the human girls' chambers, one of the pearl wall panels can be slid aside. Behind it is a hole, just big enough to crawl through.

I also plot how Kali and I will leave Eraeon. From books, I discover that there are docks five miles from Achlys Drive, where motorboats can he hired. But Kali and I won't be hiring. We'll be stealing.

I see little of Nykolas, which is just as well. One look into my eyes and he might realize that something is wrong. That I'm preoccupied with a secret agenda. I see plenty of Ziani and Nydia, who have all but moved in to my quarters, but I somehow manage not to raise their suspicions.

The day of Red Heavens dawns with pastel blue skies and balmy temperatures. The only thing I will miss about Eraeon—apart from Nykolas—is the weather. Rithelia is a frozen icescape. Our summers are mild and barely earn the title. They're nowhere near as warm as Eraeon.

There's a definite sense of excitement in the air throughout the palace on Red Heavens. Work, and even our lessons, finish at noon, as the faeries prepare for the festivities—Frieve and Filpé included.

"Enjoy your afternoon off," Frieve tells us after a class on what to expect during pregnancy. With the Choosing Ceremony so close, many of the girls will be pregnant within weeks. "You may amuse yourselves until sunset," Frieve adds, "after which you must stay in your rooms and not come out until morning."

"Why?" Ziani asks. Frieve frowns, and Ziani adds, "It's a genuine question. I just want to know what the dangers are."

"There's a lot of drunken revelry on Red Heavens," Frieve informs her. "Trust me, you do not want to be around inebriated faeries who don't like you even when they're sober."

"I heard that three males broke into the human girls' quarters last Red Heavens and forced themselves on them," Seltie says in a small voice.

"Who told you that?" Frieve asks sharply.

"I did," Ivita says, raising a hand and widening her eyes innocently. "I didn't know I wasn't allowed to tell her that. I was just trying to warn her."

More like she was just trying to scare her. Had it been Vielle or Baila who'd told Seltie that, I would be more inclined to believe that they'd had good intentions. Ivita? No.

"We have taken steps to ensure your safety," Frieve says.

"What steps?" Nydia asks.

"Wards will be placed at the entrance to your quarters. Nobody will be able to get in."

"But we'll be able to get out, if we need to?" I ask,

worrying about my plans to escape. "If we, for example, need to visit the infirmary."

Ziani and Nydia both give me probing looks. I focus on Frieve. I haven't told them I'm leaving tonight, but it's hard to believe they don't know. I read them Kali's second note, even though none of us knew what Red Heavens was at the time.

"You will each be given a call button for tonight alone," Frieve says. "If you need something urgently, you may use it and someone will attend to you. It is possible for you to leave your rooms, but that should only be done in the event of some catastrophe, such as a fire, a flood—"

"Or some faerie bypassing the wards and trying to rape us," Ziani inserts."

"Nope, use the call button in that case. If you come out, you'll only encounter more faeries who might want a taste of you. Now, dinner will be served in your rooms tonight. It will simply appear on your lounge tables. Have a good rest of the day. I will see you tomorrow."

We all begin to pack up our books. The faerie girls have wrapped gifts to carry in addition to their books. When they arrived for class this morning they greeted each other with *Happy Red Heavens* and exchanged presents.

Now, they share their plans for the night, lowering their voices as though that means we won't be able to hear them. Ivita has a rendezvous planned with two males from the Guild of Gentlemen. Kizra, one of her friends, is meeting up with a secret boyfriend for the last time before the Choosing Ceremony. Vielle is going to a wine tasting.

The other human girls and I leave them in the classroom

and head to our quarters. The palace has been decorated for Red Heavens, and it's even more breathtaking than usual.

Elaborate streamers in hues of crimson and gold, intertwined with faerie lights, adorn the ceilings, creating a magical canopy that sparkles overhead. The walls are draped with red and gold silks. Gilded lanterns hang in clusters, casting a warm glow throughout the corridors, and aurel roses, their petals a vibrant red, are meticulously arranged in ornate vases. Even the doors have been decorated. They're decked with enchanted wreaths that release a soft melody whenever someone walks past, adding to the festive atmosphere.

"They never do anything by half measures, do they?" Darna murmurs. She has been mostly quiet since Tiona and Cardice died. So has Seltie. Ziani, Nydia and I are lucky. Nobody in our little friendship group has been killed.

We pass many statues of Oriya in the hallways, some with three heads, but most with just one. Carved from black marble, the faerie god wears a long flowing gown and wings extend gracefully from his back.

"They believe the fact that no other country in the world can see Red Heavens is evidence of Oriya's favor upon Eraeon," Nydia says.

"Is Red Heavens real, or is it just Nykolas manipulating the sky?" Ziani asks.

"It's real," I reply. According to the culture books I flipped through in the library, Red Heavens was an annual phenomenon in Eraeon even before faeries settled here and began to manipulate the weather to their tastes.

When we get to our quarters, we disperse toward our

rooms. As is usual these days, Nydia and Ziani follow me into mine. Their presence has kept the dark voices whispering in my head at bay. I've told them they can't sleep over tonight, though, claiming that I just want a night on my own. They agreed, no questions asked, to leave at nine p.m.

I've heard that Queen Tarla is due back just before midnight. Apparently, her travel is in connection with rituals and rites associated with Red Heavens. I will be gone before she returns.

I unlock the door to my rooms, and we're shocked to find three faerie males in the lounge, totally making themselves at home. Camran, Neal, and Markus.

Camran beams at the sight of Ziani and holds out a wrapped gift. "Happy Red Heavens."

Ziani smiles demurely. "Ah, thank you, Camran."

I sigh and head to my bedroom. My chambers have become a meeting place for Ziani and her admirers. Camran doesn't seem to know that Neal and Markus also have... entanglements with Ziani. He seems to think he's the only one. Not that any of them can even be with her, since it's pretty certain that she'll be given to one of the princes.

Nydia follows me to my room. "Going to see Nykolas now?" she asks as I unzip my dress.

I nod. He doesn't know I'm coming. I've heard he will be participating in ceremonial rites tonight, much like the blood ritual of a few weeks ago when he was whipped to within an inch of his life. As the Crown Prince, Red Heavens will not be a night of revelry for him, but of responsibility. He's due to go into pre-ritual preparations in an hour, so I'll have to be quick.

I change into an ivory chiffon gown, then I grab the wrapped gift on my dresser.

"Have fun," Nydia tells me, sprawling out on my bed. "But not too much. Always remember, Nykolas might be nice, but he's a faerie. Think of the things he must have done in Lorthien a few nights ago."

My explanation about Nykolas making sure to only kill soldiers and not civilians didn't wash with her.

"I'll bear that in mind," I tell her.

Ziani and her admirers are still chatting in the lounge, although the tension in the air is thick enough to pierce with a dagger. They're so wrapped up in each other that none of them even notices me leaving.

I linger in the hallway, where Nykolas's 'Welcome Back' display still stands. The flowers have begun to fade, their once-vibrant colors reduced to muted, earthy tones. The cleaners wanted to clear it away, but I didn't let them. I'm sure they'll do so after I've gone.

Jaxson, I think.

His response is immediate. *What do you want?*

I cringe. I only ever try to talk to him when I want something. I don't blame him for being testy about it.

After Nykolas showed me his heart the other day, I got Jaxson to cure my magic hangover. I couldn't afford to lose whole days when I needed to focus on plotting my escape. He grudgingly complied.

I want to show Nykolas my heart without him seeing anything about you, I tell Jaxson. *Can you hide whatever you did?*

Why would I do that?

He doesn't care if Nykolas finds out? Nykolas would kill him. He's considered killing him before for much less.

You would do it because sometimes people just do nice things for other people, and you're one of those people.

Who people do nice things for?

No, who sometimes does nice things for other people? Although I'm sure the former is true too.

I'll take another piece of your heart.

Do you ever do anything without expecting anything in return?

No.

Well, you can start today.

I'll take another piece. Do we have a deal, or not?

I scowl. *We have a deal.*

~

Nykolas is in a room full of military strategists, his top army officers, and royal advisors. I always assumed the faerie princes just lounge around being pampered all day, but Nykolas is constantly busy.

He sits slightly slouched back on a throne encrusted with rubies, exuding pure power as he speaks, staring at something on the large mahogany table they're all seated at. The respect and deference with which everyone is treating him is obvious. The fact that most of them are at least twice his age, tells me Nykolas has earned that respect.

"I wouldn't go in there if I were you," says the faerie guard at the door. He was the one to tell me who all the people in the room are.

Usually, I wouldn't dare waltz into an important meeting full of powerful faeries, but I have to if I'm going to see Nykolas one last time before I leave.

I knock lightly on the door, then open it. Nykolas stops speaking as every eye turns to me. That's when I realize Jaxson is in the room too, as well as the other faerie princes. Jaxson, instead of sitting at the table with everyone else, is standing by a window across the room, silhouetted by the daylight streaming in. The rest of the princes are scattered around the table, their thrones not quite as ornate as Nykolas's.

At the sight of me, Nykolas stops speaking. Then he rises slowly. "Jaxson, take over the deliberations in my absence," he says, his eyes never leaving me.

I step out of the room to wait for him, but not before noticing the map of Prysha on the table and all the miniature figurines on it, representing the faerie army. They're plotting another attack on my country?

The door bursts open. "Riva?" Nykolas pulls me into his arms.

"I'm sorry. I know you're busy—"

"Don't you dare apologize." He sweeps me off my feet, like I weigh nothing at all, and heads down the corridor. Halfway down, he kicks open a door and carries me into the empty meeting room on the other side.

"Happy Red Heavens," I tell him as he lowers me to the floor. I hold out my gift.

Nykolas's blue eyes light up. "I shall tell my advisors, who keep reminding me of how much humans despise faeries, that you are now engaging with our customs."

I just smile.

"Thank you, Riva," he says, and I can tell he's touched. "Whatever this is, I will cherish it forever."

There's that word again. *Forever.*

"Unless, of course, it's something perishable," he adds. "In that case, I will always remember it."

"Look into my heart," I say. "I know I can't use magic to show you. But just as you can look into my mind and see my thoughts, you can look into my heart and see my emotions. Right?"

Nykolas just stares at me for a moment. Then he steps closer. "It's something you should only do if you're really sure. If you feel safe being so vulnerable with me."

"I do."

A muscle works in Nykolas's jaw. I think he's floored by my offer. "You're right," he says. "Emotions are trickier and far more nebulous than thoughts. I won't be able to sense them as clearly as you sensed mine, but I will be able to get an overall picture of what you feel for me."

I nod. "Do it."

He steps closer still, and touches his forehead to mine. He takes my hands. Interlaces our fingers. Then I sense his magic. One moment it's all around me, the next, it's inside me, cresting through my chest.

I choke on a breath as the lines between where I end and he begins blur. This is going to give me one hell of a hangover. Magic always does whenever it enters my body. And I'm loathe to ask Jaxson to cure me again.

No sooner do I have the thought, than the sweet burn of

Jaxson's magic heats my whole body, fortifying me against Nykolas's magic.

I didn't even have to ask.

Nykolas's grip on my fingers tightens and I know he's seeing...everything. In a few short weeks I have fallen for him completely. I fix my thoughts on him, so that it stirs up my emotions for him to see. His beauty. His kindness. His determination to follow his heart—whether in refusing to kill innocent citizens or make a human girl his queen. He's the sweetest, sexiest male I've ever met and I want him to know that.

"Oh, Riva," he whispers.

Then his heart is open too, and he shows me again how deep the roots of his love for me have grown. It's heady and exhilarating and overpowering.

We stand there, hand in hand, hearts laid bare to each other, lost to the world around us.

"I love you," Nykolas whispers. His lips brush against mine in a whisper of a kiss. "I love you so much, Riva."

Gently, his lips claim mine, savoring them like I'm the most delectable thing he's ever tasted. He kisses me slowly, tenderly. It turns my knees to jelly and I don't know how I remain standing.

I can still see his heart and that takes the kiss to another level. It's so much more than a dance of skin against skin. So much more than a sweet collision of tongues. It's a fusion of hearts and souls. I sense his rising passion and the flurry of desire that swirls within him when I press against him. I sense the fierce heat of his raging desire for me. Nothing in the mortal lands could ever compare to this.

When we come up for air, Nykolas brushes his thumb over my lower lip. "You blow me away," he whispers. "Every time."

He thinks the passion in my kiss was love. It was. But it was also my final goodbye.

"You know how you should always tell the people you love that you love them, in case you don't get another chance?" I ask.

His brows lift slightly. "Yes?"

Nykolas is intimidatingly sexy. I would never usually be so direct, but I know how much he wants me. He's just shown me. And that gives me the boldness I need right now.

"Well, why delay?" I murmur, brushing a lingering kiss to his lips to leave him in no doubt as to what I'm asking for.

Nykolas's eyes are pools of pure desire. "Riva..." he says warningly when I press my chest against his. But he leans in to me with a tortured groan. "The Choosing Ceremony is the day after tomorrow," he bites out. "Make me wait for you, Riva. I want us to wait."

"Life is unpredictable. Anything could happen before the Choosing Ceremony."

"Nothing is going to stop me from getting my hands on you—every part of you—that night." Nykolas shakes his head. "Forget night. Immediately after the Ceremony, we're leaving, and I'm going to do all the things I've been fantasizing about doing to you. If the humans attack that night, the army will have to fight without me. We'll go to a safe underground bunker, if we have to, and make love while war rages above ground." He gives me a dark smile. "I can't wait."

I force a smile. Because his fantasies will forever be just that. Fantasies.

So will mine.

~

At sunset, the sky turns a brilliant red.

It's so sudden, my friends and I gasp. One minute it was a serene, cornflower blue. Now, it's like the heavens are an ocean of blood, suspended far above our heads. The clouds seem to catch fire, reflecting the sun's fierce rays.

Vielle told Nydia that this was going to happen just after four p.m., and I'm glad we stepped out onto my balcony just in time.

The red sky bathes the land below with a crimson radiance. Nothing escapes the touch of its warm, red glow. Trees, grass, buildings.

"This is surreal," Nydia says.

"And mesmerizing," I whisper.

Ziani is, for once, silent. Just taking it all in.

We sit out on the balcony for two hours, watching the sky blush to deeper and deeper shades of red, until the sun dips behind a distant mountain and the stars come out to play.

When faeries appear in the gardens below, dressed in their finest clothes, some singing drunkenly, we scurry back indoors to stay out of sight.

An hour crawls by as I chat with Nydia and Ziani, the sounds of revelry bypassing my locked windows. Music vibrates the walls, punctuated by occasional sounds of shattering glass, spontaneous choruses of slurred singing, and lovers crying out in ecstasy.

We jump when there's a heavy bang against the door to my chambers. Nydia rises, but Ziani tugs her back down onto the couch. "We're not expected anywhere tonight. The rapists must have arrived."

There are more frighteningly loud bangs. "Open up," shouts a voice I don't recognize. Male. "I know there are three of you in there. I can smell you."

I step into the hallway. The door rattles disturbingly each time the faerie stranger pounds on it. Worry that it might give way fills my mind. It would be just my luck for a faerie to burst in and have his wicked way with my friends and I before leaving us for dead on the night that I'm supposed to escape.

Kali has chosen a terrible time. The faeries aren't too distracted to notice a fleeing human girl. They're wild, on the prowl, and will give chase.

Somehow, the door holds, despite more males coming to pound on it like a pack of wild hyenas. They keep up their onslaught against the door and yet it doesn't give way. The wards Frieve mentioned must be watertight.

Just as I have the thought, magic bursts through the air. I sense that Ziani is the target. I let out a scream of horror, but it suddenly fizzles out before hitting her.

"What?" Nydia asks in alarm. "What is it?"

Relief floods me as I tell them both what just happened. The wards really are rock solid, keeping us safe even from magical attacks.

I beg providence to make the males leave soon, otherwise my friends won't be able to return to their rooms for the night, and I won't be able to sneak to the tunnels.

There's another outburst of magic, and it's terrifyingly strong. It too fizzles out, but wave after wave follows. It's so distracting, I can't think straight. All foreign magic that I've never sensed before. Just when I'm certain that the continuous onslaught will drive me to despair, a distinct icy tendril drips down my spine.

"Neal is out there," I tell Ziani and Nydia. "I can feel his magic."

Ziani looks troubled. "He wants to force himself on us, too?"

Suddenly, silence descends. There are no more frantic bangs on the door. No more drunken cries for us to open up. No more attempts to crack us with magic.

"He came to get rid of them," Nydia says.

I frown. That doesn't mesh with the view I have of Neal.

"Biting him in bed the other night must have done something to him," Nydia says, slanting Ziani a teasing glance. Then she looks at me. "So you really can sense their power. That's incredible—a power in itself."

I'm so on edge in the aftermath of sensing so many attacks that I barely hear her. I go to the bedroom and flop onto the bed, my senses overwhelmed. The thought of leaving the palace, which would be dangerous on any night but is even more so tonight, drives a stake of fear into my heart.

I lie there for the next hour. Sleep beckons, but I resist it, although its pull is strong. Since the day I woke up in the hospital, back in Lorthien, I haven't had a single full night of sleep, and a deep fatigue has come to live in my bones.

Just before nine, I hear my friends leave. Disappointment settles over me at the fact that they didn't say goodbye. But then, they don't know I'm leaving. They think I just want my bedroom to myself tonight.

It's pretty unbelievable that they don't know. Didn't I read the part of Kali's note that mentioned Red Heavens? Have they just not put the pieces together.

A few minutes later, the soft chiming of the hallway clock filters into my room and my heart skips a beat. It's nine p.m. I have just fifteen minutes until I'm leaving. If I'm to get to 6 Achlys Drive by midnight, I need to give myself plenty of time.

I change, trading my ivory gown for a plain blue one—no gray as that could draw attention—and slipping my feet into flats. Then I grab the backpack that Jaxson packed for me.

The next few minutes crawl by, agonizingly slow. My heart pounds like a drumbeat—a thunderous rhythm echoing the urgency of my thoughts.

At nine-fifteen on the dot, I slip out. The circular hallway outside my room is empty. The doors to all the other human girls' rooms are shut. My breath hitches at the sight of the dents and cracks in the pale alabaster walls, a testament to the unruly revelry that unfolded earlier.

Empty liquor bottles litter the floor, their contents spilled and mingled, leaving the pungent aroma of alcohol in the air. I pick my way around bits of broken glass, moving as silently as I can.

The main hallway outside our quarters are no better.

Torn wall silks. Shreds of paper from party decorations littering the floor. Red Heavens must be a pretty expensive annual celebration. Or maybe not. They probably just fix everything using magic.

The wall silk covering the sliding panel that leads to the tunnels hangs askew. I pull it back into place then step around it. I make quick work of sliding the panel aside to reveal the hidden cavity behind it.

"Where are you going?"

I almost collapse with shock.

Nydia emerges from further down the wall silk. I press a hand to my chest. My heart is clattering like a jackhammer. "What are you doing out of your room?"

She eyes my backpack. "I could ask you the same. You're leaving, I guess."

I nod.

"To find your sister?"

"Yeah."

"As admirable and courageous as that is, it's also incredibly foolish. You really think you can survive in Eraeon outside the palace?"

"We're barely surviving inside the palace."

"Exactly," she snaps. "Out there, it'll be ten times worse. Any faerie that sees you will kill you. Or worse, they'll rape you first, *then* kill you."

"I'm willing to take the chance. I've already come this far."

"It could be a trap, Riva!"

"I don't think it is. I told you about the saying that Kali and I used to—"

"It could still be a trap. That quote doesn't mean it's her. Someone might have read it in her mind and decided to use it to fool you into thinking the notes are truly from her. As you know, the whole of Eraeon hates you. This could be some clever scheme to lure you out of the palace and murder you."

She's right. It could be. Her fear that the quote could have been stolen from Kali's mind is wild, yet plausible. But this is the whole reason why I came to Eraeon. Besides, I'm all set. I can't back out now.

"I'm going, Nydia," I say gently. "I have to."

She shakes her head. "Please don't."

But I can see in her eyes that she already knows I won't listen.

I finish sliding the wall panel aside. "I just wish I could take you and Ziani with me," I say. "I'm sorry I can't."

Nydia sighs. "Even if you could, we wouldn't come. It's too dangerous."

"Ziani knows, too?"

"Yes. She wishes you all the best. We decided not to ask you any questions so that when the faeries realize you're missing and read our minds, they'll get no information."

I smile. Now their silence about my escape makes sense. They were trying to protect me.

"Thank you," I say, meaning it with all my heart. Then I crawl through the hole in the wall.

13

Nydia slides the panel shut for me, plunging me into darkness. I barely have room to maneuver as I remove my backpack and take out the flashlight and map of the tunnels.

I begin to crawl, careful not to bump my head in the confined space. The cool stone is rough and jagged against my palms and digs painfully into my knees. My abundant skirts are a nuisance, catching and tearing as I go. What I wouldn't give for a pair of jeans right now.

After I've been crawling for about two minutes, the tunnel abruptly widens and heightens. Gratefully, I rise to my feet, casting the flashlight around. The dark mouths of two tunnels gape before me. I consult Jaxson's map. The left-hand tunnel is highlighted in red.

I hurry down it. The quicker I move through the tunnels, the more time I'll save for when I get into the streets beyond the palace and cannot move as quickly as I would like, due to having to hide from faeries.

The passage ceiling stoops low overhead, and the floor is uneven, comprised of rough-hewn stones and jutting rocks that keep snagging the hem of my skirts. The musty scent of earth and ancient stone envelops me.

My breaths echo off the damp walls as I advance. The flashlight casts elongated shadows that shift and flicker in a ghostly dance. I come to another fork, this time of three tunnels. I consult the map, then take the middle one.

The map leads me through the vast network of tunnels, and I can only hope I'm following it correctly and haven't missed a turning at any point. After about thirty minutes, the rhythmic pulse of distant music reaches my ears. It seems to grow louder with each step. I must be nearing the palace entrance.

The tunnels will take me beneath the gates and into the rolling fields beyond, allowing me to bypass palace security completely.

When the tunnel floor turns from stone to packed earth, uneven with protruding roots, I know I must be in the fields. The air grows warm and dank. I try to ignore the occasional scurrying sounds of unseen creatures.

At the next fork, I take the right tunnel. If I've followed the map correctly, this should be the final one. It isn't a long tunnel. I come to an abrupt dead-end just a few steps in.

I flick my flashlight around, wondering how to get out. The light glints off something on the wall and I step closer to investigate.

A short, horizontal, metal rod is embedded in the tunnel wall. Flicking my light upward reveals more of them, and I realize they're not rods but the rungs of a ladder. I shine the flashlight up at the tunnel ceiling, and find that there is no ceiling here. This is some kind of shaft whose top is beyond the reach of the rays of my flashlight.

I clench the flashlight between my teeth, hike up my skirts, then begin to climb. The ladder ascends into darkness, and my hands grasp each higher rung with urgency.

Before long, sweat breaks out on my forehead, and my breaths echo in the narrow shaft, growing more labored as I climb. I pause occasionally to shine my flashlight upward. On my third pause, the beam reveals a metallic grate overhead.

Almost there, I tell myself.

The thought of finally seeing Kali again propels my tired limbs. My fingers, tingling with exertion, find the last few rungs, until I'm at the top of the shaft.

Panting hard, I push against the grate, but it doesn't budge. I heave against it with all my might, to no avail.

Panic flares momentarily, then I take a deep breath, calming myself. I remove the flashlight from my mouth and shine it at the grate. It's a square slab of metal. Completely solid. No holes I can slip my fingers through for a better grip when I push upward.

Despair is setting in when I notice a small latch tucked away in one of the grate's corners. My fingers, still sore from the climb, ache as I fumble with the clasp. There's a soft click as it unlatches, then the grate slides aside.

Cool air rushes in, caressing my clammy forehead, and dim red light leaks into the shaft. I hoist myself out, emerging in a narrow alley. The grate whispers shut once

I'm through. On this side it's a concrete slab that matches all the other concrete slabs that pave the alley.

I take great gulps of fresh air. The thrill of escape courses through me, along with a pulsing fear.

I'm out of the palace.

I tug a blue silk veil from my backpack and drape it over my hair, then wrap the ends around my neck, pulling up a portion of it to conceal my lower face. I will look like all the other faerie females who veil themselves just like this as they make their way through town for clandestine dalliances during Red Heavens. Nothing about me gives me away as human. I should fit right in.

I make my way down the alley, then step into an open field. The sun is a boiling orb of golden flame, and the sky looks like miles of burning lava. It colors the landscape with hues of fiery crimson. It would be so easy to just stand there, spellbound, but I hurry through the field, heading southward. I've memorized the route to 6 Achlys Drive so that I don't draw attention by consulting my map.

As I come to the end of the field, echoes of boisterous laughter and rowdy singing fill the night. I step into a busy street lined with casinos and other entertainment centers. Crowds of faeries flock in and out of them. Although not quite as richly dressed as courtiers, their clothes are still much finer than anything I've ever seen anyone wear in Lorthien.

My gaze follows a posse of males dripping with jewelry, their makeup flawless in the bright LED lights from a nearby casino. They're stunning, each of them. I quickly avert my gaze when one glances at me.

The crowd grows denser as I go, until I have to come to a standstill. It's an effort to stay calm when I'm completely surrounded by faeries. I force steady, even breaths, despite my every nerve stretching taught with tension.

A male in front of me glances over his shoulder and eyes me for a long moment. I'm not sure if I'm just being paranoid, but I notice more faeries slant looks my way, as though sensing that I'm different.

The crowd drifts forward slightly, but nowhere near fast enough for me. I try not to think of the fact that nobody here is human. The fact that they're all strong beings with powers beyond my comprehension. Whispers of magic fill the air, but I block them out, refusing the distraction that comes with sensing them.

It's only when a faerie male glances at me, his nose twitching, that I realize why so many of them keep looking my way. It isn't just all in my head. It's my scent.

"That perfume they wear to smell like human girls is so ridiculous," I hear him mutter to the scantily-clad female hanging on to his arm.

"I know," she replies, shooting me a cool look. "She's practically doused herself with it. It's so weird."

I keep my gaze averted from them, and I'm careful not to make eye contact with anyone. Relief floods me when the crowd thins as most of the faeries flow into what is clearly the most popular casino on the street.

At the end of the street, I cross a road where traffic has come to a standstill. Their cars are sleeker than in the human lands, and they gleam like enormous gemstones. Their engines are almost silent, emitting a barely audible humming. Noting the lack of exhaust fumes, I figure they must be powered by magic.

The next street is home to businesses that have closed for the night. I cling to the shadows cast by the tall buildings.

When I've been walking for thirty minutes, the ocean comes into view. I pause, my breath stolen by the way it reflects the red sky. Its breeze-driven waves undulate all the way to the horizon like miles of sparkling rubies.

The thought of rubies brings Nykolas to my mind and I promptly push him out before melancholy sets in.

I dart down an avenue that takes me to the wide highway that runs alongside the ocean. It's a straight path now from here to Achlys Drive. I walk swiftly, side-stepping faeries, ignoring a drunken brawl that has drawn a crowd of spectators, trying not to stare in open-mouthed shock at a bunch of male strippers performing a street show.

Vendors sell spiced meats, sweetbread, and sugary treats. Their aromas fill the air, mingling with the salty scent of the ocean. I see many girls, veiled like I am, some walking alone, some in groups.

Nobody pays me any attention, but I know I won't relax until I'm away from them all. Maybe not even then.

I'm planning to give Kali the other veil in my backpack, then we'll do what we did as kids whenever we ran away from our foster parents—live by our wits. We should be able to steal a phone from some inebriated faerie as we walk the five miles to the docks further down the oceanfront. We'll use it to find the nearest human country. At the docks, we'll steal a motorboat from one of the numerous boathouses and get out of here.

It isn't much of a plan, but it's all I've got so far. If Kali doesn't think it's a good idea maybe we'll both just continue to hide in Eraeon for a while. She's been doing that for over a year now, so it's definitely possible. When the Rithelian military attacks again—which they're bound to at some point, we can try to sneak aboard one of their ships. It'll have to be sneaking, as I'm a wanted person in Lorthien.

I shake my head in frustration. That isn't a great option either. I'm probably going to have to rely on Jaxson. I really don't want to ask for his help yet again, but if I must, I will. He can get us into Lorthien without anyone knowing, and Kali and I can immediately go under the radar so that King Bastien won't know I'm back. I don't think we'll stay there, though. It'll be too risky.

My heart grows heavy at the thought of no longer being safe in the place I call home. Why work so hard to get back there if it has become as dangerous for me as the faerie land? Maybe even more so, since I have no advocate there who dresses me in precious stones to protect me.

I've lived in Lorthien my whole life, and I've done nothing deserving of death. But Kali and I will have to make a new home in a new city. Maybe even a new country far from Prysha.

My heart kicks against my ribs when I finally make it onto Achlys drive. It's a long stretch of a deserted wide road that snakes through Eraeon parallel to the waterfront for miles on end, but my destination is just two miles down.

An eerie silence blankets the drive. There are no revelers here. Only the occasional flicker of distant streetlights and the soft thud of my own footsteps disrupt the stillness.

The road is bordered on the right by huge warehouses that are shut for the night, and on the left by trees that sprout from loose, sandy earth, the ocean about half a mile beyond the trees. The giant clock glowing from the roof of a skyscraper a few streets away tells me it's fifteen minutes to midnight. Three minutes later, number six Achlys Drive comes into view.

It's a huge warehouse that, unlike the others I've walked past, doesn't have a sign out front. I figure it must be abandoned. I hide among the trees on the opposite side of the road and watch, wondering if I'll see Kali arrive, or if she's already inside, waiting for me.

The windows are concealed by metal roll-up shutters, as is the door. I hope there's some way to get inside around the back.

I release a slow exhale and go over all that I've prepared to say to Kali when I see her again. The apology I'll give her for all the terrible things I said. I'm just grateful that she's alive and I don't have to forever live with the burden of my final words to her being cutting words of anger. I get to reconcile with her. Not everyone is so lucky.

By two minutes to midnight, nobody has come. I dart from my hiding place and race across the road. My veil blows off as I dash around the side of the warehouse, and I quickly tug it back into place. The warehouse has a side entrance, but it, too, is protected by a metal, roll-up door.

At the back of the building is a boarded up entrance. I

squint up at the windows. There's one just above the canopy of the back door, and there's no shutter covering it. The glass has been smashed, leaving jagged shards protruding menacingly from the window frame. Kali must be inside, and that window must be how she got in.

I look around the warehouse's concrete backyard and spot an industrial-sized trash can. I go to try and push it to the door. It's so heavy, it takes all my energy. The wheels creak loudly in the stillness, making me cringe.

I'm completely winded by the time the trash can hits the door with a heavy crash. I make quick work of climbing onto it then planting my hands on the door canopy and hauling myself upwards. The window is easily within reach.

I climb up onto the window ledge, careful to avoid the fragments of glass. My skirts tangle as I maneuver myself inside, and instead of landing gracefully, I tumble into the pitch dark warehouse with a loud thud.

Scrambling to my feet, I take out my flashlight and flick it around. Dust particles dance in its beam. I'm in a wide, open space. The floor is coarse wood, and the air is thick and stale. Tall shelves line the walls, crammed with crates and boxes.

Silence hangs in the air like a heavy shroud. The place feels suspended in a moment of apprehension, as if the very walls are holding their breath. Or maybe that's me holding my breath.

I exhale softly then approach the door at the end of the room and try to open it. It doesn't budge. Locked. It has to be past midnight now, so Kali will be here. What if I'm in the wrong part of the warehouse? She could be somewhere downstairs, having gotten one of her faerie friends to get her past the metal doors using magic.

Worry crackles in my chest. Why didn't she say exactly where in the warehouse I should meet her? To miss each other tonight would be tragic. Maybe not for her since she must have a way to continue to stay hidden, but I don't. I need to be out of here before I'm discovered missing in the morning.

"Kali," I call quietly. My voice sounds hollow in the emptiness, and I strain to hear any response from beyond the shadows that cling to the room's corners.

I try again, louder, in case Kali is in another part of the warehouse. "Kali!"

Not a sound stirs the silence in response. I stand there, the weight of the darkness pressing in on me, wondering what to do.

Stay calm, I tell myself when panic begins to bubble close to the surface. I didn't know where to go when I went to the whispering gardens, but I figured it out. This will be the same.

I return to the window and look out. The yard below is empty. I'll give it a few minutes then I'll climb out and see if there are any other entry points to the building.

A faint click behind me makes all my muscles tense. I turn, beaming my flashlight around. There's nobody there, but I know I didn't imagine that sound.

"Kali?" I whisper, walking slowly to the center of the room where the click seemed to come from.

Suddenly, a blinding white light illuminates the room. I stumble backwards, shielding my face with my arms. Then a deafening explosion erupts, shaking the floors beneath my feet. The force of the blast throws me through the air, and debris scatter around me like deadly confetti.

I slam against a cold, hard floor, disoriented and gasping for breath but getting a lungful of acrid smoke instead. Then something heavy slams against me, knocking the air from my lungs.

No! I scream internally as darkness rushes in. I try to stand, but whatever has fallen on me is too heavy. My limbs feel sluggish, and a sharp pain throbs in my head.

The chaotic sounds of destruction fade away as my mind blinks off.

I don't know how long I've been out of it when the shrill wail of a siren pierces through my consciousness. I stir, then groan at the stabbing pain that flashes through my body. I crack my eyes open and wince at the bright lights.

As my vision slowly clears, I find that I'm pinned beneath a large metal beam. My labored breaths are inadequate against the oppressive weight. The wreckage of the exploded warehouse surrounds me, and the air is thick with dust.

Flickering blue light cuts through the haze. A distant murmur of voices reaches my ears. I strain to hear what they're saying.

"We can't touch her. It's Riva Kadiri, Prince Nykolas's...associate."

"Have you informed the palace?"

"Yes. Someone is coming to collect her."

Pure terror seizes me. I'm going to be recaptured. Dragged back to the palace. Punished.

I *have* to get away.

I struggle against the metal beam and other debris on me, desperate to free myself.

"Don't move," a voice orders. Then a bunch of faeries in black uniforms come into view. They peer at me, although they remain at a respectful distance. "You will be freed shortly."

A sharp, metallic magic bites through the air and I already know who's arrived before he materializes on a mound of rubble.

Filpé.

He's wearing a skin-tight all-in-one...thing. I do not want to know what he's been up to during Red Heavens.

"You say you have a human girl?" he demands. Then he spots me.

I expect anger. Instead, a chilling glee fills his pale, blue eyes. Frieve materializes beside him, and I'm shocked by the gaudy silver dress she's wearing, but I guess she has a life outside of being matron to the human girls. I can only hope that she will rein Filpé in when he tries to give me some heinous punishment that will take me to the brink of death.

But instead of making any move to come and get me, Filpé smiles, teeth gleaming blue in the emergency lights spilling in through a gaping hole in the wall. "I shall alert the queen," he says.

"A human girl escaping is not something to disturb the queen with," Frieve replies.

She's right, it isn't. Filpé would only bother her with this if he knew that she would be interested. He must know she wants me dead.

And by sneaking out of the palace, I have given her all the excuse she needs to kill me—especially when I have failed to break up with Nykolas.

14

A glowing, spectral image of the queen appears before Filpé. "This had better be good?" she snarls.

"I thought you might be interested in this." He points toward me and the queen's image, fashioned from light, turns.

Then the light of her spectral image begins to fade into the solid form of the actual queen. At her presence, everyone in the room drops to their knees and bows.

"Where are we?" Queen Tarla asks, her eyes not leaving me.

"Achlys Drive," Filpé says.

"This couldn't be the warehouse in which a rebel operation was discovered and disbanded two weeks ago?"

"It is that very one," Filpé replies.

I want to tell them that I know nothing about a rebel operation, but I think silence is my best option right now—until I get out from under this metal beam.

"She must be the spy," Queen Tarla says.

What?

"Jiorge," the queen murmurs softly. "Find me."

No sooner have the words left her lips than a blazing blue portal flashes to life beside her. Prince Jiorge steps through it. He looks at me and then at the queen. A few silent moments pass and I gather that they're communicating mind to mind.

Then Prince Jiorge looks at me again. "She has to be the spy."

I sense a sprinkling of Frieve's magic, then Nykolas's. When he appears from thin air, I know Frieve must have told him what is happening.

Nykolas opens his mouth to say something, then he sees me, and the blood drains from his face. The beam pinning me down is snatched away by the invisible hands of his magic and thrown aside as he hurries to me.

"You will not heal her with magic," Prince Jiorge snaps. "Allow her frail, mortal body to heal itself."

Nykolas helps me up, cool, tingling energy seeping from his hands into my body, healing me in defiance of his uncle. "There had better be a good explanation for why nobody helped her," he grinds out.

"I hope there is also a good explanation as to why she was out here, ten miles away from the palace," Queen Tarla says. "And sneaking around a well-known rebel haunt."

"Riva is not the spy, if that's what you're thinking," Nykolas replies. "I have a few leads as to who the spy is."

"Nykolas," Queen Tarla says gently. "Allow her to speak for herself."

Nykolas falls silent, and every eye turns to me.

Only then do I realize how filthy and torn my dress is. There's dirt beneath my nails. And my hair is a tangled mess. I've no idea where my veil is.

"What are you doing here?" Queen Tarla asks me.

I don't know what to say. There's no way to wriggle out of this.

Queen Tarla's magic is a subtle, rose-scented current of energy that whips toward me. The moment Nykolas's magic rises to deflect it, I know my life is over. Her son has turned against her because of me—or at least that's how she'll see it.

She turns to Nykolas brows lifted. "You will stand in the way of me reading her mind?"

"She doesn't tolerate magic well," Nykolas says. A muscle works in his jaw.

"After what she has done, her mind must be read."

"I know." Nykolas pauses. "I will read it."

The queen nods to the emergency officers. "Excuse us. And take Riva with you. Do not let her out of your sight."

The officers come and march me toward the hole in the wall. Only when we step through it into the yard do I realize that I must have fallen to ground level in the explosion.

"Why are you defending her!" Prince Jiorge sputters, once we're out of the warehouse. "Dabria is such a sweet, lovely girl who obviously adores you. She wouldn't even bother having a harem if you would pay her some attention. Yet, you're hellbent on that scheming human girl."

I can't believe everyone thinks Dabria is so nice and sweet when she only wants Nykolas for the queenhood!

"First you had to go and fall for an Aziza princess," Prince

Jiorge rages on, "and now a human. What's wrong with our faerie girls of Eraeon? They're not good enough for you, Nykolas?"

"We already know that King Bastien has a spy in Eraeon," Queen Tarla says, her tone much more measured than Prince Jiorge's. "Could it not be one of the human girls? Does what Riva has done not speak of specialized training? Not to mention the fact that she is a sentiae. I shall summon General Kunlé and hear his thoughts on the matter since you have clearly lost your objectivity."

"Your Highnesses," comes Filpé's sniveling voice. "You might want to seal us off so that nobody outside this room can overhear—"

The rest of his words are lost as the queen's magic rears to grant them privacy.

I stand in the yard with the emergency officers, one on either side of me, holding my arms. Another stands in front of me and one behind me.

I'm not a spy. I'm just a girl looking for her sister. Maybe I should come clean, because I can't have Queen Tarla read my mind. She'll see everything Jaxson did to help me, and he'll go down with me.

After a while, Nykolas steps out of the warehouse and strides toward me. Around his left wrist is the gift I gave him for Red Heavens, a bracelet I wove for him out of waxed cords and a few strands of my hair. Nykolas won't know the significance of it, but in Rithelia, women give them as tokens of love.

"Get your hands off my consort," Nykolas commands the

emergency officers, "and remain a respectable six feet away from her like you would if she were a faerie."

The emergency officers scramble to obey. A translucent blue bubble appears around Nykolas and me as he takes my hands. "My advisors, and now my kin, think you're a spy, sent by King Bastien to lure me into bed so that you can slip a dagger between my ribs while I'm in the throes of passion."

"If I was a spy, why would King Bastien sentence me to death?" I ask.

"Spies are killed all the time for many reasons. Being double agents, knowing too much, failing their mission—"

"I'm not a spy, Nykolas."

"I know. But it's going to be hard to convince everyone else, now that you've managed to sneak out of the palace and travel through Eraeon unaided. That speaks of training in stealth and knowledge of how to bypass even the toughest security measures. I want to save your life, Riva. Give me something to work with when I speak to the queen and the others. Tell me the truth. You're up to something. Tell me what it is."

I can't look him in the eyes. He's going to think everything has been a lie, when that isn't strictly the case.

"Riva," he prompts. "Please be honest with me. Why, and *how*, did you leave the palace?"

I take a deep breath then tell him everything. How Kali was snatched last year and I made sure I got kidnapped too, so I could rescue her. How I went to the forbidden north end to search the records and find out what happened to her. How I accepted his offer to return to Eraeon partly because my mission wasn't complete. And how sneaking out of the palace tonight was all about her too.

"I'm sorry," I tell him when I finish. "I should have told you..."

"I understand why you didn't," Nykolas replies. He squeezes my hands. "You're incredibly brave. Your sister is lucky to have you. Where is she?"

Pain splinters through my chest. "It was a setup. It wasn't my sister behind the notes, but wicked faeries who just wanted to kill me."

Nydia was right. This was a trap and I walked into it with my eyes wide open. Kali is gone. I'm never going to find her, and I'm going to have to live with the guilt of our final argument for the rest of my life. It's about time I accepted that.

"I'm sorry," Nykolas says. "And I will make whoever set you up sorry, too. They will die for this." His voice is low with rage, and his eyes blaze. "I can't believe I almost lost you tonight. You should have told me. I could have had the notes investigated for you."

Tears escape my eyes. I feel completely and utterly defeated. Lost. It's like Kali has been snatched from me all over again.

I think of the morning after last year's winter solstice when I realized Kali wasn't home. I'd thought maybe she'd gone to stay at one of her friends' homes. I went to work, thinking she would be at college. But the house was still empty when I got home in the evening. So I called her. She didn't answer her phone. Then I called her friends, who said they hadn't seen her since the previous day. I called her most recent boyfriend. He hadn't seen her either.

That's when I began to panic.

I called the police, and they suggested that she might have been one of the kidnapped girls. That hadn't even crossed my mind, and I refused to believe it.

I spent a week hoping she had run away, just to scare me, and would come back. Then I began to search for her myself, no longer trusting the police. It took me a month to accept that my sister, the only family I had, was gone—possibly kidnapped. And I immediately convinced myself that I could find her, bring her back, get things back to normal.

A sultry breeze brings me back to the present. I can't breathe. My chest is too tight. Nykolas catches me as I double over. He holds me wordlessly while my body heaves with great sobs. I don't want to fall apart in front of him, but tonight was my last hope of ever finding Kali.

She's gone.

No, my mind insists, because it's used to being in denial about Kali being dead. *She escaped the palace. Just because it wasn't her behind the notes doesn't mean she's dead. She's still somewhere in Eraeon.*

The thought brings me hope, but I don't know if I have the courage to grasp for hope anymore.

"Is it okay if I tell the queen what you have told me?" Nykolas asks, crouching before me and wiping the wetness from my cheeks.

I nod, because we really have no option. She, and everyone else, will want an explanation.

I sink to the ground and Nykolas remains crouched before me, wiping the tears that won't stop flowing.

A few minutes later, he speaks again. "They want to know how exactly you got out of the palace."

Nykolas must have been communicating with Queen Tarla and Prince Jiorge mind to mind.

"It's okay if you're not ready to answer right now," he adds. "I know you're upset."

"I..." I blink, feigning confusion. "I found a passageway, but I don't know how I found it, or how I navigated it so successfully. Now that I think about it, maybe someone was controlling me."

"That makes sense," Nykolas says. "They needed you to escape and come out here so that they could try to kill you. Did you sense their magic?"

I consider it then nod slowly. "Only slightly. It felt like...like silk against my skin. I don't know who it was." I'm shocked at how easily the lie rolls off my tongue.

"That's okay." Nykolas sighs. "It's not right that we bring human girls to the palace. You're all so defenseless against our magic. So vulnerable to manipulation. I'm sorry this has happened to you again. I thought that after we made an example of the last person to manipulate you, that would deter others. Clearly I will need to be more...direct." Something dangerous has crept into his voice. "Everybody involved with what happened tonight is going to die."

I study Nykolas for a moment, suddenly afraid. The way he loves me is troubling. What if I *was* a spy? He would be completely at my mercy. I shake my head, a sudden clarity coming over me. I can't be with a man I have to continually lie to. It isn't fair to him, and it's too much for me to bear.

The queen emerges from the warehouse and I quickly

pull away from Nykolas. I'm not supposed to be weeping on his shoulder and letting him comfort me. I'm supposed to be ending our relationship. "I, uh, think it would be best if we stopped seeing each other."

Nykolas frowns. "What?"

"I heard what your uncle said before the room was sealed. "Nobody wants us to be together, Nykolas."

"Who cares what people want or don't want? If we want each other that's all that matters."

"I came here for my sister—"

"You can find your sister and also be with me," Nykolas cuts in. "You can have both, you know? Your sister led you to me, and for that I'm grateful. I will help you find her."

It's tempting. Oh so tempting.

But if he finds Kali, what next? It won't change the fact that his mother, his uncle, and his betrothed hate me and want me dead. I will still have to break up with him. His love comes with too heavy a price tag.

"I'm sorry, Nykolas, but I think we should—"

"Riva," he interjects gently. "You're understandably shaken after all that has happened tonight—"

"No, Nykolas. Let me go. Please. I want to return to Lorthien."

If I don't return tonight, I will die. That much is clear from the way the queen is watching us from the other side of our little bubble. Nykolas has to send me away right now, back to Lorthien, or she'll kill me.

"I understand you were planning to escape with your sister," Nykolas says, "but you don't have to do that. You can stay. It hurts to know that you were going to leave without telling me."

I shake my head. "I'm sorry, Nykolas. Please arrange for me to leave. Tonight, please."

He looks wounded and confused. "You told me you love me. Was it all lies?"

"No, but—"

"Then don't leave me, Riva. If you go, you'll take my heart with you."

Tears threaten. "I *have* to go," I whisper.

"Why?" Nykolas asks. "Why must you go?" He pauses. "Unless someone has put you up to this?"

"No," I say quickly. "Nobody has."

Nykolas is quiet for a long moment, worry filling his eyes. "You can tell me, Riva," he says quietly. "Even if it's my own mother. The last time I was in love, mother threatened her. She was a faerie, but from Aziza not Eraeon, which mother had a problem with. This time, it's even worse, as far as she's concerned, because you're human. It's as though everyone thinks I can just switch off my feelings." Nykolas laughs shortly. "Where is the button for deactivating love? Even if there was one, I wouldn't do it. I have never been as happy as I am now, Riva. And it's all because of you. I wouldn't trade this for anything. If my mother has threatened you and demanded that you break up with me, I want to know."

"She hasn't," I lie.

The bubble around us vanishes and Nykolas rises, pulling me to my feet with him. Then he stares the queen down.

"Is everything okay, my love?" Queen Tarla asks. "Has she finally told you how she bypassed palace security?"

"You have threatened her," Nykolas says, an edge to his voice.

I shake my head desperately. "No, Nykolas. I said she didn't."

He isn't listening to me. "You threatened to kill her unless she leaves me."

Queen Tarla gives Nykolas a sad smile. "Will you never forgive me, Nykolas? I might have done that once in the past, because I thought your life was in danger—which it turned out it was—but I do not make a habit of issuing death threats to every woman my son falls in love with. If I'm suspicious of her it's simply because I want to ensure your happiness."

She's so convincing. I almost believe her myself!

What a liar.

Nykolas visibly thaws. His shoulders relax and the tightness of his expression fades into a questioning look as he turns back to me. "Don't leave me, Riva. All your concerns—we'll address them. I have to be at a ceremony in like two minutes. Just...don't do anything until I get back. Definitely don't leave. I love you. I choose you. We can make this work."

I tremble, knowing that every word that comes out of his mouth is only further sealing my fate. What does Queen Tarla want me to do? Insist, right now, that we are over, or wait until we don't have an audience? I have no idea and I'm too mentally exhausted to weigh the two options.

"She might have an explanation for what she did,"

Prince Jiorge says, joining us outside, "but whether we believe her is another matter. Her mind will be read, and even if all that she has said is true, she must still be punished for deceiving us all from day one. She is to spend a week in the dungeons."

"My bride in the dungeons?" Nykolas asks with a deadly calm.

A stunned silence ensues. They all knew that Nykolas cared for me, but not that he wants to actually make me his wife.

Queen Tarla recovers first. "Attend to your duties, Nykolas. We will discuss what is to be done tomorrow. In the meantime, I will see to it that no harm comes to her."

Nykolas strides toward the queen and kisses her cheek in gratitude. "Thank you, Mother." Then he comes and takes my hands. "My mother will protect you. I will be in rituals all night then will spend most of tomorrow passed out with pain. Think the blood rituals, but ten times worse."

I can't help a shudder. He was in a terrible state after the blood rituals a few weeks ago. He barely survived them.

"I will see you in the evening. You are to attend the Festival of Moons celebration with me. We can talk about our future after it." He looks deep into my eyes. "Okay?"

I nod. "Okay."

He leads me to the queen, giving her a grateful smile. "Nobody will be able to manipulate you with magic while you are under her care," he assures me. "She's one of the most powerful people in the kingdom."

I can't force a smile, so I just nod again, my throat closing up and panic bursting through my heart.

Nykolas vanishes into thin air and I don't dare look at Queen Tarla.

"Leave us," she says.

Prince Jiorge casts her a sly smile then disappears through a portal. Filpé and Frieve step through it too. The emergency officers scurry away around the side of the building.

"I didn't tell him," I say to Queen Tarla, shaking. I force my gaze to her beautiful, cruel face. "He jumped to conclusions, but I insisted that you didn't threaten me. I tried to break up with him, but he won't listen..."

I trail off as the cloying scent of roses fills my nose. I brace myself for a magical attack, but, instead, Dabria appears from thin air. She's practically naked in a skimpy piece of nothing, her hair tousled. At the sight of the queen, clothes appear from thin air on her body. "Your Highness?" Dabria says, bowing.

"Do with this *human* as you please," Queen Tarla replies. "And do it before sunrise."

Dabria straightens, pure bloodlust filling her eyes as she looks at me. "If I kill her, Nykolas will find out, and he'll—"

"Leave the consequences to me," Queen Tarla snaps. Then she vanishes.

Dabria releases a long, slow exhale. Then she raises her hands, a wicked smile curving her lips.

I *run.*

15

I can feel her suffocating, breath-snatching magic gathering, like a whirlwind swirling to life and spinning frantically. I know when she unleashes it. It comes after me, as though laser-guided. A tornado of certain death.

I stumble through the red-tinged darkness, darting around the side of the warehouse, racing for the wide, empty road. The tempest of Dabria's magic trails me like an ominous shadow. The air crackles with energy, white-hot and thirsty for flesh.

I'm almost at the trees on the other side of the road when I slam into an invisible barrier.

No!

"Dabria," I say turning. She isn't there. But her magic is.

A scream tears from my throat as it engulfs me, wrapping around my senses, squeezing the breath from my lungs. For a few harrowing moments, the world blurs into a maelstrom of crimson hues as my eyes flutter shut and an inferno seems to spark to life in my brain.

Just when I'm certain that my next breathless moment will be my last, the pressure on my lungs lifts and I can breathe again.

Dabria's magic withdraws, and I let out a broken cry. My bones rattle as I tremble with shock at almost dying just now. Then Dabria's magic begins to whip to life again. She's toying with me. Playing a sick game of chase.

"Just kill me," I plead, even though she isn't even there. "Kill me and let this be done with."

Her power screams toward me, but it's coming from a long distance. Maybe I can outrun it this time. It's gaining on me from my left, so I turn right and sprint down the sidewalk, my heart thrashing in my chest.

I can feel it closing the distance, its relentless pursuit sending shivers down my spine. I push my legs harder. Faster.

Suddenly, my limbs grow heavy and unresponsive, as if shackled by invisible chains, and a bout of light-headedness hits. Dabria hasn't erected an invisible barrier before me this time. Instead, she's sapping the strength and vitality from my entire being and making each step feel like I'm wading through a thick, resisting force.

When her whirlwind of power engulfs me, it sends pain like nothing I've ever felt burning through me. I can't even cry out because I can't breathe. I choke, my body convulsing involuntarily as if my entire being is being scorched from the inside out.

I have done nothing to deserve this. My only crime is winning the most coveted of hearts: Nykolas's. Inspiring love in him instead of hate.

My vision blurs and the edges of my consciousness fray like fragile threads. I feel like I'm teetering on the precipice of a vast, ancient darkness.

This is it.

I'm going to die.

I collapse to the ground, my heartbeats echoing like a distant drum in the void growing around me.

I summon one final thought. *Jaxson!*

Immediately, light rushes in. The fire in my bones is quenched. Air floods my nostrils and expands my lungs. Strength fills my body.

Thank you, I think, rising to my feet. Tears spill from my eyes. I owe Jaxson my life. I double over, shaking with horror at how close I just came to death once again.

Who is it? comes Jaxson's voice in my mind.

Dabria.

I can already feel her power building again. Spiraling toward me. Jaxson slips out of my mind, but the comforting heat of his magic lingers all over me, like a protective coating.

When Dabria's third attack hits, it's deflected completely. No pain. No suffocation. Nothing. Her magic rages around me, ferocious as a beast of prey, but I stand there, unharmed.

I let out a peal of manic laughter.

Unable to hurt me, Dabria's magic begins to drive me forward, propelling me through the night.

I laughed too soon.

I try to dig my heels in, but I'm powerless against the

force pushing me onward. I have no idea where Dabria is taking me until I make out the faint outline of trees ahead.

Fear closes its cold fist around my heart as I speed toward them. They grow more defined as I get closer, their silhouettes filling me with a strange foreboding.

Nocahya Forest.

Jaxson told me not to go in there. Said it drives human girls mad. Before I know it, I've crossed the threshold of the tree line.

Inside the forest, shadows dance in eerie patterns, and the air is heavy with silence. Red skylight filters through the branches, casting haunting carmine shapes on the forest floor.

I hurtle into the dark heart of the forest, the trees growing denser, and the shadows more oppressive. The ground beneath my feet is uneven, and the underbrush claws at my skirts, tugging at them like skeletal fingers.

The sky's feeble glow now struggles to penetrate the thick canopy above, casting a faint otherworldly glow on the twisted branches and tangled vines that reach out for me. I'm plunged into a dense thicket that seems to swallow me. Then Dabria's magic vanishes.

I sink to my knees, exhausted. Willing myself to stop trembling. But I can't. I'm completely alone in this terrifying, nocturnal wilderness, and I have no idea how to make my way out.

The thick darkness around me seems to press against my skin as if trying to gain entry to my body. My soul. It seeps into my pores and begins to spread through me, until we are one.

The moment the darkness reaches my heart, a chill washes through my body. I sigh, finding an odd comfort in whatever frightening thing is happening to me.

Suddenly, what can only be described as some kind of storm breaks out in my head. Fiery pulses run throughout my brain. I lean into it, welcoming the sweet torture; seeking the punishing pain. I deserve it for being so vile and unworthy.

I blink, recognizing this mental state. My mind is no longer my own. It's an ex-lover that has been turned against me.

I don't know if Dabria, frustrated at being unable to hurt me physically, has resorted to attacking my mind again, or if it's the forest.

It's probably the latter. This feels much worse than Dabria's mind manipulation.

I claw at the ground, fighting an invisible foe, frantic to escape myself. Then I realize what I'm doing and how irrational it is.

Stop, I order my hands. And, somehow, they obey.

I thrash my way out of the thicket then run, even though nobody and no magic is chasing me now. I'm fleeing myself, trying to outrun the dangerous thoughts that I know, instinctively, are coming. The same kind of thoughts that led to a smashed mirror and bloody fists a few days ago.

They begin as I'm gathering my skirts to keep them from tangling on roots and slowing me down.

You don't deserve Nykolas.

You don't even deserve your next breath.

You are worse than nothing.

I want to resist them, but I can't. I mash the heels of my palms against my eyes and let out a scream, trying my best to drown them out, but I can still hear them. They have broken into my mind and are shattering it from within. They're taking over my emotions, filling me with a dark rage and depthless self-contempt.

"Riva!"

A pair of powerful hands grab me and tear my hands from my eyes.

Now, I'm really afraid. I've been caught by whatever monsters dwell in the forest.

"Riva, open your eyes. It's okay."

I open my eyes and look up into Jaxson's concerned face. A light orb hovers above his head, illuminating him.

"Jaxson?" I ask, wondering if my mind, in overwhelm, has conjured him from nothing. "Are you really here?"

"Yes. I came to find you." His gaze searches mine. "I thought I would be too late."

We vanish from the forest and free-fall through a dark wind before reappearing on a clifftop in the middle of nowhere.

Up here, the air is cool and crisp, tinged with the scent of pine and earth. A panoramic view of a red-bathed valley unfurls far below us. It's like a canvas painted by gods.

The distant murmur of wind rustling through the valley's treetops is grounding—so is the feel of Jaxson's arms around me.

This is real. I'm out of the forest.

Realizing that I'm leaning against Jaxson, I pull free and take a few steps away.

He catches my arm.

"What?" I ask, noticing the flash of alarm in his eyes.

"Nothing." He releases me. "I thought—" His gaze cuts to the edge of the cliff. "Never mind."

He'd thought I was stepping toward the edge.

Just to be safe, in case such ideas do come into my mind, I back away from the edge of the cliff.

My whole body aches from Dabria's attacks, and I wish I had magic. I would heal myself. I hate having to ask someone else for help.

It's funny how that someone else is always Jaxson. Never Nykolas.

I imagine the heat of Jaxson's magic swamping my body and soothing all the pain. Fixing the scrapes, erasing the bruises, closing the wounds.

To my surprise, his fire simmers to life within me. I'm about to thank him when he lets out a gasp. Then his magic vanishes from my body. "Riva?" His dark eyes are stunned. "How did you do that?"

"Do what?"

"You snatched magic from me."

"I did?"

He looks at my arms. My dress is so tattered now that my arms are completely bare. Moments ago, they were covered in scratches, but now, they're smooth and wound-free.

I notice a cut on my right palm that hasn't completely faded. Again, I imagine the blissful blaze of Jaxson's magic infusing my hand and healing it. And it happens. My whole hand grows warm and the wound vanishes.

Jaxson is staring at me in bewilderment. I would be more

shocked if I had the capacity for it right now, but I'm too shaken. I'll process this later.

I lower my hand, sighing. My physical wounds might have been healed, but I don't know how to heal my mind.

Jaxson whispers something. It sounds like 'thief of wonder,' but that makes no sense to me, so I'm not sure.

"This must be linked to your ability to sense magic," he says more loudly, staring at me like I'm a puzzle he's trying to solve. His eyes are slightly narrowed in a mix of curiosity and caution. "It could be why you get such terrible hangovers after being hit with magic. Your body absorbs the magic instead of letting it do what it came to do then pass through." His eyes trail over me from head to toe. "I think your body wants to use it, but when the power remains inside you instead of being released, it overwhelms you—hence the hangover."

I have no idea what to think of what he's saying. I'm barely holding myself together right now. My mind is still smoldering with the flames of whatever it was that I felt in Nocahya Forest. The storm hasn't subsided yet.

The voices are still whispering.

Worthless.

You're worthless, Riva.

"This must also be why I can communicate with you mind to mind," Jaxson muses. "Despite you having no training."

I stare desperately at him, forcing myself to focus on his words and not the other words circulating in my head.

"I'm a telepath," Jaxson explains. "But thoughts can be tricky if the other person isn't one, too. Thoughts tend to be in images and it's easy to misconstrue things. But with you, I hear your voice in my head loud and clear. You must have powers."

That can't be true. "If it's so shocking that I can communicate with you mind to mind, why didn't you tell me before now?"

"Nykolas asked me not to."

"He knows I can speak into minds when I shouldn't be able to?"

"Yes, since you must have communicated mind to mind with him."

I don't know what to think about that. But if I get through this battle raging in my head, I will ask him why he didn't want me to know—assuming I'll live beyond tonight, or the next few days.

"You don't have powers per se," Jaxson says, "but it seems you can draw on the powers of others—which is a kind of power, I guess."

A sudden darkness floods my mind, and I don't realize I've doubled over until Jaxson asks me if I'm in pain. His arms are around me.

I can't speak. I can only wait for the tide of darkness to ebb slightly. Then I straighten, sweating and breathing hard.

Jaxson shifts slightly to see my face and I think he's letting go.

"No," I say, panicked. "Hold me."

"I am holding you," he murmurs. His arms tighten around me.

I barely hear him. The voices are getting louder. They

burn through my mind, growing bigger and stronger by the second.

You are nothing.

You are worthless.

I squeeze my eyes shut. Big mistake. Now, nothing exists but them.

"Riva?"

Jaxson's voice sounds miles away.

"Riva, open your eyes."

I find that I can't. I'm trapped. Falling down a bottomless black hole with no way out.

Then fire, different from the burning in my mind, licks against my eyelids and they pop open. I find that my eyes are blurry with tears. I quickly blink them away.

"Thanks," I whisper to Jaxson. He dragged me out of the black hole.

You're a filthy, disgusting creature.

Vile.

Empty.

You don't belong here or anywhere.

I clutch Jaxson's solid arms, only distantly aware of how hard my nails are digging into his flesh.

Is it true? I wonder.

Faeries hate you.

Your own people want you dead.

You don't belong anywhere.

I blink. It's getting hard to differentiate between the ugly, foreign thoughts and my own.

I look up at Jaxson. "There's something wrong with me. I'm...bad."

He just listens, his expression neutral.

"Right?" I prompt. "Do you think I'm bad?"

"It doesn't matter what I think of you." His deep voice is gentle. Quiet. "What do you think of you?"

A heavy dark feeling washes over me, bringing with it a wave of more debilitating thoughts. Before they can crash over me, I press my lips against Jaxson's and kiss him hard.

The heat of his mouth is completely distracting and it short-circuits my brain for a moment. It's long enough to wrench my mind from the grip of whatever has taken it over.

Stop kissing Jaxson, you fool, I yell at myself.

Still, it takes a supreme effort for me to tear my mouth away.

I'm breathing hard. Jaxson isn't. His midnight eyes are locked on mine. I'm glad when he doesn't say anything. I focus on catching my breath.

The burning heat of his mouth still lingers on my lips. And with how close he is, I can't help wondering about all kinds of things that I shouldn't wonder about.

Evil laughter echoes through my mind. *You think he wants you? You think anybody wants you?*

I find my lips on Jaxson's again. I kiss him with a fire that isn't normal. Isn't sane.

And he lets me.

It's only when I find myself clawing at his shirt like a wild animal that I come to my senses.

Abruptly, I step away. "I'm sorry...Stop allowing me to..."

I don't know how to complete the sentence. Shame swamps my entire being. "I'm sorry."

"Don't be, Riva."

For a few awful moments, my rapid breaths are the only sound on the clifftop. I turn to face the west where the sun has almost completely disappeared now.

Then he speaks again. "I'll give you whatever you want, Riva. So long as you're sure it's really what you want."

See, I tell the voices. *You're lying to me.*

You're a filthy—

I turn around, needing the sight of Jaxson to distract me. It works. It's been a while since I've allowed myself to really look at him. To really see him. The dim light of the crimson skies tints his golden skin and gleams in his dark eyes. He's standing with that animal-like stillness that I've come to associate with him. The breeze toys with his inky black hair. I could stare at the sculpted planes of his face forever.

Heat radiates from him—the telltale sign of his mixed blood. I step closer to him, like a moth to the flame that will be my doom.

Jaxson reaches out and tips my chin. My eyes flutter shut. When nothing happens, I open them again. Jaxson is watching me, a dangerous look in his eyes. It makes me think of a predator circling prey. But I'm the one in charge right now. Aren't I? I'm the one who started this by kissing him.

"Tell me what you want," he murmurs.

It's a quiet command that sends a thrill of something dark and wild coursing through my veins.

I clutch a handful of his shirt. "You know exactly what I want," I hiss. I refuse to give him the satisfaction of spelling it out for him.

He looks down at my hand clenched around the black silk of his oh so fancy faerie shirt.

"We can't," he says slowly. "It would be wrong. Right? Since you and Nykolas..."

I touch a finger to his lips.

It's a mistake. Jaxson sucks my finger into his mouth, his teeth nicking my fingertip. I snatch my hand away even as my pulse begins to pound. I feel completely depraved for wanting him so badly.

Jaxson huffs a dark laugh. "There's a certain sense of destiny about this. It was only a matter of time before you and I gave in to the attraction sizzling between us. It almost feels inevitable."

I want to deny my attraction to him, but I can't. He knows. I know. There's no use lying about it.

"If you're sure about this," Jaxson says, "I want you to know I will take another piece of your heart."

"I don't care," I whisper. "Make me feel better. Do whatever it takes."

My feet leave the ground as, in one swift move, Jaxson lifts me into his arms. "Anything you want, sweet Riva," he murmurs. "Anything for you."

16

We vanish from the clifftop and spiral through a dark abyss of nothingness.

When we land, it's the smell that hits me first. Fragrant earth and foliage. Jaxson sets me down, and the forest we're in registers. I'm screaming and running before I know what I'm doing. Then Jaxson is with me.

"This is not Nocahya Forest." He takes my face in his large, hot hands. "It's okay, Riva."

This isn't Nocahya Forest, I repeat to myself.

Jaxson's thumbs trace my brows almost tenderly. "I shouldn't have brought you to a forest so soon after—"

"No," I say quickly, feeling like an utter fool. "It's fine. I overreacted."

"You didn't. You've been traumatized, and your body and brain are trying to protect you. That's not overreacting. That's normal." He lowers his hands from my face. "I'm with you, okay? Hold my hand, and if you at any point feel like you can't be in here, just tell me. We'll go someplace else immediately."

I sigh through my nose then take a calming breath. "Okay."

Jaxson offers his hand. I take it and allow him to lead me through the trees. They're more spaced out than in Nocahya Forest. And it's not as dark. Red light forms dappled patterns all around us.

The ground is a carpet of moss, cushioning my steps, and a symphony of rustling leaves, chirping insects, and distant birdcalls fills the air—unlike the heavy, oppressive silence of Nocahya Forest. It helps when Jaxson creates a large light orb to brighten our way.

We come to a small clearing surrounded on three sides by trees. The fourth side is a cliff-face, with a hole carved into it. A cave.

I shake my head as the dark voices, whispers now, but still very much present, echo through my mind. Proclaiming my worthlessness.

"I come here whenever I need to escape the complexities of real life," Jaxson says, leading me to the center of the clearing. "And now I've brought the biggest complexity ever into it."

"It's beautiful," I tell him.

"Yeah; the perfect place for us to both pretend there won't be any consequences for what we're about to do." Jaxson raises my hand and twirls me around once. "You have one last chance to back out. Because if we enter that cave, you are not leaving until I'm done with you."

I think of Queen Tarla and Dabria. Of the weight of being

hated by millions of faeries. Of the fact that I might not live to see many more days.

In that moment, I make up my mind. Nykolas and I are over. I love him, but he comes with too many trappings. I don't want to be a queen. All I ever wanted was to rescue Kali and get my old life back.

"Take me into the cave," I tell Jaxson.

He makes a low growling noise at the back of his throat then tugs me forward.

The cave is much bigger than I expected from the outside. It's at least the size of what would be a large room back in Lorthien.

Soft, incandescent orbs of light flicker to life overhead, floating in the air like earthbound stars. Their gentle glow bathes the space with warm, honeyed tones.

"What's your favorite flower?" Jaxson asks, releasing my hand.

I don't even have to think. "Aurel roses."

He pauses, a strange look crossing his face. It's gone before I can figure out what he's thinking. Aurel roses appear, climbing the cave walls. Only red ones, their golden stems and thorns glinting in the orblight.

"Favorite scent?" Jaxson asks.

"Fresh red velvet cake."

The smell immediately pervades the cave, subtle and sweet.

"Is there anything you can't do?" I ask Jaxson, grateful for this reprieve from real life and all the problems I will have to face when I leave his cave.

Jaxson steps away from me, releasing the top few buttons of his shirt. "Favorite song."

I consider it for a moment. "I don't have one."

I can't even think of any songs. At Mug Shot, Grigor played nondescript instrumentals, but apart from that my life was constant work, devoid of music or any other entertainment. And I don't know any faerie songs.

"How about this?" Jaxson asks as the gentle swell of what sounds like stringed instruments whispers through the air. It's a slow, stirring melody that seems to wrap around me. There's an ebb and flow to it that feels almost spiritual and heightens my senses. If I wanted Jaxson before, the music has ignited my passion and I'm ravenous for him now.

"It's perfect." I don't recognize the strained, husky voice that just escaped my lips.

Then I stand there awkwardly, not sure what to do next or how things are going to...get started.

Jaxson stalks toward me. I try not to fixate on the sliver of golden skin on display now that he's unfastened the top few buttons of his shirt.

I try to take a step back as he reaches me, and my back hits what feels like a solid wall. I know, without looking, that he's created a magical barrier behind me, blocking off the cave's exit. There's no escaping him now. He's going to give me what I asked for.

Jaxson plants his hands on the barrier on either side of my face and stares deep into my eyes. "You've only ever had human lovers, right? Well, you're about to realize that your human men are nothing."

I choke on a breath, then force myself to relax. He has no

idea how inexperienced I am. What was I thinking, telling him I want him?

"What is it?" Jaxson asks.

I shake my head

"Tell me," he growls.

His flaming magic rears when I remain silent, and I scowl. "Don't you dare."

"Tell me, or I'll snatch it out of your mind."

"I dare you to snatch anything out of my mind," I hiss.

Jaxson's magic burns hotter. Then it vanishes abruptly.

I'm unprepared when his lips cover mine in a scorching kiss. Every thought in my head vanishes as a dizzying sensation courses through me. The barrier against my back vanishes and we fall, until my back hits something soft and cushioned on the ground.

I push Jaxson away and look around. We're on a low bed that wasn't in here before. It's decked with black velvet sheets. Red rose petals are strewn all over the floor. More light orbs fill the air, twinkling not just above us, but all around us. It's magical.

My heart begins to hammer as Jaxson trails kisses down my neck.

"Wait," I say.

He pauses, and I force myself to meet his gaze although everything within me wants to look elsewhere—anywhere but at him.

"I, uh, h-haven't had any lovers before."

Jaxson cocks a dark brow.

"You mentioned human lovers. There hasn't been any. I mean, I kissed this guy. Pete. You know, back in high school." I clamp my mouth shut, wondering why I'm babbling.

Jaxson's lips curve into a wicked smile. "So this will be your first time. Good. I'm going to blow your mind and ruin you for every other male that might try to come after me; human, faerie, demi-fae, dragon, vampire. You name it. You will compare everything to this and be left thoroughly frustrated, wanting me alone."

I don't know why I thought he would find me odd or mock me for my lack of experience. He doesn't seem to care about it at all.

He drops a kiss onto my nose, even as his hands find the zipper at the side of my dress. "Oh, sweet Riva," he says, slowly pulling it down. "I'm going to tease you until you beg me for mercy. I'm going to make you feel so damn good that you won't ever want to leave this cave."

"Talk is cheap," I whisper.

Jaxson huffs a laugh. Then his teeth are on my neck and his burning hands are slipping past the lace and silk of my dress. I arch against him, aching for his touch on my exposed flesh.

I let out a moan as his tongue sweeps over my neck and his hands push aside the thin lace of my bra. His thumbs brush my nipples and the breath catches in my throat.

"Take off this blasted dress," Jaxson growls.

I begin to tug at my neckline. Then I remember it has a button at the back. I'm reaching for it when the dress vanishes from my body along with all my undergarments. I stare at Jaxson in shock.

"I couldn't wait," he says. "No apologies."

His eyes trail over me, and I reach around for something to cover myself with. Unfortunately he didn't include blankets when he magicked in a bed.

"You have no idea how many times I've thought about you this way," Jaxson whispers, his gaze sweeping over my breasts, then lower, between my legs. "Imagined us," he whispers. "Like this."

I wonder whether to admit that I've had those thoughts too. Then I push aside my inhibitions. "Same," I whisper.

"I don't know where to start," he murmurs. "I want all of you."

Then he's trailing kisses all over my neck. I hold my breath when his lips approach my chest, but he bypasses my breasts, kissing and licking my belly. Then he trails kisses down my thighs, legs and over my feet.

By the time his lips return to mine, my breath is labored and I'm quivering with desire. His tongue plunges into my mouth and I stroke it with mine. I let out a gasp when his hands finally cup my breasts.

I arch my back, pressing my breasts against his hot hands. Still kissing me, he massages them, kneading them in a delicious circular motion that drives me wild. I kiss him harder, a wonderful pressure building in my core.

"I knew you were going to be a firecracker," he murmurs, breaking the kiss. Then he licks my right nipple. I hold my breath as his tongue plays with the erect flesh.

"Jax—" I can't complete the word as he sucks my nipple into his mouth and his hand continues to play with my other breast. Then he's trailing his hot wet tongue over the other. I dig my hands into his hair, the soft music swirling around us.

I let out a gasp when his hand slips between my legs, sliding over the throbbing sensitive flesh. The touch is deliciously invasive. For a moment, I'm torn between thrusting his hand away and rubbing harder against it.

"You're so wet," Jaxson murmurs, his breath hot against my breasts. He rubs the slick flesh between my legs.

I let out a gasp as I rock against his fingers, feeling like I'm about to explode.

"You like that?" Jaxson whispers.

I can only nod as lightning races through my veins. I move faster and his fingers rub harder, working their delicious magic. A manic pressure is building within me, desperate for release.

It's as if time stands still, and there's only the heat of his hands, kindling an ever-growing flame within me that ignites a cascade of emotions. The world around us blurs, and all that remains is the electrifying sensations. His lips cover mine again as, all at once, every nerve in my body comes alive. His tongue presses into my mouth and I lick it wildly as I cry out.

"Open your eyes," Jaxson orders.

I open them and stare at him helplessly as my body bucks and I ride the waves of pleasure flowing through me.

When it ends, he slips his hand out from between my legs and gathers me close. "What was the name of that human guy again?" he asks.

"What human guy?" I breathe, exhausted.

Jaxson smiles. "Excellent."

I lean my head against his chest. Even through his shirt, I can feel his searing heat against my cheek.

"Don't tell me you're tired," Jaxson says, a playful lilt to his tone. He runs his fingers through my curls, which must be wild right now, and drops a kiss into my hair, rocking me slightly. "We're just getting started. I'm going to show you just how good it's possible to feel."

I sigh. I haven't felt so relaxed in a long time. Maybe even ever. The way he's holding me, kissing me—I feel beautiful. Special. Desirable.

As though waiting for the perfect time to strike and ruin the moment, the dark voices creep closer, hovering on the edges of my mind.

Worthless—

My whole body tenses.

"You can still hear the Nocahya?" Jaxson asks.

I nod. I don't know how he knows. I didn't tell him.

"Ignore them." He trails his nose down my neck. "I've always wondered if you taste as good as you smell. I haven't tasted every inch of you yet."

He releases me and shifts away. I frown, thinking he's getting off the bed, then he gently pushes my legs apart and licks between them.

I suck in a breath, making a sharp hissing sound.

Jaxson lifts his head. "You don't taste as good as you smell, Riva. You taste better."

My thoughts scatter as his head lowers again and he licks and sucks. The intimate invasion is new and shocking, but oh so good. I abandon myself to it, spreading my legs wider, grabbing his head and pulling it down, thrusting upward, deeper into his mouth.

I knew Jaxson could make me feel good. I knew he could.

My stomach tightens as another explosion builds. Just when I think it isn't possible to feel any better, Jaxson slips a finger inside me, even as his lips continue to move over my sex. He slides his finger in and out, and I match his rhythm.

I didn't know it was possible to feel this way. To feel so damn wonderful. The world shifts and I let out a frenzied cry as I soar. Jaxson sucks harder, like he wants to consume me, and my blood turns to fire.

I cry out his name as I come, head spinning, heart racing. Pure unbridled pleasure courses through me, consuming every thought and leaving only raw, unfiltered ecstasy in its wake.

This time, when Jaxson comes to hold me, it's with only one arm. He hasn't removed his finger from inside me.

We stare at each other for a moment. Then I tug at his shirt. "Why are you still wearing clothes?" I whisper. "Get them off."

He just smiles and begins to move his finger inside me, sliding in and out.

My eyes flutter shut.

"Eyes on me," he whispers.

I open my eyes and stare into his dark eyes as he slowly thrusts his finger deeper inside me.

"Take your clothes off," I whisper. "I want to see you. I want you inside me."

"Say that again." Jaxson's voice is a rough growl.

"I want you inside me."

"You'll have to say please and add my name—just so there's no confusion."

"Please...Jaxson."

His eyes glint with a wicked satisfaction. Then with his free hand he begins to unbutton his shirt.

I try to be patient, but the way he's fumbling with the buttons is driving me wild. I grab his shirt and tear the flimsy silk apart. It slides off his skin revealing acres of bronzed ridges and planes. I run my hands over the chiseled muscles of his abs, unable to believe that we're here together, just like I used to imagine when we both worked at Mug Shot.

Jaxson's muscles flex as he slips his finger out of me and removes his pants.

I hold my breath as his manhood springs free. Desire makes me bold, or maybe the word is reckless, and I reach out and touch the thick, proud length of him.

"Thank you," Jaxson says, "but it's all about you tonight. Not me. Now lie back."

I obey, and he straddles me. "Ready?" he asks.

I nod, then hold my breath as he begins to slide into me. It's a strangely pleasurable pain.

"Are you okay?" Jaxson asks.

"Yes," I choke out, although I don't know if I can accommodate the sheer size, and length, of him.

"We'll take this slow, okay?" he murmurs, gently pushing in deeper.

I nod, a sweat breaking out on my forehead.

"There," Jaxson says on a sigh. He's fully in. I feel him

deep in my core. He doesn't move. He's watching my face while I adjust to the connection. To him.

Then he flips us so that he's lying down and I'm on top. "You set the pace," he says. "This is all about you."

I rock my hips, and Jaxson reaches up and grabs my breasts. I lift off him and then slide back down.

"Oh, Riva," he whispers.

I lean over him as a continue to ride him, so that my breasts are within reach of his lips, and he catches one in his mouth.

I move my hips in a slow circular motion as I slide up and down on him, savoring every bit of our lovemaking. Jaxson thrusts upwards and I gasp. The next time he does it, I'm ready, and I bear down on him. We thrust against each other again, and I let out a deep moan of pleasure.

"Riva," he whispers, his dark eyes turning liquid.

I can't believe I'm having such an effect on him. The next time he thrusts upward, I bear down harder.

We grind against each other, slowly building our pace until the fire in my thighs forces me to stop, despite how spectacular it feels.

Jaxson seems to understand why I've stopped. He flips us over again and my back presses against the plush velvet sheets. He's on top now, and being trapped under him is where I always want to be.

He drives into me. My cry is edged with a sob.

"Too much?" he asks.

I shake my head, panting. "More."

He drives into me again and I thrust against him.

"I won't come until you're ready," he tells me. "You will

tell me when you're ready for this to end because I would happily do this all night."

I can only nod.

I bite into his shoulder as he begins to move faster, unable to believe how intensely good it feels.

"Harder," I choke, and he obeys.

I cry out with every thrust, my nails digging into his back. I clench my muscles around him and he groans.

"Did you feel that?" I whisper.

"Yes," he pants.

"Did it...feel nice?"

"Too fucking nice, Riva. Don't do it again. You'll drive me—"

I do it again and he lets out a gasp and begins to thrust harder. I watch him, delighting in the sight of him losing control.

He grabs my breasts as he slams harder, faster, deeper. I clench against him, eliciting groans of pleasure from him.

I don't know how it's possible, but flames lick through my veins once more. With every breath, with every stolen touch, we inch closer to the precipice.

I cry out at the same time that Jaxson lets out a mighty roar. Together, we climax, and it's different from the last two times I came. This time, my heart catches fire, not just my body. And I don't think Jaxson has used his magic to steal another piece yet.

He collapses against me, spent, and I watch him roll onto his back.

I'm drained too, and I tell him so when he asks if I want more. Then I close my eyes.

I'm glad when he doesn't ask me to open them.

As perfect as this has been, one thing was missing. There were no 'I love yous'. And, worryingly, I realize that that's something I want from Jaxson. But maybe it's okay. I don't need him making any false promises that his country won't allow him to fulfill.

Besides, I knew going into this that he had a hidden agenda. Jaxson doesn't love me, but I guess I'm good enough, pretty enough, for him to take to his bed.

At least the dark voices have gone now.

17

My heart feels like it's been cleaved in two.

I slept with Jaxson.

I zip up my torn, burned dress with trembling hands, feeling completely empty and foolish. What was I *thinking?*

Nykolas...

I cover my mouth with my hands. Nykolas can't find out about this. But how will I face him? How will I pretend?

I shove my feet into my shoes. I *really* have to leave Eraeon now.

Jaxson is still sleeping. Buck naked. He's like a magnificent sculpture hewn from a hunk of solid gold, every contour and line chiseled to perfection. Just looking at him makes me want to...

No! I snap at myself. *Get out of here and away from him!*

Go back to Lorthien.

The ground is still strewn with rose petals, and that haunting song is still playing. The smell of red velvet cake lingers in the air.

I stumble over something on my way to the cave entrance. Jaxson's shirt. It's torn. I can*not* believe I did that. Ripping his shirt like some kind of rabid animal.

When I get outside, the sky resembles a dying log fire—mostly ashen and black with pockets of flickering fire from the last embers yet to go out. Dawn is breaking in the east.

The trees surrounding the clearing don't scare me like they did in the thick of night. I venture a little way into the forest. Wispy remnants of darkness and self-loathing loiter like cobwebs clinging to the corners of my consciousness, but my mind is thankfully silent. It wasn't the lovemaking that did that. I have a groggy memory of Jaxson trying to restore my mind with his magic while I slept.

While I slept!

I haven't slept for more than a handful of fitful hours in ages, but the warmth of Jaxson's arms was like a cocoon. I slept like a hibernating creature.

No, I reprimand myself. It was nothing to do with Jaxson's arms. It was simply the weight of my exhaustion that finally granted me a reprieve. My body hit a wall and couldn't continue without sleep so it gave in—despite all my fears and current problems.

I stop walking and turn around slowly in a full circle. What am I doing? Where do I think I'm going? I have no idea how to get back to Lorthien.

I don't know where I am right now, so I won't be able to find the docks and steal a boat. Even if I knew the way, I can't walk the streets in these rags. I'll stick out like a wilted flower in a field of vibrant blossoms. I'll be arrested for sure. Dragged back to the palace and killed.

I'm going to need Jaxson's help one last time.

I make my way back to the clearing. "Jaxson?" I ask as I enter the cave.

I blink at the empty bed. He was there a few minutes ago. I spot a small piece of paper on his pillow and go to get it.

It's covered in a neat, elegant script that gives me pause. I don't know what I expected Jaxson's writing to look like, but it wasn't this. I steel myself against my intrigue and read:

Sweet Riva,

I hope you enjoyed your walk. Have the voices gone now?

Sorry to leave without telling you. I've been summoned urgently by the palace and have arranged for Camran to come and get you in half an hour. Walk east until you reach the brook. Wait for him there. He doesn't know about us. He thinks I was at the Red Heavens rituals all night, and that you slept here alone.

I hope I haunt your thoughts today.

J.

Jaxson? I think.

There's no response.

Jaxson!

Sweet Riva, comes his deep, rumbling response. *I'm in a meeting. Nykolas is here. I need you out of my head.*

Is he okay?

Barely.

At least he survived whatever torture he endured overnight.

I have to leave Eraeon, I tell Jaxson. *Dabria wants me dead.*

I don't dare rat out Queen Tarla.

Don't worry, Jaxson replies. *She can't kill you.*

What if she isn't the only person who wants me dead? What if someone else is also trying to kill me?

I'm more powerful than anyone in the palace. I will protect you.

He vanishes from my mind, and I have no option but to find the brook he mentioned. I guess he doesn't want Camran to know about his secret hiding place.

"How am I supposed to know which way is east?" I growl.

Then I roll my eyes. *The sunrise, you idiot.*

I set off, fear stuffing my heart to bursting. I'm not supposed to still be in Eraeon. I wasn't supposed to ever set foot in the Pearl Palace again. I can't believe how things played out overnight.

I didn't find Kali.

I slept with Jaxson.

After a while, I catch sight of water sparkling among distant trees in the dim dawn light. I make my way toward it and find a meandering brook. It gurgles softly as it bubbles over the smooth stones of its bed. Since I have no way of tracking the time, I don't know how long it has taken me to find it.

I follow the path of the brook with my gaze. It winds through the trees, fading into the distance in both directions. I sigh. I don't want to leave the serenity of this place. I don't want to return to the hellish battlefield that is the Pearl Palace.

Kneeling by the water's edge, I cup my hands to rinse out my mouth, and catch my reflection in its crystalline surface.

The face staring back at me is weary and smudged with dirt. Shadows have come to live under my eyes and my hair is an unsightly tangle. I look terrible, but I also know I should look much worse considering the night I had—prior to Jaxson.

I quickly block out thoughts of what Jaxson and I did. Thoughts of his powerful male physique. Of the sweet agony of him thrusting inside me. I wanted that with Nykolas, not with him. But I guess I did want it with Jaxson at one point, before I met Nykolas.

I shake my head. That's not strictly true. Even after meeting Nykolas, there was still so much confusion in my heart about Jaxson. I don't know what I wanted, but it doesn't matter anymore. I'm leaving. I can't be with Nykolas. Can't be a faerie queen. I just need to get out of here, preferably before this evening when Nykolas is expecting me to attend the Festival of Moons celebration with him.

Jaxson, I think, even though I know he's busy.

He doesn't respond, and I don't feel his presence in my mind, but I do sense the connection between us. That gleaming, black bridge.

Get me out of here, I think. *I need to get out of here.*

The words don't fade like they usually do when Jaxson doesn't respond. They linger on the bridge, and I realize I have somehow figured out how to leave a message that he'll receive later.

Help me get back to Lorthien, I add.

I'll take my chances with King Bastien trying to find me. I

just need to get away from this mess I've created, from the hatred and death threats, from everything.

I'm sorry, Kali.

I don't know how to find you.

Camran arrives on foot after what has presumably been half an hour, looking much too chipper for my liking. His blonde hair flops over his forehead boyishly, and his sea green eyes sparkle, although they're red-rimmed from what must have been a sleep-deprived Red Heavens.

"You either had a really good night," he says by way of greeting, eyeing my dress, "or a really bad one."

It was both, I answer inwardly.

I force a smile. "How are you planning to get me back into the palace without everyone finding out I left?"

"Everyone knows you left," Camran replies. "It's all over the news, although the queen's PR Team is hard at work, disseminating the story that Nykolas gave you permission to leave the palace for Red Heavens night as you wanted to learn more about our culture."

That means she knows I'm still alive. Of course, Dabria would have told her that she couldn't kill me.

"Is that not the truth?" Camran asks. "What happened?"

"N-nothing," I say, and it's obvious from my stammer that it's a lie.

Camran doesn't push me for the truth. "A car awaits us on the clifftop."

"Car? You're not going to magic us back?"

He smiles. "It's called vaulting."

"Vaulting?"

"Yes. Many centuries ago, when faeries first awakened powers, their abilities were weak and required a lot of practice to strengthen. Some faeries, those gifted with more of the *wonder*, which is what they named the magical essence within us, discovered an ability to jump—or vault—long distances. As they built their proficiency, it turned into vanishing and reappearing. I guess they chose the word vault rather than jump because everything had to sound posh back then."

"How did they awaken powers?" I ask, wondering if it might explain what has been happening with my strange abilities.

"They were a gift from Oriya."

I barely refrain from rolling my eyes. Everything is about their blasted religion. Haven't they considered the possibility of it being a natural phenomenon, or something that can be explained with science?

"You have clearly been hanging out with Nykolas and Jaxson too much if you think we can all vault, or that those of us who can are able to vault long distances. We're twenty-three miles away from the palace. I can only vault two miles; enough to get us to the car."

I was considering trying to snatch power from him, like I did with Jaxson last night, but there's no point. Two miles is nowhere near enough to get me to Lorthien. Besides, I don't even know if I can snatch Camran's powers. I might only be able to do it with Jaxson because he's built a connection between us.

I really want to try and snatch Camran's magic, just to see if I can, but I don't dare. If it works, I will only be giving away my abilities, and it's best if nobody finds out about them.

Camran takes my hand and tucks it into the crook of his arm. "If Nykolas finds out I touched you, tell him it was for the sole purpose of vaulting safely."

His eyes are completely void of guile. I think that, along with Nykolas, Camran could be one of the noblest faeries in the land. Poor guy. Ziani is going to eat him alive.

Camran's warm, tingly magic envelops us. There's a rush of wind and a spinning sensation, then we're standing before a sleek, silver car with the royal insignia—a pair of phoenix wings that curve upward—engraved on its bonnet.

I don't know how I'm going to face the queen's wrath. I can only hope I won't see her at all before Jaxson finishes his meeting and helps me get back to Lorthien.

∽

THE PALACE IS COMPLETELY STILL when we arrive. The sun rose upon Eraeon during the leisurely twenty-three mile drive, but it seems the palace's inhabitants didn't rise with it.

Camran sees me to my rooms, claiming that it's what Nykolas would expect of him, then I'm alone. I'm glad I don't have to see Nykolas right away. He said he'll be out of it for most of the day. After the meeting he's in with Jaxson, he's probably going to pass out in his room.

My fading 'Welcome Back' flowers from Nykolas are still in the hallway. The sight of them is an almost gutting taunt. This is the last place I want to be. If I could steal Jaxson's vaulting powers remotely, I would do so.

That's an idea.

I imagine the warmth of his magic rearing to life around me and transporting me to my apartment in Lorthien.

Nothing happens.

Maybe he has to be with me physically for it to work.

There's a knock on the door as I stand in the hallway, loathe to step any further into my rooms.

"Wake up, girls," a voice calls from the other side. Frieve. "Breakfast will be served in thirty minutes."

Tears sting my eyes. I shouldn't be here. I've spent the past week planning not to be. I should be with Kali right now. Escaping. In danger, possibly, but delightedly free. Instead, I'm still trapped in this nightmare of silk and glittering gold and splendor.

I bathe for longer than usual, almost as though the scalding water can cleanse me from the guilt of what I did last night; absolve me before I have to face Nykolas.

I won't have to face him, I tell myself. *Jaxson will be free soon. Then I can disappear.*

I drain a little of the bathwater, which has grown lukewarm with how long I've been sitting here, then top it up with more hot water until the temperature is just right.

I lean my head back in my opulent tub, the scented water doing nothing to calm me. All the marble in here is giving me a headache. When I get back to Lorthien, it'll be only stone, brick and cheap wood. Nothing to remind me of the opulent Pearl Palace. I long for the gray streets and frosty weather.

Sighing, I reach out toward Jaxson in my mind, seeking the heat of his power. I can't grasp it.

Can't you vault me to Lorthien from where you are? I ask into the void between us.

There's no response.

Thoughts of the things he did to me, the things we did to each other, last night canter through my mind unbidden, and warmth that is nothing to do with the bathwater pools in my core; throbs between my legs.

Trust me, Riva. You're safe. You don't need to run away if you don't want to.

Jaxson's voice in my head startles me.

What are you doing? he asks sharply.

Nothing.

You're thinking about us. He curses softly. *I wish I could come over.*

Just his voice makes my breasts feel heavy with desire. I try to banish my arousal so that Jaxson won't sense it. But another curse from him tells me he does sense it.

In the meantime, he says darkly, *you don't need anybody else in order to find your pleasure. It is, of course, nice to have a willing partner, but you are perfectly capable of fulfilling your own needs. You have fingers.*

The thought of what he's suggesting is shocking for all of two seconds, then I wonder why I've never thought of doing that before. Exploring my own body.

I suppose I've always been too busy and too stressed to think about the more carnal pleasures—or any pleasures at all—that life might have to offer.

My hand inches slowly toward the pulsing heat between my thighs.

Jaxson's groan rumbles through my head. *Riva...you are going to be the death of me.*

I let out a moan as my fingers skim the tight, sensitive flesh between my legs. Jaxson is right. A partner is wonderful, but this feels...

What are you doing to me? Jaxson asks, his voice suddenly sounding distant as I rub my puckered nipples with one hand and stroke the slick flesh of my sex with the other.

My pleasure builds rapidly. A few firm, fast strokes later and I'm coming apart, bathwater splashing all around me.

Oh... I cry internally.

Jaxson is still with me. Silent. Then his voice whispers through my head. *That was probably the most decadent thing I've ever witnessed.*

I push him out of my mind, cheeks flaming. I don't recognize the sex-hungry, wanton woman I'm becoming.

"Riva?"

The sound of Annha's voice jolts me from my post-orgasm stupor.

"You need to get dressed."

I rise and grab my towel, then emerge from the bathroom. On my way to the bedroom, I grab a gray dress from my closet.

Annha is waiting in my room along with the makeup artist and hairstylist. "You're not wearing that," she says, scowling at the dress I'm holding.

A grand yellow ballgown with full, billowing skirts hangs from a hook on the wall.

"I'm not dressing up today," I tell her.

"You are," Annha sounds slightly panicked. "We don't have much time. You're to attend the queen's royal address in fifteen minutes."

18

"Royal address?" I ask, my heart skipping a beat. "Is that a public thing?"

"She gives an annual Festival of Moons speech on her balcony," Annha explains distractedly, guiding me onto a seat at the center of the room.

If that's the case, it isn't some ploy to kill me. At least I hope not.

Annha proceeds to help me get dry. Somehow, she and her team make me presentable in ten minutes flat. Then she opens a portal and I step through it onto a vast balcony. The gold balustrades are adorned with ivy and baby's breath, and a lectern has been set up.

Six faerie ladies in a variety of bold colors are assembled behind the lectern.

"Well it's about time," a stern-faced, white-haired woman says gesturing for me to go and stand with them. A camera hangs from a strap around her neck.

None of the ladies assembled looks at me as I approach

the right end of their little arc where a young woman in a violet dress stands.

"Not there," the photographer snaps. "Beside Dabria."

Dabria? I look at the assembled ladies. Dabria is standing second from the left. She's the very image of radiance and beauty in a bright, yet tasteful, orange dress. Nobody would believe she tried to kill me just a few hours ago. I shuffle toward her.

"You're yellow," the exasperated photographer snaps, "so you need to be on Dabria's other side, between orange and green."

Only then do I figure it out. Seriously? We're a rainbow?

I get into position, careful not to let any part of me brush Dabria, barely able to breathe comfortably beside her.

The sky is bright and cloudless, the color of Nykolas's eyes, and the air is warmer than it should be this early. There were no storms overnight while he was being tortured. Could it be that his love for me made it bearable?

Guilt pierces my heart. It was so easy to let the queen threaten me into letting Nykolas go. So easy to decide I don't want him anymore and sleep with Jaxson. I know I love Nykolas, but did I ever truly *want* him.

If everything was perfect, which it isn't, and if I was deemed an acceptable wife for him, which I'm not, it would be easier to figure out what I want. Or maybe my night with Jaxson has confused my emotions. It's as if he has grabbed my heart and shaken it like a snow globe. I need to wait for all the little snowflakes to settle, then see how I feel.

It doesn't matter, I tell myself. *I'm not wanted here.*

I think I knew from the beginning that things would never work out.

Queen Tarla sweeps onto the balcony in a figure-hugging cream dress that flares in an abundant fishtail at the hem and ripples after her as she walks. At least ten maids hurry after her, fussing over her dress and hair as she sashays across the balcony.

One of the maids waves to the center of our 'rainbow' and a throne appears from thin air. The queen comes to sit on it, and her maids arrange her skirts across the floor. Then the photographer takes pictures.

By now, I've gathered that the other women must all be either royal wives or soon-to-be royal wives. I'm the only human among them, and I've been included just to show Eraeon that the palace is fully in control of me. That contrary to any rumors they might have heard about me escaping, I'm very much still a captive womb awaiting impregnation after the Choosing Ceremony.

Which is tomorrow!

Bubbles of hysteria effervesce in my chest. I *have* to be out of here by then.

After the photos, Queen Tarla approaches the lectern, and her attendants fuss around her for another few minutes while we all stand there waiting.

Once she's ready, an oval screen materializes from thin air before her at eye level. Its surface is glossy with a gentle, ethereal glow and reflects her image. I figure it's transmitting her across the whole country.

"Cherished citizens of Eraeon," she begins, "I, and all the ladies of the royal household, bid you a Merry Moonblest."

I feel completely awkward. If I were to marry Nykolas, these are the kinds of things I would be expected to do. Stand around looking pretty. Suck up to Queen Tarla. Attend formal events. And in two years, when Nykolas ascends the throne, I will be the one giving this Moonblest address.

It's a good thing the queen, and indeed the whole of Eraeon, don't want me to marry him. I don't want to either. I certainly don't want to be queen.

"Yesternight," Queen Tarla continues, "we stood in awe as Oriya's hand painted our skies, and tonight we will rejoice as he bathes our nation in the luminous glow of three moons—evidence of the grace upon our beloved land.

"I urge you all to allow the radiance of Red Heavens to inspire within you a passion and zest for living a rich, full life, and to allow the wonder of tonight's triad moons to give you pause to reflect on all that you, and we as a people, have been blessed with."

She goes on and on, saying a whole load of nothing. Thankfully, her speech is brief. No more than five minutes.

When she finishes, the screen before her vanishes, and she stalks back into the palace, her maids gathering her skirts for her, without so much as a look at me—or any of us.

I realize Dabria is trembling. I frown, eyeing her in my peripheral vision. Now that the broadcast has ended, her smile has vanished and her color is high. It isn't hard to work out what's wrong. The queen basically ordered her to kill me, and she failed. She might be in even greater jeopardy than I am—which will likely make her even more desperate for my demise.

I do not for a second believe that being included in this

broadcast, and basically outed to the whole country as an 'associate' of one of the royal princes, means I'm safe. Nykolas must have demanded that I be part of it, and the queen probably only agreed because it would further bolster the palace's PR efforts to convince everyone that I didn't escape.

But Queen Tarla still has options. She can make some accident happen that results in my death. Or my rooms could blow up when I get back to change out of this dress. Or I could have a freak heart attack before then as I walk through the halls.

I decide it isn't a productive use of my cognition to come up with creative ways in which Queen Tarla could kill me. A portal opens before me, showing my bedroom on the other side, and Annha waiting for me. I step through it, glad to get away from them all, and eager to take off this dress.

~

At breakfast, I select food only from serving trays that other girls have taken from. I'm usually the only one who opts for oatmeal, but I avoid it, not trusting that it won't be poisoned.

They could poison my food with magic while I'm eating it.

I try to shake off the paranoia, but it's a very legitimate concern.

"Still wearing gray on the eve of the Choosing Ceremony?"

I look up from my untouched pancakes. It's Ivita. Our faerie classmates are dining with us this morning. Or, rather, they're dining in the same room as us. They're at a separate table again where much more sumptuous food is on offer.

I ignore her. It probably kills her that I've snagged Nykolas, but she needn't worry. I don't plan to be here tomorrow.

I realize, belatedly, that Ziani and Nydia are absent. Terror strikes my heart. Were they summoned last night and their minds broken into, simply because they're my friends?

I'm still silently imploding with anxiety and horror at what might have happened to them, when the door bangs open, fifteen minutes later, and Ziani saunters in, delicately fluttering an enormous fan of peacock feathers. Nydia strolls in after her.

I expect Filpé to roar at them for their tardiness, but he immediately averts his gaze. So do all the guards. The faerie girls look pissed as hell, except Vielle and Baila who continue to eat.

I'm wondering what's going on when I spot the identical ruby rings sparkling on the middle fingers of my friends' left hands.

"Riva!" Ziani cries. "You're back! How was your night learning about the traditions of Red Heavens?"

So everyone has been told the lie that's being put out there?

"It was...enlightening," I reply as they come to sit on either side of me. I can't take my eyes off their rings. "Are those from Nykolas?"

Any prince can give a female his ring to protect her, but it has to be Nykolas because rubies seem to be his stone. Queen Tarla favors diamonds, and King Xander, Onyx. I haven't noticed any of the other princes wearing rubies or sitting on thrones encrusted with them—or any other precious stone for that matter. But neither have I paid the other princes much attention.

Ziani raises her voice. "Do any of you faeries in the room have the power to create those bubble things that His Royal Highness, Crown Prince Nykolas, Heir to the Throne of Embers makes whenever he wants to visit privately with Miss Riva Kadiri of Lorthien, Prysha?"

I glance at Nydia and she has to stifle laughter. One of the guards raises his hand.

"Create one around us, please," Ziani orders.

A dull blue shield encases us immediately, nowhere near as sparkly as Nykolas's shields.

"What happened?" Ziani demands. "Why are you back?"

"I need to know about your rings first."

Nydia beams. "Nykolas's messenger came early this morning to say you've been concerned for our safety so Nykolas has declared official interest in us and is going to choose us tomorrow. He would like us to wear ruby rings in the meantime for protection. After you were included in the queen's address, disgruntled faeries could take out their anger on any of the human girls like what happened at the Official Declaration Ceremony. If they do, it won't be us."

Ziani beams. "We are now untouchable."

Their rings are much smaller than the one Nykolas gave me, evidence of who among us actually has his heart. I can't believe he's done this. Helped my friends because it was important to me. I don't think anyone has ever cared so much about my concerns.

"How do you feel about him choosing you?" I ask my friends.

"Pretty damn good," Ziani replies. "If we're going to be here for a while, we might as well live off the Crown Prince. His messenger said Nykolas will 'never summon us to his bed'. We'll get to just relax and live in peace."

"What about the other people who want you? The other princes, Camran, Markus?"

Ziani snorts. "They can't protect me like being chosen by Nykolas can. And I'm not having babies with anyone who's been forced on me." She waves a hand regally, summoning a passing server who has come to replenish the drinks on the table. The bubble around us vanishes as the server approaches. "I don't see any waffles," Ziani says. "I would like three, with maple syrup and an assortment of berries."

The server goes to do her bidding and the bubble reappears around us.

"Ziani was clearly made for this kind of life," Nydia says. "Give her a few months and she'll be as cold and ruthless as any faerie."

Ziani cackles. "Honey, I'm already worse than any of them could ever hope to be. I just don't have the magic required to unleash myself upon them all."

Nydia goes to serve her own breakfast, and I mull over what Nykolas has done for my friends. I don't need him being so sweet when I've made up my mind to leave—or when I spent last night in his cousin's arms.

Guilt wracks me for the umpteenth time. I have always prided myself on being responsible, level-headed, the kind of person who thinks things through thoroughly rather than making snap, spur of the moment decisions.

What I did overnight, and in the bathtub this morning, was none of those things.

"Are you okay?" Ziani asks.

I nod quickly.

Nydia steps back into our bubble. "So what in the world happened, Riva?"

"Yeah," Ziani says. "Camran told me that Jaxson had him pick you up from some forest. How did Jaxson know where to find you? Have you and him finally given in to—"

"Not here," I cut in, shaking my head. I can't tell them now. The faerie who created the bubble could be eavesdropping. "I'll tell you when we're alone."

"We can be alone now," Ziani says. She rises and waves to the guard who created the bubble. He promptly dissipates it. "The three of us shall have breakfast in Riva's chambers," she declares to the dining room. "Filpé, please inform the server to bring my waffles to me there."

Nydia and I rise and follow her out. As we make our way through the palace, Ziani holds up her middle finger, high and proud, making sure nobody can miss the ruby ring.

"As you can see," Nydia whispers to me, "Ziani has been milking this for all it's worth."

"Rude gestures are only going to get that ring taken off you," I say.

"What? I didn't realize this was a rude gesture here, too," Ziani says in feigned innocence that she doesn't even try to make convincing.

"Honey, that's a rude gesture *everywhere*," Nydia replies, tugging Ziani's hand down.

~

Ziani's waffles are already waiting in my lounge when we get there. So is Nydia's unfinished breakfast and my plate of untouched pancakes.

"Magic is so convenient," Ziani sighs. "I so wish I had some." She settles onto the three-seater and spreads out her abundant skirts so that they don't get wrinkled. "Anyway, I had a good Red Heavens with Markus."

Nydia sits beside me on the two-seater, neither of us is bothered about our skirts.

"I had a good Red Heavens, too," Nydia says. "I snuck into the forbidden north end. Unfortunately, I couldn't get to the royal family's magic sources. I desperately wanted to shatter them, but they're protected by all kinds of magical wards now." She shoots me a look. "I wish you'd destroyed them when you had the chance."

I stare at her, my mind caught between shock and awe.

"We're giving you some dirt on us so that you feel comfortable telling us what's going on with you," Ziani explains.

"Right. Thanks."

But neither of their 'dirt' is as bad as mine. Or maybe Nydia's is. "How did you get in?" I ask her. "Whose blood key did you use?"

"Nobody's. I used the tunnels. Thank you for that discovery. I didn't know there were tunnels."

"So, what happened last night, Riva?" Ziani presses.

I have a million questions for Nydia, but they're so anxious to hear about my night. I tell them all about my escape, tears springing to my eyes at my failure to find Kali.

Nydia slips her hand into mine and gives it a squeeze when I tell them about the explosion. She was right that the notes could be a trap, but she doesn't say 'I told you so'.

I shouldn't tell them about Queen Tarla and Dabria, but I have little to lose anymore. I tell them everything. Even about Jaxson, although I leave out what I did this morning in the bathtub while our minds were connected. I also withhold everything about being able to snatch his powers since I don't understand it yet.

Ziani and Nydia are quiet when I finish. I've shocked them. And I'm not the person who does shocking things. That's Kali. I'm the predictable, ordinary twin who always plays things safe.

"The three of us are exceedingly dangerous women," Ziani says fiercely, her waffles forgotten on the table. "And I love it!"

I search their faces for some sign that they despise me for sleeping with Jaxson when Nykolas so clearly loves me. If he finds out he might stop protecting them. I've put them in danger. But their expressions are pretty neutral.

I lower my gaze to the floor. If any faeries find out that I was unfaithful to their Crown Prince...

It doesn't bear thinking about.

I thought I would be out of here by now and never see Nykolas again. I've been detaching from him emotionally and mentally since the queen's threat five days ago.

"So what's your plan now?" Nydia asks.

"I still want to get out of here."

"Jaxson is protecting you," Nydia replies. "And the Crown Prince is in love with you. Once he chooses you tomorrow, you'll get all kinds of official protection. You're not going to die."

I wish I felt the same confidence that she does.

"You had better bring change when you become queen," Nydia continues. "Unite faeries and humans. Stop the winter solstice kidnappings."

"Me?" I laugh. "In case you haven't noticed, faeries are not exactly happy with the idea of me being with Nykolas. They don't want me as their queen. His own mother doesn't want us together either."

"Who cares what anybody wants or doesn't want?" Nydia asks. "What do you want?"

Maybe that's the problem. I don't know what I want.

I came to find Kali, not to find love. But love is making everything so complicated. Nykolas is perfect—except for the fact that he's the heir to the throne.

"I couldn't inflict myself on a nation that doesn't want me," I say. "Apart from Nykolas, nobody wants me here."

"Once again, who cares?" Nydia says. "You *are* here, and you have an opportunity to do good with the position that's coming your way."

"She might not want Nykolas," Ziani tells her. "Maybe she'd rather have Jaxson."

Nydia looks incredulous. "Last night was just a moment of weakness after Dabria's attacks, right?"

I honestly don't know. I feel like I would just be making

excuses if I were to blame it on anything but pure recklessness.

"I don't think so," Ziani says. "Have you seen the way she and Jaxson look at each other? He was a mistake waiting to happen."

"If I stay, it'll be messy," I say, glad that Ziani has enabled me to avoid Nydia's question. "Nykolas could find out, and he'll be hurt."

"You do realize he has a whole harem," Ziani says.

"Nykolas?" I ask.

"Yeah. I don't doubt that he loves you, but faeries aren't like us. They don't care about faithfulness the way most humans do. I wouldn't be surprised if he's been making use of his harem the whole time he's been falling for you. At the very least he would have made plenty use of it after the attack when you returned to Lorthien."

"If he did, that's because he was heartbroken."

"Well, you were mind-broken when you slept with Jaxson," Nydia points out. "If you can excuse Nykolas, why can't you excuse yourself?"

"You're going to have to be much more cold-blooded if you do marry him," Ziani tells me. "In case you haven't noticed, this palace is a dog-eat-dog environment. Don't let anybody have the whole of your heart, not even Nykolas. Keep some of it for yourself. And don't waste a moment feeling bad for having a good night with Jaxson. You thought you were never going to see Nykolas again."

I don't know if I can excuse myself the way my friends are. But I'll try.

"If I leave, Nykolas might stop protecting you guys," I say. "Same if I stay, but he finds out about Jaxson."

"It's sweet how you always think about other people," Ziani replies. "But maybe you should focus on your own survival and do what's right for you."

I stare at her, not understanding why she doesn't expect me to sacrifice my happiness for her protection—especially when it could mean death for her and Nydia. Protection is more important than happiness.

They're not Kali, I tell myself. Kali, being my sister, was my responsibility. Ziani and Nydia are not, and they don't expect me to act like they are.

They're true friends.

"What Ziani said about being careful even with Nykolas is right," Nydia says. "Loving him stopped you from destroying the royal family's magic sources when you had the opportunity. If you had, you wouldn't have to be so afraid of Queen Tarla, as she wouldn't have magic. At the very least you should have destroyed King Xander's magic source. Then when you got back to Rithelia, King Bastien wouldn't have tried to kill you. He would have given you a special welcome instead."

"King Bastien is hiding something," I remind her. "He has something to do with the theft of faerie immortality and he's lying to the whole country that he doesn't know why the winter solstice kidnappings are happening."

"If he *has* stolen faerie immortality," Nydia replies, "faeries should declare war and fight army to army, not steal ten girls every year."

I raise my hands. I'm not interested in the political side

of everything that's going on. There's nothing I can do about any of it. I just wanted to find Kali. And now I just need to get out of here. Preferably before having to see Nykolas again.

By the time we leave for class, I'm an even tenser bundle of anxiety.

∼

IN THE EVENING, I'm dressed spectacularly for the Festival of Moons. By now, I know I can't avoid it. Jaxson isn't responding when I reach out, and a whole host of thought messages from me are waiting on the bridge that connects our minds. I'm so annoyed I could cry.

I meet the gaze of my reflection in the mirror before me. Contrary to how I feel, my guilt isn't written all over my face. I'm the same girl on the outside, but so much has been upended on the inside.

Annha is a harried mess since it's my final night before the Choosing Ceremony. It's as though she thinks that what I wear has the power to either cinch the deal for me with Nykolas or ruin everything.

"He wants you to arrive with him," she told me when she first got here with an army of attendants to get me ready. "He wants to make an entrance. That means you have to look spectacular—worthy of being the female on his arm. Worthy of being the chosen one."

My gown is a breathtaking cascade of midnight blue silk intricately embroidered with silver. It flows around me like a river of star-strewn midnight, the silver catching the light.

The faerie who designed it, Bezaleel Onise, is with us,

making sure everything is just right. His lashes are about five inches long and he has the plumpest, poutiest lips I've ever seen.

Once the dress is all zipped and laced up, he has one of Annha's assistants turn out the lights and draw the curtains. We're all wondering why until my gown seems to come alive. It shimmers with its own luminescence. The deep blue silk glows and the silver threads are ablaze as though spun from the very stars.

"That's not all," Bezaleel purrs. "This is how you'll shine after moonrise." With a wave, velvet soft magic erupts from his fingers, and a small moon-like orb appears up by the chandeliers, shining on me. It reflects off my dress in a mesmerizing dance, and I feel like a creature of the night, draped in celestial elegance. It's a shame I can't relax enough to enjoy it.

"ZaZa," Annha breathes, "thank you *immensely* for not giving Dabria this dress."

"Dabria lost my loyalty the day she wore a hideous Moyo Abiké corset imported from Aziza," Bezaleel replies with a sniff. "I would much rather clothe the first mortal to steal a Crown Prince's heart and turn him into her lapdog. All eyes, hateful or otherwise, will be on her, and thus, on my dress."

"You can never resist a scandal, can you?" Annha says, rolling her eyes.

Bezaleel lets out a lilting peal of laughter. "I'm all about the scandals and drama, darling."

Ziani and Nydia walk in just then. They've been getting ready in the lounge which is teeming with their stylists and attendants.

"Whoa!" Ziani exclaims at the sight of my dress. "Riva, that dress! You're going to kill them dead!"

Annha switches on the lights and now I can see my friends' dresses too. Like me, they're wearing dark colors. Ziani's black dress looks lethal on her, and her hair is braided in a new pattern that piles high on her head and drips with diamonds. Nydia's earthy, umber dress is threaded with whorls of gold, and her white hair pours down her back in a sheet of curls.

A sudden blast of fanfare has us all turning toward the door.

"Everyone out," Annha says frantically, opening a portal.

They all scurry through it as a trumpeter clad in scarlet marches into my chambers and comes to a halt in the open doorway to my bedroom. My ears ring with how loudly he's blowing the trumpet. Eventually, he lowers it and in a booming voice announces, "I present His Royal Highness, Crown Prince Nykolas."

I'm sure my heart is going to break when Nykolas strolls in.

19

"Riva," Nykolas breathes. "You look beautiful!"

I find I can't look him in the eyes. "Thank you."

He's handsome as ever in a two-toned black suit that shimmers silver when it catches the light. We're almost matching.

"Did I only see you a few hours ago, just after midnight?" Nykolas asks. "It feels like a century has passed." He draws me into a hug. "I want to kiss you, but I know you have to be presentable."

I nod. However, if I wasn't wracked with guilt, I would say to hell with being presentable and kiss him.

"I have something for you," Nykolas says. He takes my hand and leads me to the full-length mirror. "Close your eyes."

I obey.

There's a whisper of a kiss on my lips. "Sorry, couldn't resist," Nykolas says.

I have to smile.

Something heavy settles on my head. Then I hear Nykolas exhale. "It's perfect," he whispers. "You can look now."

I open my eyes and my heart splinters down the middle at the sight of the diamond tiara Nykolas has placed on my head. If It were any bigger, it would be a full-blown crown. The rubies sparkling around its base will tell everyone it's a gift from him.

"It's beautiful," I whisper.

I know what he's trying to do, and so will everyone else. Diamonds are the jewels of the queen. He's hinting, not so subtly, at me, a mortal girl, becoming queen of faeries.

His own crown sparkles to life atop his head. It's one I've never seen him wear before. Gold, studded with rubies and a few onyx's—a reminder to everyone that he will soon be king.

"Ready my love?" he asks.

Before I can object to wearing the tiara and tell him we need to talk, we vanish from my room.

I don't recognize the palace entrance when we appear in it. The pearl walls and marble floors have been tinged with a silvery hue, and the ceiling has been enchanted to look like the night sky.

A doorman throws the doors open before Nykolas and me, to reveal a red carpet that spills out into the swirling dusk. Cameras flash as we step outside, my hand tucked into the crook of Nykolas's arm.

Thousands of faeries are gathered on either side of the red carpet, held back by stanchions affixed with red velvet rope. They cheer and wave small flags of Eraeon as we pose for pictures.

My breath turns to fire suddenly, scorching my nose, throat, and lungs. A burning begins in my blood, turning it lava hot.

I'm being attacked with magic.

Panic bursts through me. I don't know how to defend myself. I can't even speak, otherwise I would tell Nykolas.

I'm about to nudge him when the scent of roses fills the air, and I realize it's Queen Tarla. But looking around, I don't see her. Is she going to kill me now, in front of everyone? With Nykolas beside me?

Shimmering words appear before my eyes, hovering in the air before me. The fact that nobody else, not even Nykolas, looks at them, tells me I'm the only one who can see them. They're for my eyes only.

Gentle reminder

Break up with Nykolas tonight, or you won't live to see sunrise. Do not make a spectacle. Do it in private after the Festival of Moons celebrations.

— Queen Tarla of Eraeon.

Either she can't speak mind to mind with me, or the idea of forming such a connection with me, a mere mortal, is repugnant to her.

I gulp in a breath as soon as the burning ceases. Queen Tarla is clearly at the end of her patience. I have to do this tonight. I should have done it as soon as Nykolas walked into my room, and saved myself from having to pretend all night.

But I was still holding out for Jaxson to vault me out of Eraeon.

The few minutes we spend on the red carpet feel like an eternity in some place of torment. I'm grateful when we walk the rest of the way then step off it and onto a garden path. A flock of faeries follows behind us. They're clad in so many jewels they're like a moving mass of starry night.

Nykolas glances at me. "Are you okay?"

I nod.

"Nervous?"

"A little."

"Don't be." He gives me a wicked grin. "The Choosing Ceremony is tomorrow." His voice lowers to a devilish murmur that ties my insides up in knots. "Just think of what you and I will be doing this time tomorrow."

I force a smile. "I, uh, heard you declared official interest in Ziani and Nydia."

"Yes. Only to keep them safe, which is something I know you're concerned about. I assure you that my heart is all yours. I'll put them up in their own castles with their own security."

"That's really generous, Nykolas."

He stops walking and turns to face me. "I'll never see them, and if they want to have liaisons with other males they're free to do so. I knows it isn't the same as releasing them to return to Lorthien, but it's the best I can do for now. After my coronation, they'll be free to leave."

"Thank you," I say around a tightness in my throat. Nykolas is too good. Too wonderful.

"Do you have a harem?" I blurt as we continue down the path.

Nykolas stops again. "Look at me," he says softly.

So I do. Even though it hurts.

"Yes," he says. "But I've never touched any of them, and I won't be with anyone else when we're together. Only you, Riva. My heart, my body, my very soul, are all yours and yours alone."

The words overwhelm my guilty heart.

I need to end this.

I don't deserve him.

What I really want is to just be vaulted away and not have to break up with him; not have to look into his hurt eyes. But it's beginning to look like that isn't going to happen.

We continue to walk and I spot a crowd in the distance. Music carries over on the breeze, as well as the smell of grilled meats and baked treats.

A pack of faerie males approach us from another garden path. We reach the point where their path converges with ours at the same time, and I realize it's the other princes. Jaxson is one of them. My heart thuds at the sight of him in his bigger, wilder natural form, claws and fangs on display like many of the other males.

He's in all black, as is customary for him, but his formal dinner jacket is unfastened and he wears no shirt under it. I despise how the evening light bathes him in a soft glow, highlighting the play of shadows on his toned, rippling abs. The heat roaring through my veins is aggravating. My body just doesn't seem to know better.

Nykolas glances at me, and I realize my grip on his arm has tightened. I relax it. Force a neutral expression.

"I see you didn't die after the Red Heavens Rite and allow the crown to pass to me," one of the princes says to Nykolas.

"Nope," Nykolas replies. "I'm still very much alive."

They all begin to rib each other, except Jaxson, who is silent—and seems to be avoiding my gaze. I don't know if I'll ever get used to the sheer size of his natural form.

I reach out to him in my mind and instantly sense the bridge forming between us. *Where have you been?*

In meetings.

I want out of here.

He's silent.

If I can escape Eraeon, I can escape both the queen's threats and having to hurt Nykolas. I really don't want to have to hurt him. What I did with Jaxson last night is tearing up my conscience as it is. There's no need to break up with him and break his heart. I just want to disappear. Difficult conversations have never been easy for me.

Nykolas is laughing at something one of the princes has said, so I chance a glance at Jaxson. He's staring straight ahead, eyes strained.

I'll do anything, Jaxson. You can have another piece of my heart. I just need to get out of here.

You shouldn't do that, comes his sharp response. *Don't offer pieces of yourself. For anything or anyone.*

Why won't you help me?

His sigh is a gentle whisper in my head. *I will, but not tonight.*

Why?

The queen suspects it was me who helped you deflect Dabria's attacks. I denied it, but if you vanish, there'll be further scrutiny. Let's give it a few days.

I don't have a few days. The Choosing Ceremony is tomorrow.

Listen, my powers are locked down. Despite the fact that they couldn't prove that I helped you, I had to submit to punishment anyway. So did Camran, Vielle, and Baila—everyone who's friendly with you. They left me with only very basic abilities. I can't vault myself right now, never mind you.

I thought you said you're more powerful than anyone else here.

I am. That's why I said I submitted. I allowed them to dampen my powers. They think they overpowered me, but they didn't. I'm building my power for a reason, and I can't let any of these bastards find out just how powerful I am until it's too late.

Well, how long will your powers be dampened for? I ask.

Three days.

Great. There's no fleeing Eraeon. I'm going to have to do this Queen Tarla's way: break up with Nykolas tonight, then she will get me out of here.

Jaxson's flames flare to life around my temples, then his voice fills my mind again. *I know about Queen Tarla threatening you. She isn't going to help you leave Eraeon after you break up with Nykolas. She's planning to kill you, and she's hoping Nykolas won't care since you broke up with him.*

Frost takes over my bones. *How do you know?*

Queen Tarla's voice fills my head, and I get a sense of Jaxson eavesdropping on her and some other people who are just shapeless shadows in my mind.

We can't just send her back to Rithelia, she says. *There's every possibility that Nykolas will continue to pine for her even if she breaks up with him. The only solution is death. It's the only way he'll move on. Besides, we do not allow human girls to leave once they have set foot here. That would set a very bad precedent. She must die, but we must handle it...delicately.*

What are you thinking? comes Prince Jiorge's voice.

I'm thinking that we'll order her to be punished for rejecting Nykolas. Even Nykolas shouldn't object to that. We'll use the lava lakes when they open four days hence. Nykolas will expect her to survive, as human girls have survived it in the past. We won't tell him that we'll place her at the very center where even dragons meet their death. She will die 'accidentally' and we'll say we didn't mean for her to die and declare three days of mourning across the land. We will commiserate with him, then start planning his wedding to Dabria.

There's a round of laughter that ceases abruptly as Jaxson finishes showing me the memory.

I don't know what the lava lakes are and I hope I never find out. I should have known I couldn't trust the queen. The only reason why she hasn't killed me already is so that she doesn't get into Nykolas's bad books. As evil and twisted as she is, she seems to care about his opinion of her.

I want to refuse to break up with Nykolas and let him choose me tomorrow, just to spite her. But my conscience won't allow it. Besides, I need to just do whatever she says if I want to survive until Jaxson gets his powers back.

You say you'll get your powers back in three days? I ask him.
Yes.
Then you'll vault me off this miserable island?
I will. But Queen Tarla will probably still search for you. She

wants you dead. We'll figure something out. In the meantime, act normal, like you don't know any of this.

It isn't ideal. And we're cutting things a little close since Jaxson will get his powers back just one day before the queen is planning to kill me. But I have no other option. I have to wait.

It'll be a shame to leave Eraeon without Kali, but I have a new plan. I'm going to steal some valuables from the palace —all the trinkets in the jewelry boxes in my closet, minus the rubies. I'll sell them when I get back to Lorthien, and use the money to hire a detective.

Now that the palace knows the location of Eraeon, they will announce it publicly before long, if they haven't already. And if they don't, the detective can start by hacking whoever at the military will have the information. For the right price he or she should be able to locate Eraeon and find Kali. I won't be deserting Kali when I leave. I'll be enacting a new, more strategic plan.

We've reached the crowd now, and Jaxson and the other princes make themselves scarce, leaving Nykolas and me alone. Dabria is the first person I see. She's staring at my tiara in shock, her eyes crackling with a hatred I have done nothing to deserve.

I realize our entrance has been timed perfectly. As every eye turns toward us, the moons appear. We all look up, and I gasp at the three perfectly aligned moons shining in the indigo skies. They bathe the garden in their enchanting radiance. Each moon casts a unique hue – one a pale, brilliant amber, the one in the center a dazzling, ghostly white, while the third is tinged slightly red.

Their bewitching beams caress every petal and blade of grass, giving the gardens a whimsical, dream-like quality. The crowd of faeries, dressed in their resplendent finery, are like ethereal figures in the mystical glow. The scene is so breathtaking, it doesn't feel real. I feel like I've been transported to a whole new world where dreams and reality intertwine. Where magic swirls in the air for anyone to harness. Where everything is peaceful and perfect.

It seems to put things in perspective for me. I can either crumble in fear and bemoan the injustice of my life being at risk simply because I have captured the heart of Prince Nykolas, or I can remind myself that I chose all of this. I knew the faerie realm would be brutal and that I could very well die, but I came anyway—because of Kali.

The silence is broken by a collective gasp from the crowd. I lower my gaze from the sky and realize that everyone is staring at me. It's my dress. It's glowing in the moonlight.

Nykolas, delighted, twirls me around, and my skirts flare. Polite applause breaks out and cameras flash.

Then, as though the night isn't already bright enough, Nykolas slowly raises his hands, energy crackling all around him. I sense the flow of his watery magic swelling; a rising tide of enchantment. It sets the air humming.

The sky brightens as a dazzling moonbow appears, arching far above the moons. Its vaporous colors are like something from a fantasy.

With a sweep of his hand, Nykolas sends a breathtaking display of aurora lights dancing through the skies. They're iridescent green woven seamlessly with whispers of celestial purples and hints of indigo, and they undulate like silk curtains caught in a breeze.

I'm left completely spellbound by Nykolas's power. Judging by the awed silence in the garden, I'm not the only one.

A butler approaches us with a sweeping bow and hands Nykolas a glass of some golden, effervescent liquid. He raises it in a toast. "As we gather beneath the moons, I say eat, drink, and be merry. I command it. Merry Moonblest!"

Enthusiastic cheering and applause breaks out, then a live band, who have set up their instruments beside a row of hedges, begins to play.

Nykolas and I circulate the crowd. He doles out compliments and kind words, charming the undergarments off them all, while I stand awkwardly at his side. I murmur *Merry Moonblest* if anyone bothers to look at me, but most don't.

The moonlight is so bright, there's no need for flood lights or light orbs. Chairs are scattered all over the garden, and servers weave among the crowd, offering treats and delicacies from the grill a short distance away.

When Nykolas and I finally make it to seats, my feet are aching in my heeled shoes. I smile at the faeries in the chairs around us. I don't know any of them. They ignore me and strike up conversation with Nykolas.

I accept a glass of golden liquid from the same butler who approached Nykolas before.

"Alcohol-free and void of any other stimulants," he murmurs.

I feel like I could do with some alcohol right now, but I

smile my thanks as I accept it. He hovers at our side and I gather that he's Nykolas's, and therefore my, personal butler for the night.

A server comes to offer Nykolas and me skewers of fragrant, spiced meats, and a selection of cakes with silvery-white frosting that glows like moonlight. I set my drink on the low table beside me and fill my plate.

I eat while Nykolas chats with everyone around us. The older male sitting opposite us keeps looking at me. His golden skin is gently creased with age and his shoulder length hair is silver. I don't sense any threat from him, but his attention still makes me feel uncomfortable.

"Good evening, Riva, and Merry Moonblest," he says into a lull in the conversation.

He's the first faerie to address me directly tonight. Unfortunately, he chose a moment when my mouth is crammed with cake and I can't respond. Everyone around us watches as I rush to swallow the cake. Bad idea. I choke so hard that Nykolas quickly offers me his drink. I don't dare accept it in case it contains anything that could drive humans wild, like the ice cream I sampled last week.

I grab my own drink and ungracefully chug it back, desperate to clear my throat. Then I smile at the elder who addressed me. "M-merry Moonblest, sir."

"This is Segun, one of the palace seers," Nykolas informs me. "His sight is extraordinary. For millennia he has counseled kings on things to come and he's never wrong."

"It's a pleasure to meet you," I say, hoping Segun isn't training his magical sight on me.

"Does she know of the prophecy?" Segun asks.

Nykolas's eyes grow serious. He shakes his head.

"What prophecy?" I ask.

When Nykolas remains silent, Segun smiles and strikes up conversation with someone else.

I lean close to Nykolas. "What is he talking about?"

"At my ascension, nineteen years ago—"

"What's an ascension?"

"It's when you reach majority—become an adult."

He became an adult by faerie standards nineteen years ago? That would have been the year I was born.

"All the seers at my celebration froze all of a sudden," Nykolas tells me. "Then as one, they spoke the exact same prophecy. Here, we say, *In the mouth of two or three of the gifted, a word is established as true.* But this was all twelve of them."

"What did they say?"

"I remember it word for word." Nykolas's eyes grow distant as he accesses the memory.

He whispers the prophecy into my mind.

There comes a mortal girl of fire
And water—a thief of wonder.
To stir a prince's desire,
And make his heart her plunder.

"It's why I stayed away from human girls," Nykolas whispers. "I didn't want to be that prince. But the day you arrived, you came to me and set me on fire. I didn't even think of the prophecy until after you returned to Lorthien and I was ruminating about us and berating myself for how quickly and deeply I fell in love with you. We thought 'girl of fire' meant she would have fire powers, but now I think it might have been a reference to how we would meet."

I frown. Could this be why Nykolas loves me so wholly? Are we each other's destiny?

I reject that idea. I don't believe in their prophecies, their religion, or any of their faerie superstitions.

"It might not be about me," I tell him, my voice trembling. "It's pretty vague."

"Agreed," Nykolas whispers, "but I think it might be. You showed up and set me ablaze in more ways than one."

I can't return the smile he gives me. Can't allow myself to believe that my coming to the faerie realm was prophesied.

That's just ridiculous.

"I don't know about the water or thievery parts," Nykolas says, "but the rest of the prophecy has become pretty clear. Even Segun seems to think it's you."

I realize I do understand the water and thievery parts. I bled water instead of blood on the night of the winter solstice. And 'thief of wonder'...Jaxson said those words last night after I snatched magic from him to heal myself. Camran told me they call their magical essence 'wonder'.

It might all be a coincidence, I tell myself.

"If you're the girl in the prophecy, wonderful," Nykolas says. "If not, so what? I'm in love with you anyway. The prophecy might be about another prince and another human girl in another time."

I need to get away from Nykolas and his guilt-inducing declarations of love. I'm thinking of an excuse to walk away when Ziani, Nydia, Vielle and Baila appear in a flurry of silk, lace, and competing fragrances.

"Merry Moonblest, Your Highness," they chorus, bowing.

Except for Ziani who, after a half-hearted incline of her head toward Nykolas, grabs my hand. "Come dance with us."

"Don't be long," Nykolas says as I rise.

"I won't," I promise.

Vielle glances back as we walk away. "Nykolas can't take his eyes off you, Riva."

"Well, she is wearing the most amazing dress ever," Baila says. "It looks like a ZaZa original."

"It is," I confirm. "By the way, I heard what happened to you guys. Are you sure you're okay to talk to me? It might stir up even more suspicion."

"What happened?" Nydia asks.

Vielle lowers her voice to a whisper. "They think we blocked the magic they were using to keep track of Riva last night."

That's how they're framing the magical death blows that Dabria dealt me? I exchange a glance with Ziani and Nydia.

Vielle and Baila clearly believe I was let out of the palace yesterday and don't even suspect that I escaped. I'm not going to tell them the truth. At the end of the day, they're faeries. Nice faeries, but I still have to be careful with them.

"I'm barely powerful enough to use magic to lace up my undergarments," Baila says with a chortle. "Still, they've dampened my powers for three days."

"I'm sorry you're being punished for being friends with me," I say.

They both wave their hands dismissively. "There's plenty in this friendship for us," Vielle replies. "You have the Crown Prince's ear. It's only a matter of time before we start using you to get special favors for ourselves and our families."

I smile. They were nice to me before Nykolas fell for me.

Ziani sashays ahead of us, moving her body in ways I can only dream of doing as she steps onto the dance floor. Nydia is a terrific dancer too, swaying her hips and winding her waist to the music.

I twirl as I step onto the dance floor, letting my skirts float around me. People gape at the way my dress sparkles in the light of the moons, but I soon forget about all the eyes watching us as I copy my friends' dance moves. Kali frequented the night clubs of Lorthien while I was always too exhausted from work—and too uptight to let my hair down—so I'm surprised to find I can keep up. I'm actually enjoying myself when the music stops abruptly.

"Ooh," Baila squeals as everyone looks to the band, "it must be time for love flames."

"What's that?" Nydia asks.

"You'll find out in a moment."

20

"Love burns brighter than any flame," says the lead singer of the band. He's a handsome faerie with spiky black hair and biceps covered in silver tattoos that stand out against his deep golden skin. "Lovers, let your desire burn bright. Leave your sweetheart in no doubt."

Then he begins to croon some sentimental love song.

I almost scream when a bolt of white light spears through the air and hits the skirts of a nearby faerie lady's dress. Her skirts burst into flames. I expect people to hurry over with water to put it out, and whoever did it to be punished, but everyone bursts into applause.

A blush blooms on the lady's cheeks as she eyes the male who set her skirts ablaze. Her dress is ruined, the charred remains of her skirts barely preserving her modesty, but nobody seems to care.

The rest of the women present begin to flee around the gardens. Vielle and Baila run, too, and Ziani, Nydia, and I follow, although we have no idea why.

"What the hell is going on?" Ziani asks.

"People are allowed to make the skirts—or the jacket—of the person they desire burst into flames," Vielle explains. "It's usually males going after females with their magic, so we try to flee to make sure our skirts stay intact. Anyone who participates has to make their magic visible so that we know who burned our skirts and desires us."

"Seriously?" Ziani asks. "I would have worn prettier panties if someone had told me about this."

No sooner have the words left her lips than at least seven bolts of light in varying colors strike her skirts. Three princes and four other men that I've never seen before are closing in on us, their eyes on Ziani.

For all Frieve's and Filpé's lectures about being docile and coy, faerie males really can't seem to get enough of Ziani and her spunk.

"What do I do now?" Ziani asks Vielle and Baila.

"It's too late," Baila says. "You've been caught. Now you just strut around for the rest of the night, showing off your tattered skirts."

Nydia rolls her eyes. "This is so stupid."

Vielle nudges her. "Hey, my parents met as a result of this tradition. I wouldn't exist if Father hadn't set my mother's skirts ablaze and knocked her up that same night."

"Eww!" Nydia screws up her nose. "Nobody had better burn my—"

Her skirts erupt and she gasps, looking around in annoyance. One of the princes waves sheepishly from across the gardens, and the rest of us collapse into fits of laughter as we duck behind some bushes.

Nykolas is still sitting where I left him, deep in conversation with a group of males. It seems he's above the silliness going on.

Streams of light zip around the whole garden, hitting skirts and eliciting squeals. A faerie girl sends a bolt of pink light at the lead singer of the band and burns his jacket to tatters. Applause breaks out, and the lead singer blows her a kiss.

There's a soft thud behind us, and we spin around just in time to see two males sneaking up on us.

Vielle and Baila clearly know them, because they dash away, squealing. The males give chase with their magic, but Vielle and Baila are tricky to catch. They hide behind trees and use other people as shields. But they're caught before long and have charred skirts to show for it.

"Can you believe this?" Nydia asks. "This is so ridiculous."

"And kind of fun," Ziani adds.

We all jump as Nydia's barely there skirts burst into flames again. She doesn't even bother to check who did it.

"Whoa, who's he?" Ziani asks, eyeing up the faerie who flamed Nydia's skirts. "He's cute."

Nydia glances over her shoulder then rolls her eyes. "I don't know who he is. I've never even seen him before."

A sudden hush blankets the gardens and we peer over the bush to see why. Nykolas is standing now, a ball of crackling golden light in his hand, poised to throw. Everyone is looking around, no doubt searching for me.

Ziani shoves me out from behind the bush and I want to

throttle her. Laughter fills the air along with cries of 'run, Riva!' from many of the faerie females.

I dash through the garden, zig-zagging like I'm trying to dodge a bullet. A glance over my shoulder tells me that Nykolas's golden ball of light is streaming after me in hot pursuit. Like a laser-guided missile, it weaves around people and trees.

I skirt a row of bushes and leap over a flowerbed, drawing applause from the crowd. Then everyone gasps and I glance over my shoulder. Nykolas's light has branched into seven streams. They fly at me, and before I know it, I'm surrounded. Nowhere to turn.

"Don't do it, Nykolas," I call.

The golden streams have come to a standstill around me. Slowly, they begin to undulate toward me, and laughter rolls through the garden. Nykolas is standing in the distance watching me with a dark, satisfied smile.

Suddenly, his magic charges, and all seven streams strike my moonlit skirts, igniting them. They burst into flames that are all light and no heat. Everyone cheers, and I wonder if they're finally accepting the idea of me with Nykolas.

I make my way back toward my friends, my skirts in tatters leaving my legs exposed. I'm thankful that it isn't a breezy night, otherwise my modesty would be in jeopardy.

"You did your best," an older faerie female tells me as I pass. Her eyes are kind and her voice is gentle.

The females around her nod. "Good effort," one of them says.

"Thank you," I reply.

When I reach my friends, they're all giggling. "The way

you jumped over the flowerbed was hilarious," Baila says. "How in the world can you run that fast in heels?"

"Maybe she *is* a spy," Vielle jokes.

"Fix your crown, Riva," Ziani says.

Baila frowns. "Uh, it's a tiara, not a crown."

"Same difference," Vielle replies.

"Ugh!" Baila exclaims. "Don't say that. I hate it when people say that. What does it even mean?"

"I know," Nydia agrees. "The semantics are totally off."

The song the band is playing comes to an end, then Camran joins them, holding a fiddle. Cheering ensues.

"Can he play?" Ziani asks.

Vielle nods. "He's good."

"I'm taking song requests as usual," Camran announces. "But for my first song, I will play *Ode to the Star-flecked Night* and dedicate it to a human girl who…knows who she is."

Ziani turns abruptly so that he's out of her line of vision. Camran wasn't one of the males who burned her skirts. As a soldier and a member of Nykolas's personal guard, he can't. Not when princes want her.

Baila nudges me. "I think Nykolas is trying to get your attention."

I look over and see him waving. Nydia reaches out and adjusts my tiara for me. Then I pick my way through the crowd, heading toward Nykolas. I stop when a stream of vivid red light appears ahead of me, rushing toward my skirts.

It's from a lone figure standing in the darkness between two tall trees, their branches shading him from the moonlight.

Jaxson.

There are gasps of horror as his light almost hits what remains of my skirts. At the last moment, it zips sideways, dodging me, and hits some other girls' skirts.

Everyone releases a collective exhale of relief. I'm the only female who is entitled to only one admirer—because he's Nykolas. Anyone else who dares to admit desire for me would probably be in big trouble.

I can't help feeling like Jaxson did that on purpose, just to taunt me. I glance at the girl whose skirts he exploded. She's dark-skinned and doe-eyed. Tiny, with big, gravity-defying curls. Absolutely stunning.

Relax, comes Jaxson's voice in my head. *She asked me to blow up her skirts so that her many suitors would leave her alone. Nobody would usually dare try to take a woman I'm interested in, you see.*

The way he says 'usually' makes me wonder if he's alluding to my relationship with Nykolas. Is he trying to say he's interested in me?

I glance again at the girl whose skirts Jaxson burned. They must be pretty good friends for her to ask him to do that. Surely Jaxson would have noticed how beautiful she is.

You're jealous, he says into my mind.

So are you, I reply.

If he wasn't, he wouldn't have pulled that stunt with almost burning my skirts just now. I shove him out of my head as I reach Nykolas. I'm about to sit on my chair, but Nykolas pulls me onto his lap.

It's younger males that surround him now, and they all have a drunken glaze in their eyes. I stiffen when one of them, a male wearing a bowtie that's askew, mentions Nocahya Forest.

"You still take her there?" asks a male with cold, gray eyes that remind me of bleak winter skies.

"I've been taking her once a month," Bowtie replies. "She's stiff as a hunk of wood, but after a few minutes of being broken by the Nocahya spirits, she comes to life."

The men all laugh, and I realize that Bowtie must have a human partner if Nocahya Forest breaks her.

Nykolas isn't listening to them. He's talking to a man sitting on his right, discussing the best methods of unleashing magic at full force.

"You do that to punish her?" asks a sleepy-eyed male who is holding a bottle of wine from which he's been swigging. "Isn't that a little excessive? You don't want her to lose her mind."

"It wakes up her sexual urges," Bowtie explains. "If you don't leave them in for too long, their minds can be recovered, but the rabid, tear-your-clothes-off energy can last for up to two weeks."

Rabid, tear-your-clothes-off energy? Heat flows into my cheeks. Is that what happened to me? I was already attracted to Jaxson before Dabria ran me into Nocahya Forest, but did the forest stir up my desire?

"Ahhh," Sleepy says slowly, and the other males laugh.

"You're dragging your mortal straight to Nocahya Forest after this, aren't you?" Gray Eyes says, nudging Sleepy.

"You do have to be careful," Bowtie warns. "My last mortal jumped the bones of one of my chefs. She got so hungry for sex that she couldn't keep her legs closed."

I'm so glad Nykolas isn't listening to this.

Sleepy's eyes narrow. "She's dead now, right?"

"You bet. I killed them both. They can't use the Nocahya as an excuse. The spirits only bring out their true nature and desires, they don't force them into anything they don't already want to do."

My heart is beating too hard. I try to tune out their discussion and focus on Camran's fiddle music, but they're talking so loudly.

"Yeah, it's best to just kill them once they get like that."

"Human women can be such promiscuous little bitches."

"I'll get a new one in next year's batch, so it's no loss."

When they rise and head to the drinks table for more booze, I'm grateful that they've gone—until Jaxson comes and sits in one of their empty seats. The one directly opposite Nykolas and me. His chest and abs are still on display.

I ignore him and focus on Nykolas, who chats with the male beside him for a few more minutes. Then the male wanders off to talk to someone else, and Nykolas notices Jaxson. He nods. "Jaxson."

Jaxson nods back. "Nykolas."

"Are you enjoying yourself?" Nykolas murmurs to me.

"Yes," I say, and it's the truth. The party has been more fun than I expected.

Nykolas trails his finger up my bare thigh. "Your dress is even more magnificent now, don't you think?"

My eyes, involuntarily, snap to Jaxson. He's giving me a dark look.

I touch my nose to Nykolas's and whisper, "If I had magic, I would have burned your jacket."

"You would?"

"Yes. If I felt we could actually be together properly." I'm trying to hint that we can't be together. Trying to prepare him for the moment when I tell him I don't want him to choose me tomorrow.

All evening, I've been torn between allowing myself to enjoy these final moments with him and not wanting to lead him on.

Nykolas traces ticklish circles over my thigh. "Nobody has ever dared to burn my jacket."

I don't know if he's deliberately ignoring my hint, or if he didn't pick up on it. I decide it's a conversation for later anyway. When we're alone.

"Really?" I whisper. "Why?"

"Maybe because I'm, you know, the Crown Prince."

Suddenly, Jaxson's fiery magic swells, and I know he's going to speak into my mind. I want to resist, but that's something I haven't figured out how to do yet.

Does he know we fucked? Jaxson demands, his voice a low, throaty growl.

I twitch with shock. "Understandable," I tell Nykolas.

Does he know that this time last night you were screaming my name?

It wasn't this time last night, I reply to Jaxson. *It was much later. And it was a mistake.*

A mistake?

Yes. It was...nothing. It was nothing to you, too. You only did it in exchange for a piece of my heart.

I didn't take it. I only said that to make sure you really wanted me.

Nykolas's fingers trail higher up my thigh. Dangerously high.

Jaxson's magic whispers over my hand, and I find myself slapping Nykolas's hand away. Nykolas's eyes, which were at half mast, widen in shock.

"Sorry," I say quickly. I slap my thigh again, as though I was just trying to swat something away. I can't believe Jaxson made me slap him!

Nykolas relaxes and begins to trail ticklish circles over my skin again.

A server wanders over with a bowl of fruit. Nykolas and I decline, but Jaxson accepts an apple. He looks like he wants to pelt Nykolas with it. I don't understand what his problem is. I'm not even going to be here in three days, so what does any of this matter?

"You don't have to be presentable anymore," Nykolas murmurs to me.

"You can't kiss me here in front of everyone," I whisper back.

"Why can't I?"

"People would…it wouldn't be…" I shake my head. "You shouldn't."

Nykolas draws my face to his. I'm vaguely aware of conversations dying down—then restarting as people make a deliberate effort to ignore us. My heart grows heavy with confusion at the way Nykolas's kiss stirs my emotions.

This is the last thing I need. I'm not staying, and I'm not marrying him. I need to stop giving him hope, or he's going to be truly heartbroken when I end things later tonight.

I pull away and pretend to need a drink. The glass I was sipping from earlier is gone from my side table.

Nykolas, with a twitch of his fingers, summons his hovering butler, who immediately steps forward with a fresh drink for me.

My gaze lands on Jaxson as I sip the sweet, refreshingly cool liquid. The apple in his hand has turned to solid gold.

Shit!

He once told me he can only gild things when he's deeply angry. I glance at his face.

He looks mad as hell.

There's a loud slurping sound and I realize it's me. I've drained my glass. I set it aside, and Nykolas takes it as a sign that he can kiss me again.

This time, his kiss leaves me cold. Because a storm of other emotions are churning in my heart, all for Jaxson. His burning magic drives them. They're so intense, I feel weak.

Stop this, Jaxson.

He doesn't respond. And his magic continues to strum on my heartstrings, playing my emotions as masterfully as Camran plays his fiddle.

Please...leave me alone.

I'm not letting you fall for him, Jaxson replies.

Doesn't he know? I already have.

I'm leaving Eraeon, I reply. *You know that. I'm breaking up with him tonight.*

Doesn't mean I have to suffer the sight of you all over him. Get off his lap and get your lips away from his, or I'll make you head-butt him and slap him across the face.

What a jerk!

I know he'll do it, too.

Jaxson has to be the most infuriating person I have ever met. I pull away from Nykolas just as Camran announces the next song request.

"Ladies and gentlemen, this one is a special one," he says. "Requested by Dabria Oderon, and dedicated to Riva Kadiri."

I frown as Camran begins to play a haunting, soulful melody. It sounds familiar.

My blood runs cold as I realize why. This is the song Jaxson played last night while me made love.

"That was nice of Dabria," Nykolas says in surprise. "And you're clearly touched by the gesture. You like the song?"

I have no idea what to say.

Nykolas sways to the melody. "It's beautiful, isn't it? It's called The Ballad of Pretty Vipers. It's from a musical about an unfaithful wife who sacrifices everything to win back her husband."

Terror strikes in my heart. Dabria chose it. And dedicated it to *me*.

"Let's dance," Nykolas says, rising and pulling me to my feet with him.

My legs feel heavy and shaky as we join the other dancing couples. My thoughts are racing.

I cast my gaze around the garden, searching for Dabria. I spot her chatting with a group of ladies who are all sipping from crystal goblets. As though sensing my eyes on her, she turns, and the moment our gazes connect, I know that I'm right to panic.

Dabria, somehow, knows about me and Jaxson.

21

She can't know, I tell myself.

If she does, she would tell the queen, not make a song request. Unless she's waiting for the perfect moment to strike.

I don't want to cause Nykolas any unnecessary pain. It's going to be hard enough to break up with him. The last thing I want is Dabria telling him about Jaxson and me, and him thinking that's why I want to end things.

When Camran finishes playing the song, everyone applauds. Someone else makes a song request, but the garden has faded and I'm trapped in a private bubble of worry and guilt.

When a faerie woman asks Nykolas to dance, I'm more than happy to release him. I turn to walk away, and a dark shadow steps into my path. Jaxson. He spreads his arms. "May I have this dance?"

I step into his arms. The familiar heat of his body burns through his dinner jacket.

"Do you think she knows?" I whisper as Camran begins to play the new song and we begin to dance.

"I have no idea," Jaxson replies. "It could have been a coincidence. I'll speak to her in a moment and try to find out."

Jaxson whirls me out at arm's length then twirls me back into his arms, drawing my back against his chest. "Do you love him?" he whispers in my ear.

When I don't reply, he spins me around to face him and we continue to dance.

I lick my lips, which have suddenly gone dry. I glance up at Jaxson. He's watching me.

"What is it?" he asks.

"Will you choose me tomorrow?"

It's Jaxson's turn to not reply. His dark eyes don't leave mine as we dance. And his full lips are tightly sealed.

"I know you're not allowed a human girl," I whisper beneath the music. "But Queen Tarla doesn't want me and Nykolas to be together, so she might back you if you put in a request for me."

That way, when Jaxson vaults me out of Eraeon, she won't come looking for me and try to kill me. She'll know that Nykolas will never want me back since I belong to Jaxson.

Jaxson is still quiet, and I begin to feel like a fool. A ZaZa dress and a bit of makeup, and I start thinking I have males at my command.

Unbidden tears spark in my eyes and I try to pull away, but Jaxson holds on, not letting me go. I don't want to cause a scene so I continue to dance with him. In silence.

Eventually I ask, "What would happen if anyone found out about last night?"

"The penalty would be death."

"For both of us?"

"No. Only for you. For me it would be scourging, since you aren't the bride they want for Nykolas anyway."

The double standards are disgusting. "Dabria has another man," I whisper. "I believe she even has a harem, and nobody bats an eye."

"Dabria is a faerie and a noblewoman. You are human. You don't get to have other lovers aside from your chooser. You'd better hope Nykolas never finds out. Better yet, you'd better hope *nobody* in the palace does, because then, even if Nykolas were to forgive you and try to spare you, they would insist on your death."

My mind goes into overdrive, trying to come up with a plan, but drawing blanks. Jaxson gets his full powers back in three days, but a lot can happen between now and then.

As the song comes to an end, Nykolas steps away from his dance partner. I try to step away from Jaxson again, and he holds on.

Anger crackles through me. "What do you want from me?" I hiss. "Either stop acting like a jealous fool and leave me alone, or tell me what you want."

His throat bobs as we continue to dance. He's quiet for a long moment. I almost don't hear him when he speaks. "If I choose you, we have to be together properly. It isn't going to end when I get my powers back and return you to Lorthien. You'll be mine until I decide it's over."

"And when will you decide it's over?"

"Possibly never."

He actually looks serious.

I want to scream. "Why would you want that? Don't you want to be free to pursue some faerie girl, like the one whose skirts you burned? What do you want with me?"

"Those are my terms. Accept them, or don't." He comes to a halt, releasing my hands, then walks away.

AT ELEVEN P.M., Frieve comes to get the human girls. We have a curfew since the Choosing Ceremony is tomorrow. Ziani doesn't look very pleased about it—especially since the faerie girls who will also be in the ceremony are permitted to stay.

For the past hour, Nykolas has been in deep conversation with some rather pompous looking faeries who are dressed head to toe in furs. I decide I'll speak into his mind when I get to my chambers, and ask if we can talk.

"You must all go straight to bed when you get to your rooms," Frieve tells us as we walk back to the palace. "You will be awakened at dawn to get ready."

"Are you able to tell us who we'll be given to?" Seltie asks.

I've hardly noticed her all night. She's been much quieter since Keyta's death.

"I'm afraid not. You will find out at the ceremony."

We enter the palace via a side-entrance where Filpé is waiting with two guards. "The queen orders that Riva is to spend the night in the dungeons," he announces.

My heart sinks. I'd assumed that since they've changed the narrative about my escape, they wouldn't follow through with that.

"Riva, wait!"

At the sound of Nykolas's voice, I turn toward the door. Frieve ushers the rest of the girls down a corridor.

Nykolas appears in the doorway and hurries into the palace. A bubble sparkles to life around us as he draws me into his arms. "I just wanted to check you're okay. You've seemed a little on edge tonight." He tips my chin, trailing the pad of his thumb over my lower lip. "I guess you know that people have been plotting against you. I was hoping you wouldn't find out, but don't you worry."

Beyond our bubble, Filpe's head suddenly snaps sideways and he drops to the floor, deep blue blood spurting onto the gleaming marble floors.

Nykolas's magic hangs in the air, a powerfully chilling quality to it that I've never sensed before.

Horror and nausea twist my stomach. "You killed him!"

Nykolas, eyes cold, looks through the bubble at Filpé's body on the floor. "I have it on good authority that he has been plotting to have you killed."

I can't take my eyes off the gruesome angle of Filpé's snapped neck. Shock roils through my body. The two guards standing on either side of Filpé keep their gazes focused straight ahead as though someone hasn't just been murdered.

"I will kill everyone in the palace who is seeking your life," Nykolas says with a lethal calm. "I can assure you that you will be safe here."

He has no idea that his own mother and uncle are among those seeking my life. Filpé was merely their accomplice.

"Don't kill for me," I whisper.

"I would do worse to protect you."

I can't stand this dark side he's showing. "I don't want your protection," I blurt. "I just want out of here."

My thoughts are racing. My heart is thundering in my chest. I try to calm myself, but heat is climbing up my neck. Everything is finally catching up to me in one giant wave of debilitating overwhelm.

Kali. My almost-death in the warehouse. Dabria's magic. Nocahya Forest.

"I don't want you to choose me," I tell Nykolas. "I don't want to bear anyone's heirs or ever have children—"

"Riva—"

"Let me finish!" I snap.

Nykolas lifts a brow. "Anyone who speaks to me like that dies."

"Is that a threat?"

"Of course not. I'm telling you for your own safety. Behind closed doors, do and say what you want. But not in public if you want everyone to accept you."

I think of how Queen Tarla walks a few paces behind the king. And she's no low-born human. It's all the more reason why I can't be with Nykolas, no matter how I might feel about him. I can't stand the idea of the life I would have to lead if I were his bride. Regardless of Queen Tarla's threats, it's best that Nykolas and I break up.

"Listen," I say. "Maybe everyone else here cowers before you, but I am not one of your subjects. As you know, I didn't come here to fall in love. I came for a reason that has now fallen through—"

"Riva, tell me what's really going on."

"There's n-nothing going on."

"I know you love me. You've shown me your heart. So why are you doing this?"

Tears begin to roll down my cheeks. I don't know what to say.

Jaxson's face flashes into my mind, and I push it out. That was a mistake. I was already determined to end things with Nykolas before Jaxson happened. I tried to tell Nykolas, outside the warehouse last night, that we were over, but he wouldn't listen.

I step out of the bubble, and a guard blocks my path. "We're to take you to the dungeons." He bows toward Nykolas in apology.

"Fine," I say, wiping my cheeks. I look at Nykolas. "It's over. I'm sorry. Please don't choose me tomorrow." Then I nod to the guards. "Let's go."

I stride down the corridor, and the guards hurry to flank me.

Nykolas's voice fills my head. *If you don't belong to me, you will die. Not because that's what I want, but because that's what will happen and I won't be able to prevent it.*

I stop walking. Then I turn. Nykolas is no longer wearing his crown. He's holding it in his hands. Confusion and hurt fill his eyes.

You told me, in another palace dungeon, that you would help me escape Eraeon if my life is at risk, I reply.

He says nothing. And this time, it's him who walks away.

Would he let me die?

Maybe death is preferable, I tell myself as the guards order me to keep moving. Because if Dabria knows my secret, she will no doubt tell Nykolas—and the queen—before the ceremony.

Then, death will be the least of my concerns. In fact, they'll make me long for it like a lover's embrace.

KEEP READING

The saga continues in *A Cage of Lovely Lies*.
Scan below to start reading it now.

BECOME A VIP

Scan below to join D.T. Benson's VIP readers' group and be the first to know whenever she has a new book out.

BOOKS BY D.T. BENSON

The Gilded Thorns series

A Kingdom of Gilded Thorns

A Ballad of Pretty Vipers

A Cage of Lovely Lies

A Prince of Deadly Games - coming soon

The Ice and Shadows series

Angel of Ice and Shadows

Angel of Blood and Embers - coming soon

About the Author

D.T. Benson fell in love with books at a young age and can't believe she now gets to spend her time building her own worlds and creating her own characters.

When she isn't writing, she enjoys eating other people's cooking, listening to music, and going for long walks.

📷 instagram.com/dtbensonauthor

Printed in Great Britain
by Amazon